'Morris Gleitzman has a rare gift for writing very funny stories and an even rarer gift of wrapping very serious stories inside them' *Guardian*

'Reveals the brutality of the Holocaust in a sensitive, thought-provoking way' *Sunday Times* on *Once*

'Horrific, humorous and ultimately life-affirming. Remarkable' *Guardian*

'Funny and shocking at the same time' *Jewish Chronicle*

'One of the reasons why this humane and carefully crafted book is so readable is that the author celebrates the ordinariness and childishness even as he chronicles terrible cruelty. But prepare for shock and tears' *Sunday Times* on *Then*

'It is in preserving the essential childishness of his characters that Gleitzman manages to reveal the true horror without inducing nightmares. And he is by trade a funny writer, so yes, you will laugh. But not quite as much as you will cry' *Sunday Telegraph*

'Beautifully crafted . . . There are shocking scenes, but thanks to the elegance and humanity of Gleitzman's writing . . . the reader will respond . . . with interest and growing compassion' *Waterstone's Books Quarterly*

'An uplifting and powerful story . . . an unbearably painful narrative with deft comedic moments . . . a stand-out, hard-hitting novel' *Bookseller*

'Harrowing at times but ultimately hopeful, and full of dignity and resilience' *Big Issue*

ABOUT THE AUTHOR

Morris Gleitzman was born in England and moved to Australia at the age of sixteen. He has written for TV, stage, newspapers and magazines and is the bestselling author of over twenty books for children.

# Once & Then

## MORRIS GLEITZMAN

PENGUIN BOOKS

PENGUIN BOOKS

Published by the Penguin Group
Penguin Books Ltd, 80 Strand, London WC2R ORL, England
Penguin Group (USA), Inc., 375 Hudson Street, New York, New York 10014, USA
Penguin Group (Canada), 90 Eglinton Avenue East, Suite 700, Toronto, Ontario, Canada M4P 2Y3
(a division of Pearson Penguin Canada Inc.)
Penguin Ireland, 25 St Stephen's Green, Dublin 2, Ireland
(a division of Penguin Books Ltd)
Penguin Group (Australia), 250 Camberwell Road, Camberwell, Victoria 3124, Australia
(a division of Pearson Australia Group Pty Ltd)
Penguin Books India Pvt Ltd, 11 Community Centre, Panchsheel Park,
New Delhi – 110 017, India
Penguin Group (NZ), 67 Apollo Drive, Rosedale, North Shore 0632, New Zealand
(a division of Pearson New Zealand Ltd)
Penguin Books (South Africa) (Pty) Ltd, 24 Sturdee Avenue, Rosebank, Johannesburg 2196, South Africa

Penguin Books Ltd, Registered Offices: 80 Strand, London WC2R ORL, England

www.penguin.com

*Once* first published in Australia by Penguin Group (Australia),
a division of Pearson Australia Group Pty Ltd 2005
First published in Great Britain in Puffin Books 2006
*Then* first published in Australia by Penguin Group (Australia),
a division of Pearson Australia Group Pty Ltd 2008
First published in Great Britain in Puffin Books 2009
First published in one edition as *Once & Then* in Penguin Books 2009

3

Copyright © Creative Input Pty Ltd, 2005, 2008

The moral right of the author has been asserted

Printed in Great Britain by Clays Ltd, St Ives plc

A CIP catalogue record for this book is available from the British Library

ISBN: 978–0–141–04279–4

www.greenpenguin.co.uk

Penguin Books is committed to a sustainable future
for our business, our readers and our planet.
The book in your hands is made from paper
certified by the Forest Stewardship Council.

For all the children whose stories have never been told

*Once*

Once I was living in an orphanage in the mountains and I shouldn't have been and I almost caused a riot.

It was because of the carrot.

You know how when a nun serves you very hot soup from a big metal pot and she makes you lean in close so she doesn't drip and the steam from the pot makes your glasses go all misty and you can't wipe them because you're holding your dinner bowl and the fog doesn't clear even when you pray to God, Jesus, the Virgin Mary, the Pope and Adolf Hitler?

That's happening to me.

Somehow I find my way towards my table. I use my ears for navigation.

Dodie who always sits next to me is a loud slurper because of his crooked teeth. I hold my bowl above my head so other kids can't pinch my soup while I'm fogged up and I use Dodie's slurping noises to guide me in.

I feel for the edge of the table and put my bowl down and wipe my glasses.

That's when I see the carrot.

It's floating in my soup, huge among the flecks of cabbage and the tiny blobs of pork fat and the few lonely lentils and the bits of grey plaster from the kitchen ceiling.

A whole carrot.

I can't believe it. Three years and eight months I've been in this orphanage and I haven't had a whole carrot in my dinner bowl once. Neither has anyone else. Even the nuns don't get whole carrots, and they get bigger servings than us kids because they need the extra energy for being holy.

We can't grow vegetables up here in the mountains. Not even

if we pray a lot. It's because of the frosts. So if a whole carrot turns up in this place, first it gets admired, then it gets chopped into enough pieces so that sixty-two kids, eleven nuns and one priest can all have a bit.

I stare at the carrot.

At this moment I'm probably the only kid in Poland with a whole carrot in his dinner bowl. For a few seconds I think it's a miracle. Except it can't be because miracles only happened in ancient times and this is 1942.

Then I realise what the carrot means and I have to sit down quick before my legs give way.

I can't believe it.

At last. Thank you God, Jesus, Mary, the Pope and Adolf Hitler, I've waited so long for this.

It's a sign.

This carrot is a sign from Mum and Dad. They've sent my favourite vegetable to let me know their problems are finally over. To let me know that after three long years and eight long months things are finally improving for Jewish booksellers. To let me know they're coming to take me home.

Yes.

Dizzy with excitement, I stick my fingers into the soup and grab the carrot.

Luckily the other kids are concentrating on their own dinners, spooning their soup up hungrily and peering into their bowls in case there's a speck of meat there, or a speck of rat poo.

I have to move fast.

If the others see my carrot there'll be a jealousy riot.

This is an orphanage. Everyone here is meant to have dead parents. If the other kids find out mine aren't dead, they'll get really upset and the nuns here could be in trouble with the Catholic head office in Warsaw for breaking the rules.

'Felix Saint Stanislaus.'

I almost drop the carrot. It's Mother Minka's voice, booming at me from the high table.

Everyone looks up.

'Don't fiddle with your food, Felix,' says Mother Minka. 'If you've found an insect in your bowl, just eat it and be grateful.'

The other kids are all staring at me. Some are grinning. Others are frowning and wondering what's going on. I try not to look like a kid who's just slipped a carrot into his pocket. I'm so happy I don't care that my fingers are stinging from the hot soup.

Mum and Dad are coming at last.

They must be down in the village. They must have sent the carrot up here with Father Ludwik to surprise me.

When everyone has gone back to eating, I give Mother Minka a grateful smile. It was good of her to make a joke to draw attention away from my carrot.

There were two reasons Mum and Dad chose this orphanage, because it was the closest and because of Mother Minka's goodness. When they were bringing me here, they told me how in all the years Mother Minka was a customer of their bookshop, back before things got difficult for Jewish booksellers, she never once criticised a single book.

Mother Minka doesn't see my smile, she's too busy glaring at the Saint Kazimierz table, so I give Sister Elwira a grateful smile too. Sister Elwira doesn't notice either because she's too busy serving the last few kids and being sympathetic to a girl who's crying about the amount of ceiling plaster in her soup.

They're so kind, these nuns. I'll miss them when Mum and Dad take me home and I stop being Catholic and go back to being Jewish.

'Don't you want that?' says a voice next to me.

Dodie is staring at my bowl. His is empty. He's sucking his teeth and I can see he's hoping my soup is up for grabs.

Over his shoulder, Marek and Telek are sneering.

'Grow up, Dodek,' says Marek, but in his eyes there's a flicker of hope that he might get some too.

Part of me wants to give my soup to Dodie because his mum and dad died of sickness when he was three. But these are hard times and food is scarce and even when your tummy's stuffed with joy you still have to force it down.

I force it down.

Dodie grins. He knew I'd want it. The idea that I wouldn't is so crazy it makes us both chuckle.

Then I stop. I'll have to say goodbye to everyone here soon. That makes me feel sad. And when the other kids see Mum and Dad are alive, they'll know I haven't been truthful with them. That makes me feel even sadder.

I tell myself not to be silly. It's not like they're my friends, not really. You can't have friends when you're leading a secret life. With friends you might get too relaxed and blurt stuff out and then they'll know you've just been telling them a story.

But Dodie feels like my friend.

While I finish my soup I try to think of a good thing I can do for him. Something to show him I'm glad I know him. Something to make his life here a bit better after I've gone, after I'm back in my own home with my own books and my own mum and dad.

I know exactly what I can do for Dodie.

Now's the moment. The bath selection has just started.

Mother Minka is standing at the front, checking Jozef all over for dirt. He's shivering. We're all shivering. This bathroom is freezing, even now in summer. Probably because it's so big and below ground level. In ancient times, when this convent was first built, this bathroom was probably used for ice skating.

Mother Minka flicks her tassel towards the dormitory. Jozef grabs his clothes and hurries away, relieved.

'Lucky pig,' shivers Dodie.

I step out of the queue and go up to Mother Minka.

'Excuse me, Mother,' I say.

She doesn't seem to notice me. She's peering hard at Borys, who's got half the playing field under his fingernails and toenails. And a fair bit of it in his armpits. I can see Mother Minka is about to flick her tassel towards the bath.

Oh no, I'm almost too late.

Then Mother Minka turns to me.

'What is it?' she says.

'Please, Mother,' I say hurriedly. 'Can Dodek be first in the bath?'

The boys behind me in the queue start muttering. I don't glance back at Dodie. I know he'll understand what I'm trying to do.

'Why?' says Mother Minka.

I step closer. This is between me and Mother Minka.

'You know how Dodek's parents died of sickness,' I say. 'Well Dodek's decided he wants to be a doctor and devote his life to wiping out sickness all over the world. The thing is, as a future doctor he's got to get used to being really hygenic and washing himself in really hot and clean water.'

I hold my breath and hope Dodie didn't hear me. He actually wants to be a pig-slaughterer and I'm worried he might say something.

Mother Minka looks at me.

'Get to the back of the queue,' she says.

'He really needs to be first in the bath every week,' I say. 'As a doctor.'

'Now,' booms Mother Minka.

I don't argue. You don't with Mother Minka. Nuns can have good hearts and still be violent.

As I pass Dodie he gives me a grateful look. I give him an apologetic one. I know he wouldn't mind about the doctor story. He likes my stories. Plus I think he'd be a good doctor. Once, after he pulled the legs off a fly, he managed to stick a couple back on.

Ow, this stone floor is really cold on bare feet.

That's something Dodie could do in the future. Design bathroom heating systems. I bet by the year 2000 every bathroom in the world will be heated. Floors and everything. With robots to pick the twigs and grit out of the bathwater.

Look at that, Borys is the first one in and the water's brown already. I can imagine what it'll be like when I finally get in. Cold, with more solid bits in it than our soup.

I close my eyes and think about the baths Mum and Dad used to give me. In front of the fire with clean water and lots of warm wet cuddles and lots and lots of stories.

I can't wait to have a bath like that again.

Hurry up, Mum and Dad.

Once I stayed awake all night, waiting for Mum and Dad to arrive.

They didn't.

They haven't.

But it's alright. Nobody drives up that narrow rocky road from the village in the dark unless they're Father Ludwik. He says God helps him and his horse with the steering.

Mum and Dad were never very religious so they probably wouldn't risk it.

They'll be here once it's daylight.

What I'm worrying about now is whether they'll recognise me after three years and eight months.

You know how when you have a haircut or a tooth comes out, your parents carry on about how you must be the kid who belongs to the shoe mender down the street?

Well I've changed even more than that. When I arrived at this place I was plump and little with freckles and two gaps. Now I'm about twice as tall with glasses and a complete set of teeth.

I press my face against the cold windowpane over my bed and watch the sky start to go pale and tell myself not to be silly. I remind myself what Mum and Dad said when they brought me here.

'We won't forget you,' Mum whispered through her tears. I knew exactly what she was saying. That they wouldn't forget to come and get me once they'd fixed up their bookshop troubles.

'We'll never forget you,' Dad said in a husky voice, and I knew exactly what he was saying too. That when they come, even if I've changed a lot, they'll still know it's me.

The sun is peeping up behind the convent gates. Now it's getting light outside I don't feel so anxious.

Plus, if all else fails, I've got my notebook.

The cover's a bit stained from when I had to snatch it away from Marek and Borys in class. It was to stop them reading it and some ink got spilled, but apart from that it looks exactly like it did when Mum and Dad gave it to me. It's the only notebook with a yellow cardboard cover in this whole place, so they'll definitely recognise it if I hold it in an obvious way when they arrive.

And when they read it, they'll know I'm their son because it's full of stories I've written about them. About their travels all over Poland discovering why their bookshop supplies suddenly went so unreliable. Dad wrestling a wild boar that's been eating authors. Mum rescuing a book printer who's been kidnapped by pirates. Her and Dad crossing the border into Germany and finding huge piles of really good books propping up wobbly tables.

Alright, most of the stories are a bit exaggerated, but they'll still recognise themselves and know I'm their son.

What's that sound?

It's a car or truck, one of those ones that don't need a horse because they've got an engine. It's chugging up the hill. I can hear it getting closer.

There go Sister Elwira and Sister Grazyna across the courtyard to open the gates.

Mum and Dad, you're here at last.

I'm so excited I'm steaming up the window and my glasses. I rub them both with my pyjama sleeve.

A car rumbles into the courtyard.

Mum and Dad must have swapped it for the old bookshop cart. Trust them, they've always been modern. They were the first booksellers in the whole district to have a ladder in their shop.

I can hardly breathe.

Half the dormitory are out of bed now, pressing their noses against the windows too. Any second now they'll all see Mum and Dad.

Suddenly I don't care if everyone does know my secret. Perhaps it'll give some of the other kids hope that the authorities might have made a mistake and that their mums and dads might not be dead after all.

That's strange. The car windows are steamed up so I can't see clearly, but it looks like there are more than two people in the car. Mum and Dad must have given Father Ludwik a lift. And a couple of his relatives who fancied a day out.

I can't make out which ones are Mum and Dad.

I hold my notebook up for them to see.

The car doors open and the people get out.

I stare, numb with disappointment.

It's not Mum and Dad, it's just a bunch of men in suits with armbands.


'Felix,' says Dodie urgently, grabbing me as I hurry out of the dormitory. 'I need your help.'

I give him a pleading look. Can't he see I'm doing something urgent too? Finding out from Mother Minka if Mum and Dad sent a note with the carrot saying exactly when they'll be arriving. I've got the carrot with me to jog Mother Minka's memory.

'It's Jankiel,' says Dodie. 'He's hiding in the toilet.'

I sigh. Jankiel's only been here two weeks and he's still very nervous of strangers.

'Tell him there's nothing to worry about,' I say to Dodie. 'The men in the car are probably just officials from Catholic head office. They've probably just come to check that all our parents are dead. They'll be gone soon.'

I give a careless shrug so Dodie won't see how nervous I am about the officials. And how much I'm desperately hoping Mother Minka remembers the story we agreed on about my parents. About how they were killed in a farming accident. Tragically.

'Jankiel's not hiding from the men in the car,' says Dodie. 'He's hiding from the torture squad.'

Dodie points. Marek, Telek, Adok and Borys are crowding into the dormitory toilets.

'Come on,' says Dodie. 'We've got to save him.'

Dodie's right. We can't leave Jankiel at the mercy of the torture squad. Marek and the others have been after him since the day he arrived. He's their first new boy to torture in three years and eight months.

Since me.

Dodie shoves the toilet door open. We go in. Marek, Telek, Adok and Borys have got Jankiel on his knees. Jankiel is pleading with them. His voice is echoing a bit because they've got his head half in the toilet hole.

'Don't struggle,' says Telek to Jankiel. 'This won't hurt.'

Telek's wrong. It will hurt. It hurt when they did it to me three years and eight months ago. Having your head pushed down a toilet hole always hurts.

'Wait,' I yell.

The torture squad turn and look at me.

I know that what I say next will either save Jankiel or it won't. Desperately I try to think of something good.

'A horse crushed his parents,' I say.

Now the new kid is staring at me too.

I grip my notebook hard and let my imagination take over.

'A great big plough horse,' I continue. 'It had a heart attack in the mud and fell onto both his parents and it was too heavy for him to drag off them so he had to nurse them both for a whole day and a whole night while the life was slowly crushed out of them. And do you know what their dying words to their only son were?'

I can see the torture squad haven't got a clue.

Neither does the new kid.

'They asked him to pray for them every day,' I say. 'At the exact time they died.'

I wait for the chapel bell to finish striking seven.

'At seven o'clock in the morning,' I say.

Everyone takes this in. The torture squad look uncertain. But they're not pushing anybody down the toilet, which is good.

'That's just one of your stories,' sneers Telek, but I can tell he's not so sure.

'Quick,' says Dodie. 'I can hear Mother Minka coming.'

That's a story too because Mother Minka is down in the courtyard with the head office officials. But Marek and the others look even more uncertain. They swap glances, then hurry out of the toilets.

Dodie turns wearily to Jankiel.

'What did we tell you?' says Dodie. 'About not coming in here on your own?'

Jankiel opens his mouth to reply, then closes it again. Instead he peers past us, trying to see down into the courtyard.

'Have they gone?' he says.

Dodie nods and points towards the dormitory.

'Borys is putting mud in your bed,' he says.

'I mean the men in the car,' says Jankiel.

He looks almost as scared now as he did with the torture squad.

'They'll be gone soon,' I say. 'Mother Minka's dealing with them.'

Jankiel starts to look a bit less nervous, but only a bit. I find myself wondering if he's got secret alive parents too.

'Thanks for saving me,' he says. 'That was a good story about my parents being crushed.'

'Sorry if it brought back sad memories,' I say.

'Nah,' says Jankiel. 'My parents froze to death.'

I stare at him. If that's true, it's terrible. Their bath must have been outdoors or something.

Jankiel glances down at my notebook.

'Do you make up lots of stories?' he asks.

'Sometimes,' I say.

'I'm not very good at stories,' he says.

As we go out into the dormitory I find myself wondering if

Jankiel is Jewish. He's got dark eyes like me. But I don't ask him. If he is, he wouldn't admit it. Not here.

Dodie stays with Jankiel, who's peering nervously out the window again, and I head off, hoping that Mother Minka has got rid of the officials so I can ask her about Mum and Dad.

As I hurry down the stairs I glance out the window myself.

In the courtyard Mother Minka is having an argument with the men. She's waving her arms, which she only does when she's in a very bossy mood.

I stop and stare.

What's that smoke?

It's a bonfire. The men are having a bonfire in the courtyard. Why are they doing that? It can't be for warmth, the sun's up now and it's going to be a hot day.

I can see why Mother Minka's so angry. The smoke is going into the chapel and the classrooms and the girls' dormitory.

Oh no, I've just seen what the men are burning.

That's terrible.

If Mum and Dad saw this, they'd be in tears.

The other nuns are down there in the courtyard, and some of them have got their faces in their hands.

I'm feeling very upset myself.

The men are burning books.

Once I saw a customer, years ago, damaging books in Mum and Dad's shop. Tearing pages out. Screwing them up. Shouting things I couldn't understand.

Mum was crying. Dad was furious. So was I. When customers are unhappy they should ask for a refund, not go mental.

These men are just as bad. They're hurting books cruelly and viciously and laughing about it.

Why?

Just because Mother Minka is a bit bossy? That's no reason to destroy the things she loves most in the world except God, Jesus, the Virgin Mary, the Pope and Adolf Hitler.

Wait a minute, those wooden boxes the men are flinging around are book boxes from our library.

I get it.

Mother Minka was complaining to us library monitors only last week that the library was very messy and needed a tidy-up. She must have got sick of waiting for us to do it and called in professional librarians in professional librarian armbands. They've reorganised the library and now they're burning the books that are left over.

No wonder Mother Minka is so upset. I bet she didn't give them permission to do that.

Me and Mum and Dad would have taken those books. We love all books, even old and tatty ones.

I can't watch any more.

I turn away from the smoke and flames and hurry down to Mother Minka's office. Rather than risk mentioning Mum and Dad out there, I'll wait for her to come back inside.

I stand by her desk.

Suddenly a voice yells at me. It's not Mother Minka, it's a man's voice, and he's shouting in a foreign language.

I turn, trembling.

In the doorway stands one of the librarians. He's glaring at me very angrily.

'This isn't a library book,' I say, pointing to my notebook. 'It's my notebook.'

The librarian scowls and takes a step towards me.

I'm confused. Why would Mother Minka call in foreign librarians? Perhaps people who don't speak Polish are faster library tidiers because they don't get tempted to read the books before they tidy them.

Mother Minka hurries into the room. She looks very unhappy. I'm starting to think this isn't a good time to ask her about Mum and Dad.

'What are you doing here?' she demands.

I can't tell her the truth in front of the librarian, so I try to tell her that I've come down to make sure none of the sparks from the fire blow in and singe her furniture or stationery. But at this moment, with her and the librarian glaring at me, I can't get the words out.

'Um . . .' I say.

'I remember now, Felek,' says Mother Minka. 'I asked you to come down and collect your notebook. Now you've got it, go back upstairs.'

I stare at her, confused.

Why is she calling me Felek? My name's Felix.

I don't wait to try and work it out. I head for the door. The librarian is still scowling at me. Mother Minka is still looking very stern. But also, I see as I brush past her, very worried.

Suddenly she grabs my ear.

'I'll take you myself,' she says.

She drags me along the corridor, but instead of dragging me upstairs, she pulls the kitchen door open and bundles me inside.

I've only been in the kitchen a few times before, to trim mould off bread as a punishment for talking in class, and I'd forgotten what a great soupy smell there is in here.

I don't have a chance to enjoy it today.

Mother Minka has shut the door behind us and is crouching down so her face is level with mine. She's never done that before, ever.

Why is she acting so strangely?

Maybe whoever trimmed her bread for dinner last night didn't do a very good job. Dodie says eating bread mould can affect your brain.

'This must be terrible for you,' she says. 'I wish you hadn't seen what they're doing out there. I didn't think those brutes would bother coming all the way up here, but it seems they go everywhere sooner or later.'

'Librarians?' I say, confused.

'Nazis,' says Mother Minka. 'How they knew I had Jewish books here I've no idea. But don't worry. They don't suspect you're Jewish.'

I stare at her.

These Nazis or whatever they're called are going around burning Jewish books?

Suddenly I feel a stab of fear for Mum and Dad.

'When my parents sent the carrot,' I say, 'did they mention when they'd actually be getting here?'

Mother Minka looks at me sadly for a long time. Poor thing. Forgetting my name was bad enough. Now she's forgotten what Mum and Dad told her as well.

'Felix,' she says, 'your parents didn't send the carrot.'

I desperately try to see signs of bread-mould madness in her eyes. It must be that. Mother Minka wouldn't lie because if she did she'd have to confess it to Father Ludwik.

'Sister Elwira put the carrot in your soup,' says Mother Minka. 'She did it because she . . . well, the truth is she felt sorry for you.'

Suddenly I feel like I'm the one with bread-mould madness burning inside me.

'That's not true,' I shout. 'My mum and dad sent that carrot as a sign.'

Mother Minka doesn't get angry, or violent. She just puts her big hand gently on my arm.

'No, Felix,' she says. 'They didn't.'

Panic is swamping me. I try to pull my arm away. She holds it tight.

'Try and be brave,' she says.

I can't be brave. All I can think about is one awful thing.

Mum and Dad aren't coming.

'We can only pray,' says Mother Minka. 'We can only trust that God and Jesus and the Blessed Mary and our holy father in Rome will keep everyone safe.'

I can hardly breathe.

Suddenly I realise this is even worse than I thought.

'And Adolf Hitler?' I whisper. 'Father Ludwik says Adolf Hitler keeps us safe too.'

Mother Minka doesn't answer, just presses her lips together and closes her eyes. I'm glad she does because it means she can't see what I'm thinking.

There's a gang of thugs going round the country burning Jewish books. Mum and Dad, wherever in Europe they are, probably don't even know their books are in danger.

I have to try and find Mum and Dad and tell them what's going on.

But first I must get to the shop and hide the books.


Dodie opens his eyes wide even though we're kneeling in chapel and meant to be praying.

'Jewish?' he says. 'You?'

I nod.

'What's Jewish?' he says.

It's too risky to try and explain all the history and geography of it. I've already spent most of this prayer telling Dodie about Mum and Dad and why I have to leave. Father Ludwik has just turned round and he's got eyes like that saint with the really good eyesight.

'Jewish is like Catholic only different,' I whisper.

Dodie thinks about this. He gives me a sad look.

'I'll miss you,' he whispers.

'Same here,' I say.

I give him the carrot. It's fluffy and a bit squashed, but I want him to have it because he hasn't got a mum and dad to give him one.

Dodie can't believe it.

'Is this a whole carrot?' he says.

'When I come back to visit,' I say, 'I'll bring more. And turnips.'

I wait till everyone's gone into breakfast, then I creep up to the dormitory to pack.

I pull my suitcase from under my bed and empty it out. The clothes I was wearing when I arrived here are much too small for me now, so I stuff them back into the suitcase and slide it back under the bed. Best to travel light.

All that's left are the books I brought from home and the letters Mum and Dad wrote to me before the postal service started to have problems.

I put the books on Dodie's bed. They're my favourite books in the whole world, the William books by Richmal Crompton that Mum and Dad used to read to me. William was their favourite when they were kids too, even though Richmal Crompton isn't a Jewish writer, she's English. I used to think Mum and Dad were translating the words into Polish themselves, but then I found out somebody had already done it.

I've always loved the William stories. He always tries to do good things, and no matter how much mess and damage he causes, no matter how naughty he ends up being, his mum and dad never leave him.

Dodie knows I'd never give these books away for ever. When he finds them on his bed he'll know I'll be back for a visit.

I pick up my notebook, tear out a clean page and write a note.

*Dear Mother Minka,*

*Thank you very much for having me. Please don't worry, I'll be fine.*
*If possible, can Dodie have my soup?*

*Yours faithfully,*
*Felix*

I put my notebook and pencil and letters inside my shirt.

I'm ready.

I peer out the window. The sun is shining brightly. The Nazis have gone. The courtyard is empty except for a pile of smoking ash and a few charred books.

If I'm quick, I can be out of here before everyone finishes breakfast.

I hurry past the other beds, trying not to feel sad about going, and I'm just about to leave the dorm when somebody steps in through the door and blocks my way.

Jankiel.

'Don't go,' he says.

I stare at him, my thoughts racing. He must have overheard me telling Dodie about leaving. I remember him asking me about making up stories. He must want me to stay and teach him how to make up stories himself.

I can see he's desperate, the poor kid. Desperate for something to keep the torture squad's mind off stuffing him down the toilet.

'You know how to make up stories already,' I say.

'What?' he says.

'Stories,' I say. 'Half of Saint Jadwiga dorm's still blubbing over that story you told them while we were queuing for chapel. About all the different ways you tried to get the dead horse off your parents. Cranes. Tugboats. Balloons. That was brilliant. Some of those girls were looking at you in that weepy adoring way nuns look at Jesus.'

'Really?' says Jankiel, sounding pleased.

'Here,' I say, pulling out my notebook. 'Here's what a story looks like written down. Practise as much as you can and you'll be fine.'

I tear out a page for him. It's the story where Mum and Dad hack their way through the jungle to a remote African village and help mend some bookshelves.

'Thanks,' says Jankiel.

He looks so confused and grateful I know he won't mind if I excuse myself and hurry off.

I'm wrong. As I move past him he suddenly looks desperate again and grabs my arm.

Oh no. If I try and fight him to get away and he starts yelling, every nun for a hundred miles around will come running.

'Don't go,' he says. 'It's too dangerous.'

I know what he means. If the nuns see me sneaking out I'll be history, but I've got to risk it.

I pull myself out of Jankiel's grip.

'There are Nazis everywhere,' he says.

'I know,' I say. 'That's why I have to go.'

Jankiel screws up his face and stares at the floor.

'Look,' he says, 'I can't tell you what the Nazis are doing because Mother Minka made me swear on the Bible that I wouldn't tell anyone. She doesn't want everyone upset and worried.'

'Thanks,' I say. 'But I know what they're doing. They're burning books.'

Jankiel looks like he's having a huge struggle inside himself. Finally he gives a big sigh and his shoulders slump.

'Just don't go,' he says. 'You'll regret it if you do. Really regret it.'

For the first time I feel a jab of fear.

I squash it.

'Thanks for the warning,' I say. 'That vivid imagination of yours is going to be really helpful when you need to make up more stories.'

He doesn't say anything. He can see I'm going.

I go.

Once I escaped from an orphanage in the mountains and I didn't have to do any of the things you do in escape stories.

Dig a tunnel.

Disguise myself as a priest.

Make a rope from nun robes knotted together.

I just walked out through the main gate.

I slither down the mountainside through the cool green forest, feeling very grateful to God, Jesus, the Virgin Mary, the Pope and Adolf Hitler. Grateful that after the Nazis left this morning, the nuns didn't lock the gate. Grateful that this mountainside is covered in pine needles rather than tangled undergrowth and thorns.

Mother Minka took us out on an excursion once, to look for blackberries. Dodie got tangled in thorns. He cried for his mum, but she wasn't there.

Only me.

Stop it.

Stop feeling sad about him.

People who feel sad make careless mistakes and get caught. They trip over tree roots and slide down mountains on their heads and break their glasses and the nuns hear them swearing.

I slither to a halt and listen carefully, trying to hear if Father Ludwik and his horse are on the mountain road looking for me.

All I can hear is birds and insects and the trickle of a stream.

I push my glasses more firmly onto my face.

Mum and Dad are the ones who need me now.

I think about getting to the shop and hiding our books and finding a train ticket receipt which tells me where Mum and Dad are and which train I have to catch to find them.

I think about how wonderful it'll be when we're all together again.

I have a drink from the stream, and head down the mountain through beams of golden sunlight.

You know how when you haven't had a cake for three years and eight months and you see a cake shop and you start tasting the cakes even before they're in your mouth? Soft boiled buns oozing with icing. Sticky pastries dripping with chocolate and bursting with cream. Jam tarts.

I'm doing that now.

I can smell the almond biscuits too, even though I'm crouching in a pigpen and there's a very smelly pig sticking its snout in my ear.

Over there, across that field, is Father Ludwik's village. It must be, it was the only village I could see as I was coming down into the valley. One of those buildings must definitely be a cake shop. But I can't go any closer, not wearing these orphanage clothes. Father Ludwik has probably put the word around that an escaped orphan is on the loose. Plus Nazi book burners could be in the general store buying matches.

The pig is looking at me with sad droopy eyes.

I know how it feels.

'Cheer up,' I say to the pig. 'I don't want to waste time in that village anyway.'

I need to get to my home town. And the good news is I know it's on a river that flows near here. When Mum and Dad drove me to the orphanage in the bookshop cart, we travelled next to the river almost the whole way to the mountains.

The pig cheers up.

It snuffles the sore patches on my feet.

'You're right,' I say. 'These orphanage shoes hurt a lot. I need to get some proper shoes from somewhere, ones that aren't made from wood, and some proper clothes, and directions to the river.'

The pig frowns and I can see it's trying to remember where the river is.

It can't.

'Thanks for trying,' I say.

Thinking about cakes has made me hungry. I didn't have breakfast this morning and now it's past lunchtime.

I look wistfully at the pig's food. It's grey and lumpy like Sister Elwira's porridge. My mouth waters, but there's not enough in the rusty trough for both of us. I can see the pig is happy to share, but I don't feel I should. The pig is stuck here and this is all it's got.

I'm lucky. I can get food anywhere. I'm free.

Thank you God, Jesus, Mary, the Pope and Adolf Hitler for answering my prayers.

A house.

I'm sorry I started doubting you while I was lost in the fields. And blaming you for the scorching sun and lack of puddles to drink.

This is perfect. A house on a deserted road without any nosy neighbours or police stations close by. And on the wall next to the front door is one of those carved metal things that religious Jewish families in our town have on their houses.

I knock.

The door swings open.

'Hello,' I call. 'Anyone at home?'

Silence.

I call again, louder.

Still no reply.

I wish I had Mother Minka with me for advice about what to do next, but I don't and I'm desperately thirsty, so I go into the house, hoping the owners aren't deaf and unfriendly.

If they are, it doesn't matter, because they're not here. All three rooms in the place are empty. The people must have left in a big hurry because there are two half-eaten meals on the kitchen table and one of their chairs has fallen over.

I pause, listening carefully.

What's happened? Where are the people?

I pick the chair up.

The kitchen stove is still burning and the back door is wide open.

I stick my head out. The garden and the fields next to it are all empty.

In the distance I hear faint gunshots.

Of course. That explains it. They're out hunting. They must have seen some rabbits, grabbed their guns and gone after them in a big hurry.

They probably won't be back for ages. When Father Ludwik goes rabbit hunting he's usually gone for hours.

On the kitchen table is a jug of water. I drink most of it. Then I eat some of the potato stew on each plate. I leave a bit in case the people are hungry when they get back.

In one of the other rooms are some clothes and shoes. None of them are for a kid, but I guess you can't have all your prayers answered in one day.

I take off my orphanage clothes, put on a man's shirt and trousers, trim the ends off the arms and legs with a kitchen knife, and use the bits of cloth to wedge around my feet in a pair of man's shoes.

Then, while my clogs and orphanage clothes are burning in the kitchen stove, I tear a page from the back of my notebook and write a note.

> Dear People Who Live Here,
> Sorry. I know stealing is wrong but I haven't got any money. And my mum and dad's books are in great danger. I hope you understand.
> Yours faithfully,
> Felix

I can't find a single map in the house, but it doesn't matter. I think I know which way the river is now. In the distance I can hear more gunshots. Dad read me a hunting story once, about how deer and foxes and rabbits prefer to live near lakes and rivers. So the hunters from this house are probably over near the river.

Thanks, Dad.

I eat one more mouthful of the potato stew and cut a piece off a loaf of bread and put it inside my shirt with my notebook and letters. I find a hat and put it on and clean my glasses and lace up the shoes as tightly as I can.

Then I set off along the road towards the gunshots.


This is just like a story I wrote once.

The two heroes (Mum and Dad) come to a lonely crossroads. They're not sure which way to go to get to their destination (the cave of a troll who wants to buy a full set of encyclopedias). So they use their ears for navigation. They listen carefully until, in the distance, they hear the troll noisily eating farm animals, and that tells them they have to turn left.

I'm doing the same standing here at these crossroads. I'm listening really hard. But I'm having trouble hearing any more gunshots because here it's the countryside that's noisy. Birds chirping in the trees. Insects chattering in the sunshine. Fields of wheat rustling in the breeze.

Sometimes real life can be a bit different to stories.

I adjust my hat, which keeps slipping down over my ears.

Wait a second.

Over there.

Gunshots.

Thank you God and the others.

I head along a road that's wider than the last one. This one's got wheel tracks in the dust. Not the usual smooth cartwheel tracks with hoof marks between them. These are the jagged tracks of rubber truck tyres.

I hope a truck comes along soon because now that I'm wearing ordinary clothes and I don't look like a runaway orphanage kid, I can ask for a ride.

A horse cart would be fine too.

Anything to get me to the river and our town and our books more quickly.


At last, a truck.

I stand in the middle of the road and wave my hat.

As the truck gets closer I see it's a farm animal truck packed with people. They're standing in the back, squashed together.

That's strange, they don't look like they've got many clothes on. Why would half-naked people be packed into a truck like that?

I get it, they must be farm workers going on holiday. They're so excited about having a swim in the river that they've undressed already. I don't blame them, this sun's really hot.

I'm still waving but the truck isn't slowing down. It's speeding up, driving straight at me.

'Stop!' I yell.

The truck doesn't stop.

I fling myself off the road into the long grass. The truck speeds past, spraying me with dust and grit and engine fumes.

I can't believe it. That truck driver was so busy daydreaming about his holiday, he didn't even see me.

Wait a minute, there's another one coming. This one's painted in brown and grey splotches. I think it's an army truck.

This time I wave from the side of the road, just in case.

'Hey,' I yell. 'Can I have a ride?'

There are soldiers sitting in the back. Some of them see me and point. One raises his rifle and pretends to aim at me.

That's very nice of him, giving a country kid a thrill, but I'm not a country kid, I'm a town kid and I need to get home urgently.

'Please,' I yell.

This truck doesn't slow down either. As it passes it hits a hole in the road and all the soldiers bounce up into the air.

Suddenly there's a loud bang.

I fall back into the long grass.

I'm stunned with shock. I've been shot at. The soldier shot at me. The bullet whizzed so close to my head I can still hear it buzzing in my ear.

I roll over and lie as flat as I can in case any of the other soldiers have a go.

None of them does. I start to breathe again. It must have been an accident. The bounce of the truck must have made the gun go off.

I have another thought.

That poor soldier. Tonight in the barracks he'll hardly be able to swallow his dinner he'll be so upset. All he wanted to do was play a little trick and now he thinks he's shot an innocent kid.

I scramble to my feet and wave at the truck, which is disappearing down the road.

'Don't worry,' I yell. 'I'm alright.'

But the truck has vanished into the dust cloud from the first truck, so the soldier doesn't see me and they don't give me a ride.

What bad luck.

For me and him.


At last, the river.

After walking such a long way, it's so good to kneel on the cool stones, stick my face in the water and have a drink.

This river is beautiful. The water is gleaming gold in the sunset, and the warm air smells damp and fresh, and there are millions of tiny insects turning happy floating cartwheels in the soft light.

Last time I was here, when I was six, I must have been too young to notice how beautiful Poland is in summer. Though there is another reason why I love this river so much now.

It's going to lead me home.

I stand up and look around.

The little road beside the river is still here, just like I remember it. The road that goes all the way to our place. Shame it's too narrow for trucks, but you can't have everything.

I'm feeling really good now, even though I'm a bit hungry because I'm trying to make my bread last and one mouthful wasn't a very big dinner.

I've still got a lot more walking to do, but in my heart I feel like I'm almost home. And I don't feel so anxious about the Nazi book burners because I've worked out what they're doing. They're burning books in the villages and remote orphanages first, before winter comes, so they don't get cut off by the snow. Which means they probably haven't done any of the towns yet, so I'll be in plenty of time to hide our books.

What's that noise?

Boy, gunfire's loud when it's so close. That lot startled me so much I almost fell into the water. The hunters must be just round that bend in the river.

Another burst of gunfire, a long one.

And another.

Sunset must be when loads of rabbits come out. Or perhaps the hunters are just using up their bullets to save carrying them home.

I'm glad I'm not going in that direction. I'm glad I have to head this way, the same way the river's flowing, away from the mountains.

Look at that. The river has suddenly turned red. Which is a bit strange, because the sunset is still yellow.

The water's so red it almost looks like blood. But even with all those gunshots, the hunters couldn't have killed that many rabbits.

Could they?

No, it must just be a trick of the light.

Once I walked all night and all the next day except for a short sleep in a forest and all night again and then I was home.

In our town.

In our street.

It's just like I remember. Well almost. The street is narrow like I remember and the buildings are all two levels high and made of stone and bricks with slate roofs like I remember, but the weird thing is there are hardly any food shops.

At the orphanage I used to spend hours in class daydreaming about all the food shops in our street. The cake shop next to the ice-cream shop next to the roast meat shop next to the jelly and jam shop next to the fried potato shop next to the chocolate-covered licorice bullet shop.

Was I making all that up?

Something else is different too.

Dawn was ages ago but there's nobody out and about. Our street used to be crowded as soon as it got light. People doing things and going places even though they were still yawning. Farm animals complaining because they didn't like being on the cobbles. Kids pinching things from market stalls.

This is very different.

The whole street is deserted.

I walk along from the corner wondering if my memory is wrong. That can happen when you're hungry and tired and your feet hurt because your shoes are too big.

Perhaps I'm confused. Perhaps I'm remembering all the stories I've made up about our noisy crowded street. Perhaps I made the crowds up too.

Then I see it.

Our shop, there on the next corner, and I know I haven't made that up.

Everything's the same. The peeling green paint on the door, the metal post for customers to lean their bikes on, the front step where Szymon Glick threw up as he was leaving my fifth birthday party.

And there's not a single Nazi burn mark anywhere on the shop.

I feel very relieved, but a bit weak from hunger as well and I have to stop and hold onto the wall of Mr Rosenfeld's house.

Now I'm so close to home, I'm starting to feel sad.

I wish Mum and Dad were here instead of away somewhere persuading their favourite author to write faster, or trying to sell books on gun safety to soldiers.

I take a deep breath.

I haven't got time to be sad. I've got a plan to carry out. Hide the books before the Nazis get here. Then I'll have plenty of time to find a railway receipt and be reunited with Mum and Dad.

First I've got to get into the shop.

I walk over and try the door. It's locked. I'm not surprised. Mum's dad was a locksmith before he was killed in a ferry-sinking accident. Mum's very big on locks, except on toilet doors in ferries.

I peer in through the shop window. If I have to smash my way in, I must make sure the flying bits don't damage the books.

I stare for a long time. I have to because when you're shocked and horrified and feeling sick, your eyes don't work very well, even with glasses.

There aren't any books.

All the books in the shop are gone.

The shelves are still there, but no books.

Just old coats. And hats. And underwear.

I can't believe it. The Nazis can't have burnt the books already or the lock would be broken and there would be ash and weeping customers everywhere.

Have Mum and Dad changed their business to second-hand clothes? Never. They love books too much. Mum's not interested in clothes, she was always saying that to Mrs Glick.

Have I got the wrong shop?

I kneel at the front door.

It is the right shop. Here are my initials where I scratched them in the green paint the day before I went to the orphanage so the other kids around here wouldn't forget me.

What's going on?

Have Mum and Dad hidden the books?

Suddenly I hear voices coming from our flat over the shop. A man and a woman.

Thank you God and the others.

'Mum,' I yell. 'Dad.'

Mum and Dad stop talking. But they don't reply. They don't even open the window. I can see their faint shapes, moving behind the curtains.

Why aren't they flinging the windows open and yelling with joy?

Of course. It's been three years and eight months. My voice has changed. I look different. Plus I'm wearing a rabbit hunter's clothes. They'll recognise me once they see my notebook.

The shop door is locked, so I race round the back and up the steps.

The back door of the flat is open.

'Mum,' I yell, bursting in. 'Dad.'

Then I stop in my tracks.

While I was running up the steps part of me feared our kitchen furniture would be gone, just like the books. But it's all here, exactly where it was. The stove where Mum used to make me carrot soup. The table where I had all my meals and my bread-crumb fights with Dad. The fireplace where Mum and Dad used to give me my bath and dry my book if I dropped it in the water.

'Who are you?' snarls a voice.

I spin round.

Standing in the doorway from the living room, glaring at me, is a woman.

It's not Mum.

Mum is slim with dark hair and a gentle pale face. This woman is muscly with hair like straw. Her face is angry and red. Her neck and arms are too.

I don't know what to say.

'Get out,' shouts the woman.

'Grab him,' says a man who isn't Dad, coming in from the bedroom. 'We'll hand him over.'

I back towards the door.

The man comes at me.

I turn and run down the steps. Halfway down I crash into a kid coming up. As I scramble over him I see his face. He's older than he was, but I still recognise him. Wiktor Radzyn, one of the Polish kids from my class when I went to school here.

I don't stop.

I keep running.

'Clear off, Jew,' yells Wiktor behind me. 'This is our house now.'

They've stopped chasing me.

I crouch in my secret hiding place at the edge of town and listen.

No more yelling.

The crowd that was after me must have given up. They mustn't know about this hollow sentry space in the ancient ruined castle wall. When Dad showed me this place years ago he told me it was our secret, so I never told anybody and he mustn't have either.

Thanks, Dad. And thank you God and the others that I wasn't able to fill it up with books like I'd planned, or there wouldn't be room for me in here.

Through the arrow slit I can see the town people walking back towards their homes. Now they're gone, I'm shaking all over.

31

Why do they hate me and Mum and Dad so much? They couldn't all have bought books they didn't like.

And why is the Radzyn family living in our place?

Have Mum and Dad sold it to them? Why would they do that? The Radzyns aren't booksellers. Mr Radzyn used to empty toilets. Mrs Radzyn had a stall at the market selling old clothes and underwear. Wiktor Radzyn hates books. When he was in my class, he used to pick his nose and wipe it on the pages.

I lean against the crumbling stone wall of my little cave and have a very sad thought. Wiktor has my room now. My bed and my desk and my chair and my oil lamp and my bookshelf and my books.

I think of him lying on the bed, blowing his nose on one of my books.

Then I have a much happier thought.

America.

Of course.

The visas for America must have come through. The ones Mum and Dad tried to get before I went to the orphanage. That's why they've sold the shop, so they can open another one in America. Dad told me a story about a Jewish bookseller in America once. The bookshelves there are solid gold.

Oh no.

Mum and Dad must be on their way to the orphanage to pick me up. Doesn't matter. They won't leave without me. I can be back at the orphanage in two days, two and a bit to allow for walking up the mountain.

Of course, that's probably where all the books are. Mum and Dad have taken them up to Mother Minka so she can buy the ones she wants before they ship the rest off to America.

Phew, I'm feeling much calmer now.

It all makes sense.

I wipe the sweat off my glasses, repack my rags and my feet into my shoes, and wriggle out through the thick undergrowth covering the entrance to the sentry space.

Then I freeze.

Somebody's behind me. I just heard the grass rustle.

I turn around.

Two little kids are staring at me, a boy and a girl, barefoot in the dust.

'We're playing grabbing Jews in the street,' says the little boy.

'I'm a Jew,' says the little girl. 'He's a Nazi. He's going to grab me and take me away. Who do you want to be?'

I don't say anything.

'You be a Nazi,' says the little girl, squinting at me in the sunlight.

I shake my head.

'Alright, you be a Jew,' she says. 'That means you have to be sad 'cause the Nazis took your mum and dad away.'

I stare at her.

She gives an impatient sigh.

'All the Jew people got taken,' she says. 'My dad told me. So you have to be sad, alright?'

Relax, I tell myself. It's just a game.

But panic is churning inside me.

'He doesn't want to play,' says the little boy.

The little boy's right, I don't.

I stand outside Mr Rosenfeld's house, doing what I've been doing for hours. Hoping desperately that the little girl is wrong.

Little kids are wrong quite a bit in my experience. There was a little kid at the orphanage who thought you could eat ants.

That's why I've waited until dark and crept back into town. Mr Rosenfeld is Jewish. If he's still here, that'll prove all the Jewish people haven't been taken away.

I knock on Mr Rosenfeld's door.

Silence.

I knock again.

Silence.

That doesn't mean he's not here. He could be reading and

concentrating very hard. Or asleep with lots of wax in his ears. Or in the bath and naked.

I knock again, louder.

'Mr Rosenfeld,' I call softly. 'It's Felix Salinger. I need to ask you something. It's urgent. Don't be shy if you're in the bath, I've seen Dad undressed.'

Silence.

Hands grab me from behind. I try to yell, but one of the hands is over my mouth. I'm dragged backwards over the cobbles, into the alley next to Mr Rosenfeld's house.

'Are you crazy?' hisses a man's voice in my ear.

It's not Mr Rosenfeld.

I squirm round and look up.

I can't see the man's face in the dark.

'They're all gone,' he says. 'Rosenfeld, your parents, all of them.'

I want him to stop. I want him to tell me it's just a story.

I try to bite his hand.

'They've all been transported to the city,' he says.

I try again. This time my teeth sink in a bit. The man pulls his hand away. And clamps it back on, harder.

'That's why those weasel Radzyns are living in your house,' says the man. 'That's why Rosenfeld's favourite brown hat is for sale in their shop. And most of the other things he left behind.'

Fear stabs through me. He's right. I did see Mr Rosenfeld's hat in the shop.

I squirm round again.

The moon has come out.

I can see the man's face. It's Mr Kopek. He used to empty toilets with Mr Radzyn.

'You shouldn't be here,' says Mr Kopek. 'Bad time for you lot around here. If I was one of you I'd go and hide in the mountains.'

Suddenly he lets go of me.

'If they get you,' he says, 'we never spoke.'

I understand what he's saying.

34

'Don't worry,' I reply. 'The Nazis won't be interested in me. I haven't got any books. I lent all mine to a friend.'

Mr Kopek stares at me for a moment, then stuffs something under my arm and hurries away down the alley.

I'm too shaky to stay standing up, so I sit down on the cobbles. I take the package from under my arm. It's wrapped in grease-proof paper. Inside is a piece of bread and a bottle of water.

I don't understand. Why are some people kind to us Jewish book owners and some people hate us? I wish I'd asked Mr Kopek to explain. And also to tell me why the Nazis hate Jewish books so much that they've dragged Mum and Dad and all their Jewish customers off to the city.

I tell myself a story about a bunch of kids in another country whose parents work in a book warehouse and one day a big pile of Jewish books topples onto the kids' parents and crushes them and the kids vow that when they grow up they'll get revenge on all Jewish books and their owners.

It doesn't feel like a very believable story.

It'll have to do for now, though. Perhaps while I'm on my way to find Mum and Dad I'll be able to think up a better one.

I carefully wrap the bread and the bottle of water again.

I'll need them.

It's a long journey to the city.

Once I walked as fast as I could towards the city to find Mum and Dad and I didn't let anything stop me.

Not until the fire.

I slow down, staring at the horizon.

The fire is miles away, but I can see the flames clearly as they flicker in the darkness. They must be huge. If that's a pile of burning books, there must be millions.

I stop.

I wipe my glasses and try to see if any Nazis are over there. I can't. It's too far away to see people, let alone armbands.

I can hear trucks or cars, though, and faint shouting voices.

Part of me wants to run away, just in case. Another part of me wants to go closer. Mum and Dad might be there. This might be where all the Jewish book owners have been taken, so the Nazis can burn all their books in one big pile.

I go closer.

I don't want to stay on the road in case I bump into any Nazis who are running late, so I cut across some fields.

One of the fields has cabbages in it. As I get closer to the fire, the cabbages are starting to get warm. Some are starting to smell like they're cooking. But I don't stop and eat any.

I can see what's burning now.

It's not books, it's a house.

I still can't see any people, so I stuff the bread and water inside my shirt and take my hat off and pee on it and put it back on to keep my head from blistering and go even closer in case there are some people inside who need to be rescued. I wrote a story once about Mum and Dad rescuing an ink salesman from a burning house, so I know a bit about it.

Blinking from the heat and the glare, I reach the wire fence that separates the house from the fields. The wire is too hot to touch. I wriggle under it.

The lawn is covered with dead chickens. Poor things, they must be cooked. That's what I think until I see the holes in them.

They've been shot.

The owners must have done it to put them out of their misery.

Then I see the owners.

Oh.

They're lying on the lawn next to the chickens, a man and a woman. The man is in pyjamas and the woman is wearing a nightdress. They're both in the same twisted positions as the chickens and both lying in patches of blood.

I want to run away but I don't. Instead, I pick up a chicken feather and hold it in front of the woman's mouth and nose. It's how you tell if people are dead. I read it in a book once.

The feather doesn't move.

It doesn't move with the man either.

I'm shivering in the heat. I've never seen real dead people before. Real dead people are different to dead people in stories. When you see real dead people you want to cry.

I sit on the lawn, the flames from the house drying my tears before they're halfway down my face.

These poor people must be Jewish book owners who couldn't bear to let the Nazis burn their books so they put up a struggle and to pay them back the Nazis killed them and their chickens and set fire to their whole house.

Please Mum and Dad, I beg silently.

Don't be like these people.

Don't put up a struggle.

It's only books.

Behind me part of the house collapses, bombarding me and the poor dead book owners with sparks and burning ash. My skin stings. My clothes start to smoulder. I roll across the lawn to put them out. And stop with my face close to another person.

It's a girl, about six years old, lying on her side.

A little kid. What sort of people would kill a little kid just for the sake of some books?

A horrible thought grows in my throbbing head. What if us Jews aren't being bullied just because of books? What if it's because of something else?

Then I notice that the little girl isn't bleeding.

Gently I roll her over.

The fire behind me is burning bright as day and I can see that the girl's pyjamas don't have any holes in them at all. Not from ash or bullets. The only medical condition I can find is a big bruise on her forehead.

I grab a feather and hold it in front of her face, but I don't need to because when I crouch closer I can hear the snot rattling in her nose.

It's loud, but not as loud as the car engine noise I suddenly hear in the distance.

I peer over towards the road.

Coming along it fast are two black cars. They look just like the Nazi cars that came to the orphanage.

The Nazis must be coming back here to the scene of their crime to get rid of the evidence. I've read about this type of criminal behaviour in stories.

I haul the unconscious girl up onto my back and stagger through the smoke and sparks towards the fence. The hot wire burns my arm as I squeeze through, but I don't care. I just want to get me and this poor orphan safely hidden in the cabbages.


'What's your name?' I ask the girl for about the hundredth time as we trudge along the dark road.

Actually it's just me doing the trudging. She's still on my back, her arms round my neck.

As usual she doesn't reply. The only way I know she's awake

and not unconscious is when I look over my shoulder at her and see the moonlight gleaming in her dark eyes.

This is killing me. The longest I've ever carried anyone before was Dodie in the piggyback race on sports day. That was only once around the playing field.

I try to take my mind off the pain in my arms by thinking about good things.

Mum's smell.

The way Dad's hair falls into his eyes when he's reading.

How at least this kid isn't getting overexcited like Dodie and kicking me in the ribs.

The pain in my arms is still bad. I wonder how much longer I can keeping going without dropping her.

Then I see something.

Is that a haystack?

It's a bit hard to tell because the moon's gone behind a cloud, but I'm pretty sure that big dark shape behind that hedge is a haystack.

Suddenly I can't resist it.

I know it's risky. The Nazis could be coming along here any time. But I can't go on. My legs are hurting too now.

'I need a rest,' I say to the girl.

She doesn't reply.

I push through the hedge and drag armfuls of hay off the haystack with one arm and make a bed on the ground. I lay the girl down on it as gently as I can and put some hay over her to keep her warm. Then I lay down next to her. I don't bother with top hay for me, I'm too tired.

The girl stands up and starts crying.

'Where's my mummy and daddy?' she wails.

It's the first thing she's said since she stopped being unconscious and it's the thing I've been dreading most.

'I want my mummy and daddy,' she howls.

At least I've had plenty of time to make a plan.

'I want mine too,' I say. 'That's why we're going to the city.'

Keep her hopeful, that's the plan. She's had a nasty bang on the head. I can't tell her the terrible news while she's not well. Later on, when she's feeling better and I've found Mum and Dad, that'll be the time to let her know her parents are dead. Because then Mum can do it. And then we can take her to live with Mother Minka.

'Who are you?' sobs the girl.

'I'm Felix.' I say. 'Who are you?'

'I want Mummy,' she wails.

'Don't yell,' I beg her. 'We have to be quiet.'

She carries on wailing. I can't tell her that the reason we have to be quiet is because the Nazis might hear us. That would terrify her. So I make something up.

'Shhhh,' I say. 'We'll wake the sheep.'

Then I remember there aren't any sheep. The fields are all empty.

Still sobbing, the girl looks at me like I used to look at Marek when he tried to tell me his parents were professional fighters who died in a wrestling accident.

I get up and go over to her and kneel down so my face is level with hers. I put my hand gently on her arm. I wish my hand was bigger, like Mother Minka's.

'I'm scared too,' I say quietly. 'I want my mum and dad too. That's why we're going to the city.'

I gently touch her forehead, next to the bruise.

'Does it hurt?' I ask.

She nods, more tears rolling out of her eyes.

'My mum's very good with hurt heads,' I say. 'When you meet her tomorrow she'll make it stop hurting.'

'Your hat smells,' says the girl, but she's not sobbing so much.

I flop back down on the hay.

'If you lie down and have a rest,' I say, 'I'll tell you a story about your mummy and daddy taking you on a picnic.'

The girl looks at me. She sticks her bottom lip out.

'We don't go on picnics,' she says. 'Don't you know anything?'

'Alright,' I say. 'You and your mummy and daddy flying in an aeroplane.'

'We don't fly in aeroplanes,' she says.

I sigh. I feel really sorry for her. It's really hard being an orphan if you haven't got an imagination.

I try one more time.

'Alright,' I say. 'I'll tell you a story about a kid who spends three years and eight months living in a castle in the mountains.'

She gives me that look again.

I give up. I roll over and close my eyes. I've done my best. I'm so tired I don't care any more.

Then I feel her lying down next to me.

I sigh again. A promise is a promise. I roll over and face her.

'Once,' I say, 'there was a boy called William –'

'No,' she interrupts, pointing to herself. 'I'm a girl. My name's Zelda. Don't you know anything?'

Once I woke up and I was at home in bed. Dad was reading me a story about a boy who got left in an orphanage. Mum came in with some carrot soup. They both promised they'd never leave me anywhere. We hugged and hugged.

Then I really wake up and I'm in a haystack.

Hay stalks are stabbing me through my clothes. Cold damp air is making my face feel clammy. The early morning sun is hurting my eyes. A young girl is shaking me and complaining.

'I'm hungry,' she's saying.

I feel around for my glasses, put them on, look at her groggily, and remember.

Zelda, the girl with the dead parents.

And the bossy attitude. She made me tell her the castle in the mountains story about ten times last night, till I got it right.

'I need to do a pee,' she says.

'Alright,' I mumble. 'First a pee, then breakfast.'

We both do a pee behind the haystack. Then I unwrap the bread and water. Zelda has a drink and I have a sip. I break her off a piece of bread and a smaller one for me. She needs extra because she's injured. The bruise on her forehead is dark now, and there's a lump.

'Your hat still smells,' says Zelda.

I open my mouth to explain why firefighters often have smelly hats, then close it again. Best not to remind her that her house has burnt down.

'Sorry,' I say.

Zelda is frowning and screwing up her face, and I don't think it's just because of my hat.

'Are you alright?' I ask.

'My head hurts,' she says. 'Don't you know anything?'

'It'll feel better when we get to the city,' I say. I don't mention Mum's healing powers this time in case it makes her wail for her parents again.

My head hurts too.

It's hot and throbbing. Last night when it started hurting I thought it was just overheated from the fire. But it can't be that now because my skin is cold and clammy.

I'm hearing things too, which can happen when you've got a fever. I can hear voices and footsteps and the rumble of cart-wheels. I must still be half-asleep, dreaming about our street on market day.

No I'm not.

I'm wide awake. The sounds are real. They're coming from the road on the other side of the hedge.

'Stay here,' I whisper to Zelda.

'What is it?' she says, alarmed.

'I'll be back in a minute,' I say. 'Then we'll go to the city.'

'To see our mums and dads,' says Zelda.

I run to the hedge, wriggle into the leaves and branches, and peer out at the road. And gawk in amazement. The road is crowded with people. Men and women and kids and old people. A hundred or even more. They're all walking wearily in the direction of the city. Most of them are carrying bundles or bags or suitcases or cooking pots. A few are carrying books.

Each person is wearing an armband over their coat or jacket. Not a red and black armband like the Nazis had at the orphanage, these are white with a blue star, a Jewish star like on some of the Jewish houses at home. Must be so these travellers can recognise the other members of their group. We used to have paper saints pinned to our tops on sports day so everyone could see which dormitory we were from.

A sudden loud noise makes me shrink back into the hedge.

Several soldiers on bikes with motors are driving up and down, yelling and waving at the people in a foreign language.

The soldiers have all got guns. None of the people have. The soldiers seem to want the people to go faster.

With a jolt I understand.

These soldiers are Nazis. This straggling crowd of people are all Jewish book owners, all being transported to the city.

Are Mum and Dad here?

I lean forward again, trying to see, but before I can spot them I hear a sound behind me.

A scream.

Zelda.

I struggle out of the hedge, almost losing my glasses. I jam them back on and almost faint at what I see.

Zelda is standing by the haystack, rigid with fear. Next to her, pointing a machine gun down at her head, is a Nazi soldier.

'Don't shoot,' I scream, running over to them.

The soldier points his gun at me.

I freeze. With a stab of panic I see my notebook lying in the hay at his feet. It must have fallen out of my shirt. The Nazi soldier must have seen it. He must think we're Jewish book owners. Disobedient ones, like Zelda's parents.

My throat goes dry with fear.

'That isn't really a book,' I croak. 'It's a notebook. And it isn't hers, it's mine. And I wasn't trying to hide it. I was planning to hand it over as soon as we get to the city and find the place where the books are being burnt.'

The soldier stares at me like he doesn't believe what I've just said.

Desperately I try to think of a way to make friends with him.

'Sorry I just shouted at you,' I say. 'I'm from the mountains where you have to shout and yodel to make yourself heard. Can you yodel?'

The soldier doesn't reply. He just scowls and waves his gun towards the hedge.

I grab Zelda by the hand, and my notebook, and the bread and water.

Zelda is trembling just as much as me.

'Come on,' I say to her gently. 'He's telling us we have to go to the city with all the other people.'

'To see our mums and dads,' says Zelda to the soldier.

You know how when you're looking for your mum and dad in a straggling crowd of people trudging along a dusty road and you speed up and get to the front and then slow down and drop to the back and you still can't see them even when you pray to God, Jesus, the Virgin Mary, the Pope and Adolf Hitler?

That's happening to me.

My head is throbbing and I feel squashed with disappointment.

I try to cheer myself up by thinking how Mum and Dad have probably already arrived at the city and are having a sit down and taking the weight off their feet.

It doesn't cheer me up much. The Nazi soldiers on the motorbikes are still yelling at everyone. I hope Mum and Dad haven't got noisy cross soldiers like these. Mum gets very indignant when people are rude, and sometimes she tells them off.

Zelda doesn't look very happy either.

'My feet hurt,' she says.

Poor thing. She's only wearing fluffy bedtime slippers. The soles aren't thick enough to protect her feet from the stones on the road.

I bend down and pull some of the rag stuffing out of my shoes.

'Come on,' I say to Zelda. 'Piggyback.'

She jumps on my back.

'Hold on tight,' I say, and start walking again so the soldiers won't yell at us for lagging behind.

Some of the other kids walking with their mums and dads give Zelda jealous looks. I don't blame them. Some of them are only about three or four. Their mums and dads are too weary to talk to them, let alone carry them.

45

I can see Zelda wants to stay on my back till we get to the city. I wish she could, but I feel too ill.

I take her slippers off, wind the rags round her feet and put her slippers back on.

'There,' I say. 'That should help.'

I put her back down.

'It feels funny,' she says after a few steps.

I try to think of something to help her get used to it.

'All the great travellers in history had rags round their feet,' I say. 'Christopher Columbus who discovered America, he had rags round his feet. Doctor Livingstone in Africa, he did. Hannibal the Great, he did too. So did his elephants. In the future, by the year 1960, I think they'll make shoes with rags already in them.'

Zelda gives me one of her looks.

'By the year 1960,' she says, 'people won't need shoes. They'll have wheels instead of feet. Don't you know anything?'

'Sorry,' I say. 'I forgot.'


'Why do those people look so sad,' asks Zelda.

I've been expecting her to ask. She's been staring in a concerned way at the people walking with us. An elderly woman near us is crying and Zelda's been looking at her a lot.

I'm not sure what to say.

Zelda squeezes my hand even tighter than usual.

'Well?' she demands. 'Why do they?'

I know why the people look sad. They've been walking for hours and they're tired and hungry and worried about their books and parents, just like us. We probably look sad to them.

But I don't say this to Zelda. When a little kid doesn't even know her parents are dead, you've got to try and keep her spirits up.

'They're feeling sad because they haven't got rags in their shoes,' I say to her. 'They'll be much happier when we get to the city.'

I'm about to tell Zelda about the rag shops that are probably in the city when I see something out of the corner of my eye.

The elderly woman has just fainted at the side of the road. She's lying in the dust. Nobody is stopping to help her. Not the other Jewish people, not the soldiers, not me.

I can't give anyone else a piggyback. I can't even lift Zelda, the way I feel now.

'What's wrong with that lady?' asks Zelda.

I tell her that the lady is just having a rest, and after we've gone a farmer will come and take the lady home and she'll live happily on the farm with his family and become very good at milking cows and in the year 1972 she'll invent a machine that milks them automatically and also makes butter.

Zelda thinks about this.

'In 1972,' says Zelda, 'cows will make their own butter. Don't you know anything?'

I'm tempted to say, 'No, I don't. Not any more.'

I look around at the tired hungry sick Jewish people staggering along the road. An awful question has been throbbing in my head for ages now. It's the question I first thought of when I saw Zelda lying on her lawn.

Why would the Nazis make people suffer like this just for the sake of some books?

I need to try and find an answer.

'Excuse me,' I say to a man walking nearby. 'Are you a book lover?'

The man stares at me as if I'm mad. His grey sagging face was miserable before, but now he looks like he's close to tears. He looks away. I feel terrible. I wish I hadn't asked.

Not just because I've made a suffering Jewish man feel upset at the sight of a crazy kid. Also because I've got a horrible suspicion I know the answer to the question.

Maybe it's not just our books the Nazis hate.

Maybe it's us.

Once I spent about six hours telling stories to Zelda, to keep her spirits up, to keep my spirits up, to keep our legs moving as we trudge through the rain towards the city.

At least the rain is washing my hat, but my head is still hot and throbbing. Every time a Nazi soldier yells at me or at another person in our soggy straggling group, my head has stabs of pain.

Me and Zelda have eaten our bread and we're both hungry. As we trudge on I keep my eyes open for food. Nothing, just dark wet trees and big fields full of mud and wet grass.

I keep thinking about Mum and Dad and hoping they're not this hungry, but worrying about them only makes my head throb more.

'Why have you stopped the story?' says Zelda.

'Sorry,' I say. I'm telling her a story about how much fun kids can have in the city, but my imagination is as tired and hungry as my body, and my shirt's wet and I'm worried my notebook is getting ruined.

Zelda is looking annoyed. I don't blame her. Her pyjamas are as sodden as my shirt.

'Keep going with the story,' she says. 'William and Violet Elizabeth are in the big cake shop at the zoo. Remember?'

'I remember,' I say. 'Did I tell you about the elephants? The ones that float in by parachute with the extra supplies of cakes?'

'Yes,' says Zelda crossly. 'Don't you know anything?'

I'm being distracted again. Another straggling crowd of Jewish people have appeared out of a side road and are walking with us now. They look terrible. Some of them have got bigger bruises than Zelda.

48

Zelda's so exhausted she hasn't even asked me about them, but I can see she's noticed and she's as concerned as I am.

Somehow I find the energy to carry on with the story.

'William and Violet Elizabeth eat another six cakes each,' I continue. 'Then suddenly a zoo keeper rushes in, upset and yelling. A vicious gorilla has escaped and is on a violent rampage across Poland.'

'Across the whole world,' says Zelda.

'Yes,' I say, glad I've got her mind off the bruised people. 'So William and Violet Elizabeth come up with a plan to capture the gorilla.'

'Violet Elizabeth comes up with most of it,' says Zelda.

'Alright,' I say. 'The plan is, they go to a luxury hotel and get a luxury hotel room and put lots of things in it that gorillas like. Bananas. Coconuts. Small roasted monkeys.'

I can see Zelda isn't happy with this.

'Why do they put the things in a hotel room?' she asks.

'Because,' I say, 'luxury hotels in cities are made of a modern invention called concrete which is super strong. Even a gorilla can't bash his way out when he's locked in a concrete room.'

'The gorilla might be a girl,' says Zelda.

I look at her wearily.

'He might,' I say. 'Anyway, William and Violet Elizabeth send a message to the gorilla about the hotel room, then hide in the wardrobe with a big net.'

'And toys,' says Zelda.

I look at her, puzzled.

'Gorillas like toys,' she says.

I know I should be agreeing with her, but I don't, partly because I'm not sure if gorillas do like toys, and partly because what I'm seeing ahead of us is suddenly making it hard for me to speak.

One of the people in our group, the man who isn't a book lover, has started yelling at the soldiers, screaming hysterically. Suddenly a soldier hits the man in the face with a machine gun.

The man falls down. The soldiers start kicking him. People cry out. I almost do myself.

Instead I step between the man and Zelda so she won't see. I put my arm round her shoulder and walk as fast as I can, talking loudly to distract her.

'William and Violet Elizabeth's plan is a big success,' I say, 'because when the gorilla hears about the toys, he rampages straight to the hotel.'

'I think it's a silly plan,' says Zelda.

I'm struggling to stay calm. Behind us I can still hear the poor man grunting as the soldiers kick him.

'Tell me a better plan,' I say.

'Well,' says Zelda. 'Violet Elizabeth and William dig a big hole, like those people over there, and the gorilla falls into it.'

I look over to where Zelda is pointing. In a patch of forest near the road a big crowd of people, hundreds it looks like, are digging what looks like a huge hole.

I stare, confused.

It's hard to see because of the trees, but the people don't look like farm workers. Some of them look like children. Some of them look very old. Some of them look like they might be naked. And I think I can see soldiers pointing guns at them.

'What are they doing?' says Zelda.

I wait for my imagination to come up with something.

It doesn't.

'Maybe a gorilla has really escaped,' says Zelda.

She puts her arm round my waist. I keep mine round her shoulders.

Some of the people in our group are stopping, trying to see what's going on in the forest. The soldiers are yelling at us to keep moving.

We trudge on through the rain.

'The gorilla has a friend,' says Zelda. 'A kind man. He doesn't want the gorilla to be captured, so he tells the army to leave the gorilla alone and they hit him with a gun.'

50

I look down at Zelda. I can tell from the sadness on her face that she did see the man being hit.

I squeeze her tighter.

'That's a good story,' I say. 'And when the man gets better, he and the gorilla go and live happily in the jungle and open a cake shop.'

'Yes,' says Zelda quietly.

She doesn't look as though she totally believes it.

I don't either.

The city isn't anything like it is in stories.

The wide streets are dirty and the tall buildings, five levels high some of them, have all got Nazi flags hanging off the balconies and out of the windows.

Army trucks and tanks are parked everywhere and lots of soldiers are standing around telling each other foreign jokes and laughing.

There's no sign of a zoo and I haven't seen a single cake shop or rag shop and the local people are really unfriendly. Lots of them are standing on the footpaths yelling unkind things at us as we straggle past.

Dirty Jews.

Stuff like that.

Of course we're dirty. We've been walking for nearly a whole day in the rain.

I'm looking around for Mum and Dad, but I can't see them. Zelda is doing the same. I hope I find mine before she realises hers aren't here.

Where are you, Mum and Dad?

I must try and be patient. That's what Mum used to tell me when I was little and I got upset because I couldn't read any of the words in Dad's big book about two thousand years of Jewish history.

This is hopeless. There are too many people. I've never seen so many people in one place. And all the Jewish people look as unhappy as us, huddled and weary in dark damp coats and blankets trying to ignore the rude things the city people are shouting at us.

'I don't like the city,' says Zelda.

I wish I knew what to say.

I wish I could tell her a story to make us all feel better. But I'm too exhausted and my feet are too blistered.

We're heading for a big brick wall built right across the street. That's a very strange place to build a wall. There's a gate in the wall with soldiers guarding it and the people ahead of us are going through the gate.

No they're not, not all of them.

The soldiers are grabbing some of the Jewish people. They're giving them buckets and scrubbing brushes. They're making them kneel down and scrub the cobblestones.

This is terrible.

The city council should pay people to clean the streets, not make visitors do it while the locals stand around laughing.

I hope Mum and Dad didn't have to do this.

Oh no, what now?

This is even more terrible.

Soldiers are grabbing Jewish kids and throwing them into the back of a truck. It looks like no kids are allowed through the gate. People are screaming and crying as their kids are snatched away.

What's going on?

Why are the Nazis separating the kids from the adults?

I don't want to be separated, I want to stay here and find Mum and Dad.

I pull Zelda over to the side of the street. I look around for an alley we can run down. The local people are pointing at us and yelling at the soldiers that we're Jews and we're escaping.

What was that noise?

Gunshots.

Everyone is screaming.

Over by the wall two people are lying on the ground bleeding.

Another man is wrestling with a soldier, trying to get to a kid that another soldier is holding. The soldier with the kid points a pistol and shoots the man.

Oh.

The screaming is even louder now, but I can still hear Zelda howling in fright.

I try to cling onto her. Too late. Somebody is dragging her away from me.

A Nazi officer with a bored look on his face is holding her by the hair and pointing a gun at her.

'Please don't,' I croak.

I wait for my imagination to come up with a reason I can tell him why he mustn't shoot her, but my head is burning and everything is spinning round and I fall down shouting but not words.

The cobblestones hurt my face. Gunshots hurt my ears. I start crying. I don't know what to do.

I haven't got any more stories.

Once I lay in the street in tears because the Nazis are everywhere and no grown-ups can protect kids from them, not Mum and Dad, not Mother Minka, not Father Ludwik, not God, not Jesus, not the Virgin Mary, not the Pope, not Adolf Hitler.

Then I look up and see that I'm wrong.

Here's one doing it now.

A big man in a scuffed leather jacket has his hand on Zelda's shoulder and is pleading with the Nazi officer in a foreign language. I think he's speaking Nazi. Which is strange because he's wearing a Jewish armband.

The Nazi officer lets go of Zelda's hair and raises his gun and points it at the man's head.

The man doesn't weep or grovel. He lifts up the leather bag he's carrying, which is also fairly scuffed, and holds it in front of the Nazi officer's face.

Why is he doing that?

The Nazi officer glances at the bag, still looking bored. He raises his other hand, grabs a tuft of the man's beard and twists it hard with his leather glove. The man stands there and lets him.

The local people watching all laugh and cheer.

The man looks sad, but ignores them.

After a very long twist, the Nazi officer turns and walks away. He goes over to the crowd of Jewish people who are still crying and shouting because some of them have been shot and their children are still being put into the truck.

He goes up behind a woman and points his gun at the back of her head.

I try to scramble up so I can go over and stop the Nazi officer.

I can't stay on my feet. I'm too dizzy. I fall back down onto my knees.

The Nazi officer shoots the woman.

Oh.

Zelda screams.

The man turns her away from the horrible sight and starts to take her off through the crowd of gawking locals.

'No,' yells Zelda. 'I'm not going without Felix.'

She struggles and kicks. The man turns and stares at me. He looks very weary, as if having his beard twisted and seeing innocent people being shot to death is bad enough and the last thing he needs is a kid who can't stand up and has just started vomiting.

I try to tell him I'm looking for my mum and dad, but more vomit comes out and the whole street goes spinning away from me.

I wake up with a painful light flickering in my eyes.

It's a candle flame.

Mother Minka always has a candle when she comes into the dormitory at night to give Marek a detention for going to bed with no pyjamas on or to whack Borys for throwing Marek's pyjamas out the window or to –

I sit up in panic.

Am I back in the orphanage?

I don't want to be. I need to find Mum and Dad. I need to warn them. I need to –

A big hairy hand pushes me gently back down. It's not Mother Minka's.

A man with a beard is looking down at me, frowning. I've seen him somewhere before.

'Are you Father Ludwik?' I say.

My throat hurts. My skin is burning.

The man shakes his head. He wipes my face with a damp cloth.

'Try and rest,' he says.

I can see now he isn't Father Ludwik but I don't know who else he could be. Then I remember. The man with the magic bag. But he's not speaking Nazi any more.

Suddenly a girl is looking down at me too.

'He's Barney,' she says. 'Don't you know anything?'

I know who the girl is, but before I can say her name everything spins away again.

I wake up in darkness.

Panic smothers me.

'My notebook,' I yell. 'I've lost my notebook.'

My throat still hurts. My whole body feels cold. Except my head. It's on fire.

Somebody lights a candle.

A silver heart is glinting in front of my eyes. It's on a chain, hanging from the girl Zelda's neck as she looks down at me, concerned.

'He thinks he's lost his notebook,' she says.

The man who's not Father Ludwik is also looking down at me, also concerned.

'Your notebook is safe,' he says.

'So are your letters,' says Zelda. 'We threw your hat away.'

'Here,' says the man. 'Drink.'

He puts a metal cup to my lips. I sip some water. It makes me cough, which makes my head hurt a lot.

'Is Felix going to die?' whispers Zelda to the man.

The man doesn't say anything, just looks more worried.

Now my head feels even worse. I have to find Mum and Dad. They know how to make me better.

I remember the Nazis have got them.

Panic swamps me again.

If only Mum and Dad hadn't put me in that stupid orphanage. If only they'd let me stay with them. I could have protected them. Somehow.

I want to sit up, to ask the man to help me find them, but I'm so weak and giddy I don't know where up is.

Far off I can hear Zelda demanding to know if I'm going to die.

'Please,' I whisper to the darkness. 'Find my parents.'

I hope the man can hear me.

'They're in danger,' I croak. 'Really bad danger. Don't believe the notebook. The stories in the notebook aren't true.'

I wake up to the sound of someone crying.

It's not me.

'I want to go home,' sobs a kid's voice.

Zelda?

No, it's a boy.

I open my eyes. A few thin needles of daylight are stabbing through the dark. They make my eyes sting but I don't feel like I'm burning up any more and my head doesn't hurt so much.

I put my glasses on but I can't see much in the gloom. My bed is a sack stuffed with something soft. Next to me is another sack bed with a crying boy on it. He looks about five.

The man who's not Father Ludwik crouches down and gives the boy a hug.

'I want to go home, Barney,' sobs the boy.

'I know,' says the man.

'I miss them,' says the boy.

The man gently smooths the boy's hair.

'I know, Henryk,' he says. 'One day you'll be with your mummy and daddy. Until then I'll look after you, I promise.'

The boy sniffs, but he's stopped crying.

'Cry some more if you want to,' says the man. 'Ruth will hold you.'

A girl about my age with curly hair steps forward and puts an arm round the boy.

The boy wipes his face on his sleeve.

'I've finished now,' he says.

Barney turns to me and puts his hand on my forehead.

'Good,' he says. 'Much better. You're doing well, Felix.'

He hands me a metal cup with something hot in it.

Soup.

I put the cup down, roll over angrily and close my eyes.

This man Barney is an idiot.

You don't tell a kid he'll find his parents one day. One day doesn't mean anything. If you don't know when they're coming, you let the kid go and look for them now.

I want to shout at the man, but I don't because Dodie reckons it's pointless shouting at idiots, plus it would probably hurt my throat.

Instead I ignore the man's hand on my back and try to tell myself a story to cheer myself up. A story about a kid who finds his parents in a city and takes them to a desert island with cake shops where they live happily ever after.

It's no good.

When I close my eyes all I can see is Nazi soldiers shooting people, including kids who just want a lift on a country road.

What if Mum and Dad waved to an army truck on their way to the city?

I don't want to think about it.

If you tell yourself stories like that you could end up crying.


'Felix.'

A hand is shaking me gently. I keep my eyes closed for a while, then open them.

Barney is crouching by my bed. He's holding my notebook.

'Felix,' he says. 'Do you mind if I read one of your stories to the others?'

I put my glasses on and look around, squinting in the candle-light.

My bed is surrounded.

There's Barney and Zelda and the little boy who was crying and the girl with the curly hair. There's also a boy a bit younger

58

than me who's chewing the end of a piece of wood, a girl a bit older than me with a bandaged arm, a toddler with half its hair missing, and a boy about my age who's blinking his eyes non-stop and hugging the dirtiest teddy bear I've ever seen.

'Just say if you don't want me to,' says Barney. 'We understand if your stories are private. But Zelda has told us what a good storyteller you are, and a few people here have got missing parents, and I think they'd enjoy hearing one.'

'I would,' says the girl with the bandaged arm.

'I would,' says the little boy who was crying.

'I would,' says the girl with curly hair.

'No,' I say.

They all look at me, disappointed.

'Felix,' says Zelda crossly. 'We all want to hear your stories. Don't you know anything?'

Barney puts his hand on my shoulder.

'That's alright, Felix,' he says gently. 'We understand.'

I can feel myself shaking and I know why. The stories in my notebook are stupid. While I was writing them, Mum and Dad were being chased all over Europe by the Nazis. And being captured.

'Those stories are obviously very important to you,' says Barney.

No they're not, I think bitterly. Not any more.

'Anyway,' says Barney. 'We're very glad to have you and Zelda living with us. Aren't we everyone?'

'Yes,' says the girl with the bandaged arm. So does Henryk and the girl with the curly hair and the toddler. The chewing-wood boy just keeps chewing his wood and the blinking boy just keeps blinking.

As I look around at their faces I can see how disappointed they are not to be hearing a story.

Too bad.

'Zelda,' says Barney. 'How about you telling us a story?'

Zelda sits up straight and smooths her tattered dress down

over her knees. I'm glad to see she's not still wearing her damp pyjamas.

'Once upon a time,' she says, 'two children lived in a castle in the mountains.'

She pauses, gives me a look to show me she's still cross, then continues.

'Their names were Zelda and William . . .'

Once I was living in a cellar in a Nazi city with seven other kids when I shouldn't have been.

My fever has gone.

I shouldn't be lying in bed, I should be out looking for Mum and Dad.

'Felix,' says Zelda, jumping on my sack. 'Wake up. It's time to wake up. Are you awake?'

'Yes,' I say. 'I am now.'

'You have to get up,' says Zelda. 'You have to tell us a story.'

I don't reply.

'You have to,' insists Zelda. 'Barney said I'm not allowed to any more. He said I start too many arguments. He's wrong, but that's what he said.'

I get up. I'm desperate to pee. While I was sick Barney let me pee in a bottle, but he must have taken it.

'Where's the toilet?' I say.

Zelda points. Through the gloom of the cellar I can just make out some wooden steps going up in one corner. Behind the steps is a bucket.

I stagger over to it. It's half full and pongs, but I'm desperate.

While I go, Zelda comes over and watches. I want to turn away, but I don't. Orphans deserve a bit of fun.

'Hurry up,' says Zelda. 'We're bored. We want a story.'

When I've finished I look around the cellar, but I can't see the others. There are needles of light pricking through the gloom and I can see several sack beds but no Barney and no other kids.

'Where's Barney?' I say.

'He's out getting us food,' says Zelda.

'Where are the other kids?' I say.

Zelda doesn't reply. I can see she's trying not to giggle. And trying not to look at a big untidy pile of coats in the middle of the cellar floor. The pile of coats seems to be giggling too.

Suddenly the coats fly up into the air. Huddled on the floor in a circle are the other kids, hands over their mouths, laughing themselves silly. Well, most of them are. The wood-chewing boy is just chewing his wood.

I'm not sure what's going on.

'It's a tent,' says Zelda. 'A story tent. Don't you know anything?'

The kids are all laughing at me now.

Suddenly I feel cross. Don't *you* know anything, I want to yell at them. Our parents are out there in a dangerous Nazi city. The Nazis are shooting people. They could be shooting our parents. A story isn't going to help.

But I don't. It's not their fault. They don't understand what it feels like when you've put your mum and dad in terrible danger. When the only reason they couldn't get a visa to go to America is because when you were six you asked the man at the visa desk if the red blotches on his face were from sticking his head in a dragon's mouth.

'Story,' says little Henryk, clapping his hands.

The others are looking up at me hopefully.

'Sorry,' I say. 'I haven't got time for a story right now. I have to go out.'

'You can't,' says Zelda. 'We're not allowed to.'

I ignore her. I look for the exit. The cellar has stone walls and a stone floor and no windows. The ceiling is made of wooden planks. The long needles of daylight are coming in through gaps between them. Up there must be the way out.

I climb the steps. At the top is a square door in the ceiling planks. The bolt is pulled back. I push the door, but it won't open.

'It's locked on the other side,' says the older girl with the bandaged arm. 'Barney locks it.'

I thump the door in frustration.

62

'Shhhh,' say most of the kids.

'We have to be quiet,' says Zelda. 'We're hiding.'

'Who from?' I say as I come down the steps. As soon as I say it, I remember the Nazis putting kids into a truck and I know it's a stupid question.

'Adolf Hitler doesn't like Jewish kids,' says the girl with the curly hair.

'Adolf Hitler?' I say, surprised. 'Father Ludwik says Adolf Hitler is a great man. He's in charge of Poland. He's the prime minister or the king or something.'

Zelda gives me her look.

'Adolf Hitler,' she says, 'is the boss of the Nazis. Don't you know anything?'

I stare at her.

'It's true,' says the blinking boy, blinking harder than ever.

I stare at all the kids, who are all nodding.

If they're right, this is incredible. I wonder if Father Ludwik has heard about this?

'That's why we have to hide,' says the girl with the bandaged arm. 'All the other Jewish kids around here have been taken away by the Nazis. Adolf Hitler's orders. And they never come back. The only kids left are the ones hiding like us.'

'Can we get on with the story now?' says Zelda.

I sit on the floor with them, my thoughts in a daze. Suddenly I'm thinking about another story. The one Mum and Dad told me about why I had to stay at the orphanage. They said it was so I could go to school there while they travelled to fix up their business. They told it so well, that story, I believed it for three years and eight months.

That story saved my life.

Zelda and the others are dragging the coats over our heads and making a tent.

'Tell us another story about the boy in the castle,' says Henryk.

'His name's William,' says Zelda.

'Shhh,' says the girl with the curly hair. She's brushing it with a hairbrush, over and over, which looks pretty painful. She smiles at me. 'Let Felix tell us.'

I try to think of something to tell them. Something to take our minds off our worries. Something to make us forget that the most important man in the whole of Poland hates us and our parents and our books.

'One morning,' I say, 'William wakes up in his castle. In his breakfast soup he finds a magic carrot.'

'A magic carrot,' interrupts Zelda. 'That means he gets three wishes.'

'It doesn't have to be three wishes,' says the blinking boy. 'It could just be one wish.'

'It's three,' says Zelda indignantly. 'If he holds the carrot right.'

I sigh. I'm not in a story mood. My brain is buzzing with too many other things.

'Look,' I say. 'Let's not have another fight. Why doesn't everybody just take it in turns to say what they'd wish for if they had a magic carrot.'

'I'd wish for my mummy and daddy,' says Zelda. 'Three times.'

'Apart from parents,' says the girl with the bandaged arm.

Everyone frowns and thinks hard.

'Tidy hair,' says the girl with curly hair, still brushing it non-stop.

'Your hair is tidy, Ruth,' says the girl with the bandaged arm. 'You've got lovely hair.'

Ruth gives a little smile but carries on brushing.

'What about you, Jacob?' says the girl with the bandaged arm to the blinking boy.

Jacob blinks hard. 'My dog,' he says.

'Me too,' says Henryk. 'And my grandma's dog.'

The girl with the bandaged arm gives the toddler a cuddle. 'What would you like, Janek?'

'Carrot,' says the toddler.

Everyone laughs.

'I'd wish to be alive,' says the girl with the bandaged arm.

Everyone laughs again, except me and the wood-chewing boy.

I don't get it.

'Her name's Chaya,' says Ruth, still brushing. 'It means alive in Hebrew.'

'Your turn,' says Chaya to me.

I can't think of anything except for Mum and Dad. And wishing Zelda's parents were still alive. But I can't say that either. I signal to the wood-chewing boy to have his go.

He doesn't reply. He doesn't even look at me. He just keeps on chewing the end of the piece of wood in his hands.

'You'd like the rest of your house, eh Moshe?' says Chaya gently.

Moshe nods as he chews, not looking up.

'Come on, Felix,' says Zelda. 'You have to have your turn. Use your imagination.'

I wait for my imagination to come up with something.

Anything.

It doesn't.

All I can think of is that if Adolf Hitler hates Jewish kids, perhaps God and Jesus and the Virgin Mary and the Pope do too.

'He's not going to tell us,' says Ruth.

'Come on,' says Henryk. 'Let's have a lice hunt.'

The kids throw the coats off and go and sit in the needles of daylight and start searching through each other's hair and clothes.

All except Zelda.

'You're mean,' she says to me.

'Sorry,' I say.

I flop down on my bed. My imagination doesn't want to be bothered with stories, not now. All it wants to do is plan how I'm going to get out of this place and find Mum and Dad before Adolf Hitler's Nazis kill them.

Once I escaped from an underground hiding place by telling a story. It was a bit exaggerated. It was a bit fanciful. It was my imagination getting a bit carried away.

It was a lie.

'Barney,' I whisper, tugging his sleeve as he creeps up the cellar steps.

He spins round, startled, and nearly drops his candle. He thought I was asleep like the other kids.

'I need to come with you,' I whisper.

Barney frowns.

I start to explain why I have to go with him.

He puts his finger on his lips and signals for me to follow him up the steps. I climb after him through the doorway in the ceiling. And find myself in a huge room full of dusty old machinery.

Barney puts his leather bag down, gently lowers the trap door and locks it with a padlock.

He sees me looking around and points to the machinery.

'Printing presses,' he says. 'For printing books. Not now. Before.'

I know what he means. Before the Nazis went right off books. And Jews.

'So,' says Barney quietly. 'Why do you need to come with me?'

I take a deep breath.

'I need to find my parents,' I say. 'Urgently. Because of my rare illness.'

Barney thinks about this. He gives me a look that I'm fairly sure is sympathetic.

This is going well.

'Mum and Dad have got my pills,' I say. 'For my rare illness. If I don't take the pills, my rare illness will get worse and I could die.'

Barney thinks about this some more.

'What exactly is this rare illness?' he asks.

Suddenly I realise what he's concerned about. The other kids catching it. And him.

'Don't worry,' I say. 'It doesn't invade other people.'

Barney's eyes are twinkling in the candlelight. He almost looks amused. I feel indignant. People shouldn't be amused by other people's rare illnesses.

'If I don't find Mum and Dad and take those pills in the next two hours,' I say, 'I'll get warts growing inside my tummy and my pee will turn green.'

I stop myself saying any more. I may have gone a bit too far already.

Barney is actually smiling now.

'Zelda's right,' he says. 'You are a good storyteller.'

Poop, I did go too far.

Barney suddenly looks serious.

'She also told me,' he says, 'that you haven't seen your parents for nearly four years.'

I feel myself blushing in the candlelight. What a stupid story-telling mistake. That was as stupid as Father Ludwik telling us Adolf Hitler is a great man.

Desperately I try to think of a way to make the story better. Would Barney believe me if I tell him that I only have to take the pills once every four years?

I don't think so. This is pathetic. I can't tell a decent story to save my life any more. Or Mum and Dad's.

Barney puts his hand on my shoulder and I wait to be escorted back down into the cellar.

But that doesn't happen. Barney hands me the candle, picks up his bag and steers me towards a big rusty door in the wall of the printing factory.

'I'm glad you want to come with me, Felix,' he says.

'Why?' I say, surprised.

Barney suddenly looks very serious.

'I have to confess something,' he says. 'I read one of the stories in your notebook.'

I stare at him, stunned. He just doesn't seem like the sort of person who'd read a private notebook without permission.

'I'm sorry,' he says. 'But I wanted to find out what I could about your parents.'

Before I can say anything about my stories being dumb and not true, Barney grips my shoulder and looks me right in the eyes.

'You're a very good storyteller,' he says.

I don't know what to say.

Before I can think of something, Barney goes on.

'The reason I'm glad you're coming with me, Felix,' he says, 'is because I need your help.'

We pause in the doorway of the printing factory while Barney looks up and down the dark street.

In the moonlight I can see his leather jacket has a small hole in the back. I wonder if it's a bullet hole.

Did Barney get shot once?

Did his family?

Is that why he's looking after other people's kids in a secret cellar?

It might not be a bullet hole. A candle flame could have done it, or a rat. Barney might be a teacher or something. The Nazis might have burnt all the books in his school so he brought some of the kids here to hide them.

'This is the dangerous part,' whispers Barney, still squinting up and down the street. 'If anyone sees us leaving this building, we're sunk.'

Or he could be a sailor.

'Come on,' says Barney. 'All clear. Let's go.'

*

The streets of the city are filthy, scraps of paper and rubbish everywhere. Some of the buildings have got bits missing from them. The whole place is deserted. I know it's night and everything, but we haven't seen a single person apart from a couple of dead bodies on a street corner.

I manage not to cry.

Barney makes us cross over to the other side, but it's alright, I've already seen they aren't Mum and Dad.

'Where are all the other people?' I say.

'Indoors,' says Barney. 'There's a curfew. That means everybody has to stay indoors after seven at night.'

We go down a narrow laneway with tall apartment buildings on both sides. I can't see a single person through any of the windows. I read once that cities have electric lights, but there doesn't seem to be much electricity going on around here.

Finding Mum and Dad isn't going to be easy, even if I can slip away from Barney while he's concentrating on getting food.

'What happens if people don't do the curfew?' I ask.

'They get shot,' says Barney.

I look at him in alarm. I can tell from his voice he's not joking.

He holds up his leather bag.

'We'll be alright,' he says.

I wonder what's in the bag. Money, maybe. Or something the Nazis need. I hope it's not guns they could use to shoot Jewish booksellers.

I change the subject.

'Why is there a curfew?' I ask.

Dad taught me to use every new word as much as possible after hearing it for the first time.

'This is a ghetto,' says Barney. 'It's a part of the city where the Jews have been sent to live. The Nazis make the rules here.'

I think about this.

Barney knocks on a door, and while we wait he turns to me with a serious expression.

69

'Felix,' he says. 'You might not be able to find your parents. I know that's a hard thing to hear, but you might not.'

It is a hard thing to hear.

Luckily he's wrong.

'The Jewish people who've been brought to the city,' I say, 'are they all in this ghetto or are there other ghetto curfew places as well?'

Barney doesn't answer.

Perhaps I didn't say the new words right.


A woman leads us into a back room in the apartment. There are several people in the room, all wearing coats and all standing around a bed. The man lying on the bed is wearing a coat too, and holding his head and groaning.

'Lamp, please,' says Barney.

Somebody hands Barney an oil lamp. He bends over the bed and looks into the man's mouth. The man groans even louder.

I glance at the other people. They don't look very well either, though none of them are groaning.

Barney opens his bag and takes out a bundle of metal poles and leather straps. He fits the poles together using little metal wheels to make a kind of robot arm. From his bag he takes the foot pedal from a Singer sewing machine like Mrs Glick used to have. He connects the poles to the pedal with the leather straps.

My imagination is in a frenzy. Is Barney going to show these people how to mend their clothes? Their coats are fairly ragged. Or is this a machine he's invented that helps people grow food in their own homes? There are lots of damp patches on these walls and these people do look very hungry.

After all, this is 1942, so anything's possible.

'Salt water,' says Barney.

While a couple of the people get water from a bucket, Barney attaches a short needle to the end of the robot arm and pedals the sewing machine thing with his foot. The straps make the needle spin round very fast with a loud humming noise.

Suddenly I realise what Barney has just put together.

A dentist's drill.

Barney gives the man in the bed a glass of salty water and a metal bowl.

'Rinse and spit,' he says.

The man does.

I stare in amazement. I take my glasses off and wipe them on my shirt and put them back on.

Barney is a dentist.

Mum went to a dentist once. Me and Dad met him in his waiting room. He was very different to Barney. He was a thin bald man with a squeaky voice who didn't do house calls.

'Felix,' says Barney. 'Over here, please.'

I jolt to attention. Barney wants me to help him. I've never been a dentist's assistant before. Will there be blood?

I squeeze through the people until I'm next to Barney. He's taken the top off the lamp and is holding the tip of the drill in the flame. Heat kills germs, I've read about that.

'Felix,' says Barney as he dips the drill tip into the water the man has spat into the bowl. 'Tell the patient a story, would you?'

The water bubbles as the drill cools. My brain is bubbling too, with confusion.

A story?

Then I get it. When Mum went to the dentist, she had an injection to dull the pain. Barney hasn't given this patient an injection. Times are tough, and there probably aren't enough pain-dulling drugs in ghetto curfew places.

Suddenly my mouth feels dry. I've never told anyone else a story to take their mind off pain. And when I told myself all those stories about Mum and Dad, I wanted to believe them. Plus I didn't have a drill in my mouth.

This is a big responsibility.

'Open wide,' says Barney.

He starts drilling.

'Go on, Felix,' he says.

The groans of the patient and the grinding of the drill and the smell of burning from the patient's mouth make it hard to concentrate but I force myself.

'Once,' I say, 'a boy called William lived in a castle in the mountains and he had a magic carrot.'

The patient isn't looking at Barney any more, he's looking at me.

'If the boy held the carrot right,' I go on, 'he could have three wishes. About anything. Including parents and cakes.'

Barney knocks on another door. A big door at the front of a big building.

'This one will be different,' he says to me. 'But you'll be fine.'

'I hope so,' I say.

My feet blisters are hurting and I'm a bit worried by the Nazi flag flapping over our heads.

Barney puts his hand on my shoulder.

'You did a really good job back there,' he says. 'Poor Mr Grecki was in a lot of pain, but your story helped him get through it. Well done.'

I feel myself glowing, which I haven't done for years, not since the last time I helped Mum and Dad dust the bookshelves and straighten up the folded-down corners of pages.

It's true, Mr Grecki was very grateful. He and his family looked very sad when I asked them if they'd seen Mum and Dad and they said they hadn't.

The door opens.

I nearly faint.

Glaring at us is a Nazi soldier.

Barney says something to him in Nazi language and points to our dentist bag. The soldier nods and we follow him in. As we climb some stairs, Barney whispers to me.

'This patient is German. Tell him a nice story about Germany.'

Suddenly I feel very nervous. I don't know much about

Germany. I think I read somewhere that it's completely flat and has a lot of windmills, but I could be wrong.

'I don't speak German,' I mutter to Barney.

'Doesn't matter,' says Barney. 'Say it in Polish and I'll translate.'

The soldier leads us into an upstairs room and I feel even more nervous.

The patient is a Nazi officer. Not the one who did the shooting when we arrived in the city, but he could be a friend of that one. He's sprawled in an armchair holding his face, and when he sees us he scowls and looks like he's blaming us for his toothache.

Barney sets up the drill. He doesn't ask for salt water. I think this is because the Nazi officer is swigging from a bottle. Whatever he's drinking smells very strong. He's doing a lot of rinsing but no spitting.

I don't understand. Why is Barney drilling a Nazi's teeth? And why doesn't the German Nazi army use its own dentists? Perhaps the officers don't like them because they're too rough and they use bayonets instead of drills.

Barney picks up a lamp and looks inside the Nazi officer's mouth.

That's amazing. I've never seen that before. The lamp is connected to a wire. It must be electric.

'Go on, Felix,' says Barney.

He wants me to start. My imagination goes blank. What story can I tell to a Nazi officer in a bad mood? I want to tell a story about how burning books and shooting innocent people makes toothache worse, but I'd better not risk that.

The soldier comes back in with a bulging cloth bag. Poking out the top is a loaf of bread with hardly any mould on it and some turnips and a cabbage.

'Thank you,' says Barney as he starts the drill.

I understand. This is why we're giving this Nazi dental treatment when we could be giving it to a poor Jewish person.

To earn food.

I think of the kids back in the cellar. I didn't tell them a story before, but I can tell one for them now.

'Once,' I say to the Nazi officer, 'two brave German book-sellers, I mean soldiers, were hacking their way through the African jungle. Their mission was to reach a remote African village and help mend a, um, windmill.'

Barney translates.

I start making up the most exciting and thrilling story I can, with lots of vicious wild animals and poisonous insects who say nice things about Adolf Hitler.

The Nazi officer seems to be interested. Well, he's not shooting anybody. But he could at any moment.

I try hard to stop my voice wobbling with fear.

I want to do a good job so this patient will be as grateful as the last one was. So that afterwards, when the drilling and the story are over, he'll feel warm and generous towards me.

That's when I'll ask him if he knows where Mum and Dad are.

Once a dentist stopped me from asking a Nazi officer about my parents and I was really mad at him.

I still am, even after a sleep and a long sit on the bucket.

I want to break this stupid toothbrush he made for me into tiny pieces. That's why I'm scrubbing my teeth so hard.

The Nazi officer was smiling by the time I was halfway through the story. By the time I'd described how the two German soldiers turned the windmill into a giant water pump and built a lake for the African kids to go ice skating on, he was laughing. He made me carry on with the story even after Barney finished drilling.

At the end the Nazi officer asked me to write the story down so he could send it home to his kids.

Of course I said yes.

I told him it would be in Polish and it would take me a couple of days. The Nazi officer didn't mind at all, just asked me to drop it round when it's finished. I don't think he's a friend of the other Nazi officer, the murderer. I think when he hears about what's happened to Mum and Dad he'll want to help them.

But before I could start telling him, Barney grabbed me and the bag of food and we left.

'Too dangerous,' Barney told me in the street, but he wouldn't say why.

This toothbrush is unbreakable. It's only wood and bristles, but Barney must have some dentist's secret of making it really strong.

'Felix,' says a muffled voice.

I look down.

Zelda has joined me at the teeth-cleaning bowl. Her mouth is already foaming with Barney's home-made toothpaste that he makes from chalk dust and soap.

'When you went out with Barney last night,' she says, 'did you find our parents?'

I don't know what to say.

Her eyes are shining hopefully above the foam and suddenly I feel terrible. Here's me moaning about waiting two days to have a conversation with a Nazi officer, and poor Zelda still doesn't even know her parents are dead.

Her face falls.

'You didn't find them?' she says.

I shake my head.

We look at each other. I try and think up a story about how parents aren't really that important, but I can't because they are.

'I know a place we can see them from,' says Zelda.

I smile sadly. At least she's learning how to use her imagination.

'Up there,' she says.

I look up to where she's pointing. A needle of daylight, bigger than the others, is coming in through a crack where one of the walls meets the ceiling.

'Jacob says that from up there he can see outside into the street,' says Zelda.

I sigh. Everyone's a storyteller these days.

'It's true,' says a voice behind me.

Jacob is climbing off his sack bed, blinking very indignantly. Several of the other kids are waking up too.

'It's easy,' says Jacob. 'You make a pile of beds and climb up. I did it last night.'

'He did,' says Zelda. 'But he wouldn't let me.'

I look at them both. I can see they're telling the truth. When people lie, their toothpaste foam droops.

'Let's do it now,' says Zelda excitedly.

I peer over at the other side of the cellar. Barney is still in bed, snoring. When he's been out at night he usually sleeps pretty late.

'Alright,' I say.

It's worth a try. And not just for me. It might be good for Zelda, too. She might see an aunty or uncle or something.

'I can't see my mummy and daddy yet,' says Zelda. 'Can you see yours?'

'Not yet,' I say.

I get a firmer grip with my bare feet on the wobbly pile of beds, hold Zelda's arm tighter so we don't both fall, press my glasses harder against the crack in the wall and try to see something that isn't feet and legs. That's the problem with looking out into the street at ground level, you don't get to see the tops of people.

It's very confusing. I can see hundreds of feet and legs milling around out there. With this many Jewish people in Poland, how come Mum and Dad's shop didn't do better?

'I can see my mummy's feet,' yells Zelda. 'Over there, in her brown shoes.'

'Shhh,' calls Chaya from down below. 'You'll wake Barney.'

'It's alright,' says Jacob, his voice strained from helping Chaya prop up the pile of beds. 'Barney's a heavy sleeper.'

Zelda's eyes are pressed to the crack in the wall.

'Over there,' she squeaks. 'Mummy's feet.'

I know how she feels. I thought I saw Dad's dark green trousers. Until I saw another pair. And then three more.

I try to see if any of the feet and legs look as if they're doing the sort of things that Mum and Dad do, like carrying big piles of books or having discussions about books or reading somebody else's book over their shoulder.

I can't tell. The feet and legs could be doing anything. I can identify those two pairs of legs over there. They belong to two men who are wrestling on the ground over a piece of bread. And those there belong to another man who's just collapsed and is lying on the cobbles while people step over him. But the rest of the feet and legs could belong to anybody. The only thing I can tell for sure is that none of them belong to kids.

I press my nose to the crack in the wall and try and get a whiff of Mum's perfume.

Nothing.

I cram my ear to the crack to try and hear Mum and Dad's voices.

All I can hear is trucks arriving and people yelling. Some of them sound like German soldiers.

Suddenly all the feet and legs are scattering and running away.

'Mummy,' yells Zelda.

She's jiggling up and down. The pile of beds underneath us is toppling.

'Look out,' yells Jacob.

I plummet towards the floor.

Luckily the beds break my fall. So does Jacob. When my head stops spinning and I find my glasses, I help him out from under a sack. And almost step back into Barney, who is standing there, hands on his hips, glaring at us.

I can't give him my full attention yet, not till I've made sure Zelda is alright. If she landed on this stone floor . . .

Phew, there she is, crawling around on her hands and knees.

'Where are my slippers?' she's saying. 'I need to put my slippers on so I can go and see Mummy.'

I look at how desperately she's searching and suddenly I know I have to tell her. I don't want to, and I don't know how to, but I have to. The poor kid can't go on like this. She needs to know the truth.

'You're sure they were both dead?' says Barney quietly as we watch the other kids put the beds back into position and Zelda put her slippers on.

I nod.

I tell him about the feathers I held under their noses.

'They'd been shot,' I say. 'So had the chickens.'

I try not to think about the blood.

78

Barney frowns.

'You're right,' he says. 'Zelda does need to know.'

I wait, but he doesn't say anything else.

'Will you tell her?' I say.

Barney frowns some more.

'I think it's better if you do it,' he says. 'You've both been through a lot together and she trusts you. And you were there.'

That's what I've been dreading he'd say.

'I don't know how to,' I say quietly.

Barney looks at me. I haven't noticed before how red his eyes are. Must be because he works at night a lot.

'Just tell her the story of what you saw,' he says. 'You don't have to make anything up.'

'Alright,' I say.

I wish I could make things up for Zelda. I wish I could tell her a happy story. About how my glasses were affected by the heat of the fire, and how her parents aren't really dead, and how they're just having a holiday on a desert island with a cake shop, and how they'll be coming back for her as soon as their suntans are completed.

But I can't.

I tell Zelda the story of what I saw.

She doesn't believe me.

'No,' she yells, throwing herself onto her sack.

Barney puts his hand gently on her shoulder. The other kids watch silently, their faces sad.

I tell her again, still without making anything up.

This time she doesn't yell. For a long time her body shakes in Barney's arms without any sound at all.

I'm trembling myself, partly at the memory of what I saw, and partly because, for Zelda, my story has made her parents dead.

Now several of the other kids are crying too.

Ruth stops brushing her hair and lets her tears run down her face.

'Once,' she whispers, 'some goblins hit my dad with sticks. They hit him with sticks till he died.'

Barney reaches over and squeezes her hand.

Jacob is sobbing too.

'Nana was burned,' he says, tears trickling through his blinks. 'I got home from school and they were all burned. Nana and Popi and Elie and Martha and Olek.'

Henryk stands up and kicks his bed.

'I hate goblins,' he says. 'They killed Sigi and cut his tail off.'

Chaya puts her good arm round him and holds him while he sobs. She lowers her gentle face and speaks quietly.

'Once a princess lived in a castle. It was a small castle, but the princess loved it, and she loved her family who lived there with her. Then one day the evil goblins came looking for information about their enemies. They thought the princess knew the information, but she didn't. To make her tell, the goblins gave the princess three wishes. Either they could hurt her, or they could hurt the old people, or they could hurt the babies.'

Chaya pauses, trembling, staring at the floor. I can see how hard it is for her to finish her story.

'The princess chose the first wish,' she says quietly. 'But because she didn't know any information, the goblins made all three wishes come true.'

We're all crying now. Moshe is still chewing his wood, but tears are running down his face too.

A whole cellar full of tears.

I take Chaya's hand for a while. Then I go over and Barney lets me hug Zelda. I can feel the sadness shaking her whole body.

All around me poor kids are crying for their dead families.

My tears are different.

I feel so lucky because somewhere out there I know my mum and dad are still alive.

Once I told Zelda a story that made her cry, so I lay on her sack with her for hours and hours until she fell asleep. Then I started writing down the African story for the Nazi officer until I fell asleep too.

Now Barney is shaking me.

'Felix,' he whispers. 'We've run out of water. I need you to help me find some.'

I sit up and put my notebook inside my shirt. I reach for my shoes and the rags to pack around my feet.

'Try these,' says Barney.

He hands me a pair of boots. I stare at them in the candle-light.

They're almost new. I've never had an almost new pair of boots before. When I was little Mum and Dad used to get my shoes from other families with bigger kids who liked reading.

I put the boots on.

They fit.

'Thanks,' I say. 'Where did you get them?'

I can see Barney doesn't want to tell me. I remember something he once said.

'You don't have to make anything up,' I add.

Barney smiles.

'I bought them,' he says. 'Three turnips.'

I stare at him, horrified. Three turnips is a fortune. We could have made soup for all of us with three turnips.

'Water hunters need good shoes for running,' says Barney. 'In case the water tries to get away.'

I look down at Barney's shoes. They're both split open and wound round with rope.

Barney sees me looking.

'Alright,' he says quietly. 'I'll tell you the truth. I got you the boots because everybody deserves to have something good in their life at least once.'

I don't know what to say. That is one of the kindest things I've ever heard, including in stories.

'Thanks,' I whisper. 'But . . .'

I'm confused. Surely Barney knows I've got lots of other good things in my life. More than anyone else in this cellar, probably.

Barney locks the trapdoor and I follow him through the dark printing factory, an empty bucket in each hand, my feet snug and grateful in my new boots.

As we get close to the big rusty door, Barney suddenly blows out the candle and puts his finger on my lips.

I can hear it too. Voices and footsteps out in the street.

It's after curfew time. Everybody's meant to be indoors.

We creep over to a window. Barney rubs a small patch on the dusty glass and we peep out.

The street is crowded with people, all trudging in the moonlight, all in the same direction. Jewish people, I can tell by the armbands on their coats. Some are carrying bags and bundles. They're so close I can hear their voices, even through the glass.

'Yes, but where?' says a woman wearing a scarf.

A man with his arm round her rolls his eyes. He looks like he's done it before, so he's probably her husband.

'I don't know exactly,' he says. 'The countryside. Does it matter where? For each day's work we get a loaf of bread and sausage and marmalade. That's all that matters.'

The husband and wife are too far away now and I can't hear them any more because their voices are mixed up with all the others.

A man with a loud voice is passing the window.

'Please,' he's saying. 'Which is it? Russia? Romania? Hungary? You must know where we're going.'

I shrink back. The person he's talking to is a Nazi soldier.

'Countryside,' says the soldier. 'Beautiful. Much food. Easy work.'

I look at Barney, to see if he's thinking what I'm thinking.

The Nazis are taking the Jewish people to the countryside to work. Farming, perhaps, or looking after sheep. Anything to get their minds off books, probably.

That means Mum and Dad will be going there.

'Barney,' I whisper. 'Can we go too? Zelda and Henryk and all of us?'

Barney looks as though this is the worst idea anybody has ever had in the history of the world.

'No,' he says.

'But it could be great,' I say. 'A farmer could let us live in his barn and we could make cheese and sell it.'

Barney isn't even listening, just peering out of the window.

The street outside is empty now. I can hear the last of the Jewish people and the Nazi soldiers fading into the distance.

'Come on,' says Barney, unchaining the big door. 'We've got water to find. Let's go.'

In the cool night air my thoughts are clear.

I don't say anything more about the countryside. I know what I'm going to do. Once me and Barney have found some water and got it back to the cellar, I'm going to finish writing my African story and give it to the Nazi officer and ask him which bit of the countryside Mum and Dad have been taken to.

Then I'm going to wake Zelda up and we'll go there on our own.

I don't believe it.

Barney just walked into an apartment without knocking. He just looked around the stairwell to make sure nobody was watching, pushed the door open and barged in.

Lucky the stairwell was deserted.

'Is this your apartment?' I ask him.

'No,' he says. He's saying that a lot tonight.

He stops in the hallway. His shoulders slump. I see what's caught his eye. On the floor is a Jewish candlestick, the type that holds a row of candles. It's completely squashed, as if somebody's stamped on it.

'This place belongs to friends of mine,' says Barney quietly.

I understand. They must have gone to work in the countryside and forgotten to lock up.

I follow Barney into a room. It's an unusual sort of room. I need a moment to take it all in.

The big leather chair.

The two sinks.

The robot-arm drill.

Now I understand. It's a dentist's surgery.

'See if the water's on,' says Barney.

I don't waste time. I take my buckets over to one of the sinks and turn the tap. Nothing.

'It's off,' I say.

Barney is rummaging in cupboards and stuffing things into his pockets. Metal syringes. Packets of needles. Small bottles filled with liquid.

'That's not water, is it?' I say, puzzled.

Barney looks at me and I get the feeling he wishes I hadn't seen what he's doing.

'It's a drug,' he says. 'Dentists use it to stop their patients feeling pain.'

'I know,' I say. 'My mum had it once.'

Barney comes over and crouches down so his face is level with mine.

'I don't want you or any of the others to touch this,' he says, holding up one of the little bottles. 'It's very dangerous. Only dentists should touch it.'

'Why is it dangerous?' I ask.

'If a person takes too much,' says Barney, 'they go into a very deep sleep and never wake up.'

Something about the way he says it makes me shiver. But at least his patients will have something else to dull their pain when I'm in the countryside with Mum and Dad and Zelda and can't tell them stories.

I remember why we're here.

'I'll look in the other rooms for water,' I say.

'There's a bathroom down the hall,' says Barney.

We go into the bathroom and straight away I can see we're in luck. The bath is full of water. I scoop some out with one of my buckets.

'Hang on,' says Barney, taking the bucket from me and tipping the water back. 'Somebody's had a bath in that. It's dirty. Better not risk it.'

I stare at the water, confused.

That's not dirty. It's just a bit soapy with a few hairs in it. One person's been in that, two tops. If Barney wants to see dirty water he should go to an orphanage on bath night. There's not even any grit in this as far as I can see.

'See if there's any food in the kitchen,' says Barney. 'I'll fill the buckets from this.'

He's lifting the lid off the toilet cistern. Which I have to admit is a good idea. Two buckets of clean water at least.

I go down the hall to the kitchen, wondering why there are cooking utensils on the hall floor.

In the kitchen things are even worse. The floor is covered with broken plates and bits of cooked food. I crouch down, wondering if Barney is going to be fussy about food that's been on the floor.

Then I realise there's someone else in the room.

Oh.

It's a little kid, about two, in a high chair.

I can't tell if it's a girl or a boy because there's too much blood on the little body.

Oh.

I scream for Barney.

He comes running in and he almost falls over himself when he

85

sees the poor horrible sight but then he grabs me and drags me out into the hall.

'It's a little kid,' I sob. 'They shouldn't shoot little kids.'

'Shhhh,' says Barney. He sounds like he's sobbing too. He pushes my face into his coat.

'Why didn't the parents do something?' I sob. 'Why didn't they take their kid to the countryside?'

Barney is shaking. He hugs me very hard.

'Sometimes,' he says, his voice shaking as well, 'parents can't protect their kids even though they love them more than anything in the world. Sometimes, even when they try their very hardest, they can't save them.'

I can feel Barney's tears falling onto me. For a while he doesn't say anything, just strokes my head.

I stroke his hand.

Something tells me he needs it too.

'Your mum and dad loved you, Felix,' says Barney. 'They did everything they could to protect you.'

Loved? Why is he saying that as if it's in the past?

'I'm going to find them,' I say. 'I'm going to live in the country-side with them.'

I feel Barney give a big painful sigh.

'There is no countryside,' he says quietly. 'The Nazis aren't taking anyone to the countryside. They're taking Jews away to kill them.'

I stare up at him.

What?

That's the stupidest story I've ever heard. Didn't he hear what the Nazi soldier said to the Jewish people outside the window?

I kick and struggle to get myself out of his grip so I can go and find Mum and Dad before the Nazis take them to the country-side. But Barney is holding me too tight. His arms are too strong. I can't get away.

'It's true, Felix,' he says. His voice sounds like he's at a funeral.

'How do you know?' I yell at him.

'Somebody escaped from one of the death camps,' he says. 'This man came to the ghetto to try and warn the rest of us.'

My head is hurting.

Death camps?

'You're making this up,' I yell at Barney. 'If it was true, you would have warned the people leaving tonight.'

I feel his chest heaving for a long time before he answers.

'They wouldn't have believed me,' he says. 'They didn't believe the man from the death camp. Not even after the Nazis killed him. And I need to be alive so I can take care of you and the others.'

It's on Barney's face, I can see it.

He's telling the truth.

Oh Mum.

Oh Dad.

My imagination goes into a frenzy, trying to think up ways for them to escape, places for them to hide, reasons why none of this has happened to them.

Every time I start to think of something I remember the poor little kid in the kitchen.

Barney is still holding me tight and I can feel the metal syringes in his coat pocket pressing against my cheek.

Suddenly I want him to stick one of the syringes into me so I can go into a deep sleep and never wake up and never feel this bad ever again.

Once I loved stories and now I hate them.

I hate stories about God and Jesus and Mary and that crowd and how they're meant to be taking care of us.

I hate stories about the beautiful countryside with much food and easy work.

I hate stories about parents who say they'll come back for their children and never do.

I roll over on my bed. I push my face into my sack so I can't hear Barney over at the other side of the cellar, reading some stupid story to the others. I never want to hear another story. I never want to write another story. I never want to read another book. What good have books ever done me and Mum and Dad? We'd have been better off with guns.

'Felix,' says a faint voice in my ear.

It's Zelda.

I ignore her.

'Are your parents dead too?' she asks.

I don't answer.

I feel her put something round my neck. It's her silver chain with the little heart on it.

'This is to make you feel better,' she says.

I don't want to feel better.

I don't want to feel anything.

I just want to be like the Nazi officer, the murderer one. Cold and hard and bored with people.

Zelda strokes my head.

I try to ignore that too. But I can't. There's something wrong. Her hand is hot.

Very hot.

I sit up and look at her. Her face is pale. But when I touch her cheek, her skin is burning.

'I've got a temperature,' she whispers. 'Don't you know anything?'

Then her eyes go funny and she flops down onto the floor.

'Barney, quick,' I yell, my voice squeaky with panic. 'Zelda's sick.'

'I don't like you going out alone,' says Barney.

I can see he doesn't. I've never seen him look so worried. All day while we took it in turns to wipe Zelda's hot skin with wet rags, Barney was telling us she was going to be alright. But ever since the other kids got exhausted and went to bed, he's been looking more and more worried.

'Chaya can't run with her bad arm,' he says. 'Jacob and Ruth and Moshe get too scared outside, and the others are too young.'

'I'll be alright on my own,' I say.

'I can't leave Zelda like this,' says Barney, dipping the rag into the bucket of water and pressing it gently to her face. 'But she needs aspirin. If we can't get her temperature down in the next few hours . . .'

He stops because Zelda's eyes flutter open.

'I'm hot,' she croaks.

I lift her cup to her white lips and she swallows a little.

'There'll be aspirin in the dental surgery we were in last night,' says Barney.

I don't say anything.

I try not to think of what's in the kitchen of that apartment.

'But if you don't want to go back there,' Barney says, 'you'll find empty apartments in most of the buildings. And you'll almost certainly find aspirin in one of them. In a bathroom or kitchen or bedside drawer.'

I nod. I know about aspirin. Mother Minka used to get headaches from praying too much.

'Are you sure you can do this?' asks Barney.

'Yes,' I say.

I know what Barney was going to say before Zelda opened her eyes. If we can't get her temperature down in the next few hours, she'll die.

I must find her some aspirin.

And there's something else I must bring back for her as well.


I slip quietly out of our building without anybody seeing me.

The ghetto streets are different tonight.

They're just as dark and scary and full of litter as always, but not so deserted. Nazi trucks are zooming around. German soldiers are running in and out of apartment blocks. In the distance I can hear shooting.

I creep into an empty apartment.

No asprin.

I try next door.

Yes. A whole jar.

But I haven't finished yet. There's something else I need to find.

All the apartments in this block seem to be empty. I can hear Nazis down the street but I haven't seen a single Jewish person.

I creep down yet another apartment hallway, holding the candle out in front of me so I don't trip over any of the toys or ornaments or smashed photos on the floor.

More gunshots in the distance.

This will have to be the last apartment. If I don't find it here, I'll have to give up.

I close my eyes as I step into the kitchen. I open them slowly. After last night I won't ever be able to go into a kitchen with my eyes open again.

This one's alright, except for a big dark stain on the floor that could be just gravy.

I ignore it and start opening cupboards.

Nothing in the top ones.

I bend down and start opening the bottom ones. Zelda's locket chain keeps getting caught on the cupboard doors. I toss it over my shoulder so it hangs down my back.

Two cupboards left.

Please God, Jesus, Mary and the Pope, if you're still on our side please let this be the one.

Yes.

There, lying next to a mouldy potato, something that will help Zelda just as much as the aspirin.

A carrot.

I know I should get out of this apartment as fast as I can. I know I should sprint down the stairs into the street and hurry along the darkest back alleys to the cellar so Zelda can have her aspirin and her carrot soup.

But I can't just yet.

Not now I've seen this bedroom.

It's exactly like the room I used to have at home.

The wallpaper is the same, the reading lamp is the same, the bookshelves are the same. The one thing that's different is that there are six beds crammed in here.

These kids have even got some of the same books.

I clamber over the beds and squeeze onto the floor and take a book from the shelf. *Just William* by Richmal Crompton. It's still one of my favourite books in the whole world. And probably one of Dodie's by now. As I open it I try not to remember Mum and Dad reading it to me.

Instead, I read a bit to myself. About William's dog. He's called Jumble and he's a mixture of about a hundred different dogs and William loves him even when he pees in William's new boots.

Mum and Dad said I can have a dog like Jumble one day.

Stop it.

Stop thinking about them.

William is training Jumble to be a pirate. That's what I love about William. He always stays hopeful, and no matter how bad things get, no matter how much his world turns upside down, his mum and dad never die.

Not ever.

I know I should be getting back, but I can't get up at the moment. All I can do is stay here on the floor, with *Just William* and Zelda's carrot, thinking about Mum and Dad and crying.


What's that noise?

It's dark. The candle must have burnt down. Oh no, I must have fallen asleep here on the floor.

The noise again, thumping. A dog growling.

Jumble?

No, there's somebody in the apartment.

Several people. Boots thumping. Torches flashing. Men shouting in another language.

Nazi soldiers.

Where can I hide?

Under the beds. No, every story I've ever read where somebody hides under a bed they get caught.

I know. Under the books.

I lie next to the bookcase and tilt it forward so all the books slide off the shelves and onto me. With one hand I arrange books over all the bits of me that feel uncovered. It's not easy in the dark. I pray to Richmal Crompton that I haven't missed any bits. Then I slide my hand under the pile and stay very still.

Bang.

The bedroom door is kicked open.

Torchlight stabs between the books.

I hold my breath. I can hear someone else breathing. Then footsteps, leaving the room.

I wait.

More banging and shouting in other rooms. Dogs barking. Getting further away. I think they've gone.

I wait more.

I can't hear them at all.

I scramble out from under the books. I strike a match and find *Just William* for Zelda and the others. Then I run. Down the hall. Out into the stairwell. Down the stairs. Skidding on the clothes and shoes that have been chucked around everywhere. Jumping over the cooking pots. And the musical instruments.

Oh no, I've tripped.

I'm falling.

Ow.

Quick, get up. I don't think I'm hurt. I've got my glasses. The carrot and the asprin are safe in my pocket. *Just William* is still in my hand.

That wasn't as bad as it could have been. Except for the torchlight that's suddenly dazzling me from the doorway of one of the ground floor apartments.

It's a Nazi soldier.

He's yelling at me. He's got a pile of clothes and stuff in a box clutched to his chest. He's aiming his torch at me and coming closer.

I put my hands up to show I'm not armed.

The soldier tucks his torch under his chin.

Why does he need a spare hand?

For his gun?

No, to grab *Just William* from me. He stares at it, frowning. He puts it in his box. Now he's staring at something else. On my chest. Zelda's locket, which is smashed and hanging off the chain in two halves. He peers at it, breathing smelly drink fumes out of his hairy nostrils.

Then he lets go of it and turns and sticks his head back into the apartment and starts yelling. I think he's calling to someone else. A William fan, maybe.

I don't wait to find out.

The gate to the back alley is open. I fling myself through it and run down the alley and into the next one, weaving from alley to alley, not stopping, going for the narrowest ones I can find, the ones not wide enough for a tank to squeeze down, or a troop carrier, or a Nazi soldier loaded up with stuff he's been looting.

I only stop when I suddenly find myself in a wide street, bright with moonlight, empty and silent.

I crouch down next to a wall, gasping for breath, and have a look at Zelda's locket to see what the soldier found so interesting.

One half of the locket is empty.

In the other half is a tiny photograph. A man and a woman standing in front of a Polish flag. Zelda's parents, they must be. Her poor dead parents. The woman has hair a bit like Zelda's, only shorter, and a face a bit like Zelda's, only older.

I rub some Nazi finger grease off the photo and see Zelda's father more clearly and the clothes he's wearing and I almost stop breathing even though I'm still desperate for air.

Zelda's father is wearing a uniform.

A Nazi uniform.


Thank you God, Jesus, Mary, the Pope and Richmal Crompton. I thought I was never going to find my way back, but I know where I am now.

This is the street next to where our cellar is.

If I can get past that corner without any Nazi patrols coming along, I'll be in our cellar in no time and Zelda can have her carrot soup and aspirin.

I know what you're thinking, God and Richmal and all the others. If Zelda's dad's a Nazi, does she deserve carrot soup and aspirin?

Yes.

She can't help what her father did. Plus he's dead now and so's her mum and I don't know if she's got any other living relatives but after what we've been through together that makes me one and I say yes.

Oh no. I can hear trucks. And soldiers shouting. And dogs barking.

Where are they?

I look around desperately.

They're not in this street.

I crouch by the building on the corner and peer into our street.

Oh.

The trucks are parked in front of our building.

Oh.

Nazi soldiers are aiming guns at the printing factory doorway. Dogs are straining on leads and snarling. Not dogs like Jumble. These are all dogs with only one type of dog in them.

Killers.

Somebody must have tipped the Nazis off. A disgruntled dental patient probably.

How can I warn Barney and the others? How can I get in there without being seen and help Barney find a secret way out that the Nazis don't know about and get the kids out in disguise if necessary and . . .

Too late.

I can hear other soldiers shouting and other dogs barking, inside the printing factory.

I can hear kids screaming.

It doesn't matter any more who sees me.

I run towards the cellar.

Once the Nazis found our cellar. They dragged us all out and made us walk through the ghetto while they pointed guns at us.

'Barney,' I whisper. 'Where are they taking us?'

Barney doesn't answer for a while. I know why. He's got little Janek on his chest and Henryk holding his hand and the other kids huddled around him and some of them are close to tears and he doesn't want to upset them any more. Ruth has lost her hairbrush. The Nazis wouldn't let Jacob bring his teddy bear. At least Moshe has still got his piece of wood to chew.

'We're going to the railway station,' says Barney at last.

'Will there be water there for Zelda?' I ask.

'Yes,' he says.

I hope he's right. She's on my back, hot and limp, and dawn's just starting, and if we can't give her the aspirin soon she's going to burn up.

'Is the station far?' I ask Barney.

'Cheer up everyone,' says Barney, ignoring me. 'It's a beautiful summer day. We're going on an outing. Let's all enjoy it. Has everyone got their toothbrush?'

The other kids all hold up their toothbrushes.

The Nazi soldiers are staring. They probably haven't seen unbreakable toothbrushes before.

'I've lost my toothbrush,' whispers Zelda in my ear.

'It's OK,' I say. 'You can borrow mine.'

This makes me extra glad I was able to get into the cellar and grab Zelda and my stuff before the Nazis dragged me back out. Even though Zelda is pretty heavy and I think the station probably is a long way. When grown-ups go cheerful on a trip it means you won't be getting there for ages.

It can also mean when you do get there you'll be killed.

I tilt my head back and give Zelda a kiss on the cheek so she won't know I'm having scary thoughts.

One thing is puzzling me.

If the Nazis are going to kill us, why didn't they shoot us in the cellar? It would have been much easier for them. Now they have to march us through the streets in the hot sun. They look really grumpy in their thick uniforms.

I get it.

They must want other people to see us. Other Jewish people hiding in the buildings along these streets. Peeping out and seeing us and knowing it's hopeless and deciding they might as well give themselves up.

I straighten up and try not to look hopeless.

You know how when things are really bad and you feel like curling up and hiding but instead you take deep breaths and the air reaches your brain and helps you think better?

That's happening to me.

I've just thought of a way of saving Zelda's life.

'Zelda,' I whisper. 'Can you see I'm wearing your locket round my neck?'

'Yes,' she says.

'I want you to take it off me and put it on you,' I say.

She doesn't touch it.

'I gave it to you,' she says.

'Please,' I say. 'This is very important.'

She hesitates.

'It's a lovely gift,' I say. 'It makes me feel not quite so bad about my mum and dad. But now I want to give it back to you. Please let me.'

Zelda hesitates some more. Then I feel her hot little fingers reaching for the chain.

*

The railway yard is crowded with Jewish people standing and sitting in queues, waiting to get onto a train that stretches so far along the track I can't see the front of it or the back.

'Wow,' says Henryk. 'I've never been on a train before.'

Several of the other kids say they haven't either.

'We'll all be going on it soon,' says Barney. 'Who's excited?'

The kids all say they are, except for Moshe who just chews his wood and Zelda who just clings to my neck.

I'm glad the other kids are excited because it means they haven't seen what I can see now that I've wiped my glasses.

Nazi soldiers with dogs are pushing people onto the train really roughly. It's not a normal sort of train. The carriages are like big boxes with sliding doors. Some people don't want to get on and the Nazi soldiers are hitting them with sticks and whips.

Halfway along our queue a woman collapses onto the ground.

A Nazi soldier steps over to her and shoots her.

Oh.

'No,' screams Ruth.

'Make a tent,' says Barney. 'Everyone make a tent.'

Chaya and Jacob and Barney take their coats off and we all huddle together and the others put their arms into the air and Barney throws the coats over us.

I can't put my arms up because I'm holding Zelda on my back.

Barney reaches into his coat pocket above our heads and takes out the water bottle Mr Kopek gave me. It's been filled again. Barney passes it to the others.

'Just one sip each,' he says. 'Felix, did you get the aspirin?'

I nod.

Barney takes Zelda into his arms.

'Crush two into powder,' he says.

I grind the aspirin into my palm with my thumb. Barney makes sure each person only has a small sip of water and that there's some left in the bottle.

'Put the powder into the water and shake it up,' he tells me.

I do. I hand the bottle to Barney. He puts it to Zelda's lips.

'This won't taste nice,' he says. 'But you must drink it.'

She does, screwing up her face.

While she's busy drinking, I huddle closer to Barney.

'Look at this,' I say.

I show him the locket round Zelda's neck. He stares at the photo of her parents. Even in the hot gloom of our tent I can see he knows what it means. Chaya does too.

'I hate Polish people who join the Nazis,' she mutters.

Barney sighs. 'The Polish resistance must have killed them,' he says softly.

I don't know what resistance means, but this isn't the time to learn new words. There's something much more urgent we need to do.

'We must tell someone,' I say.

Barney nods.

'Stay in the tent,' he says to the others. 'We'll be back soon.'

Barney and Zelda and me crawl out of the tent.

I squint around the railway yard, looking for someone to tell, someone who can save Zelda.

Suddenly I see him.

Thank you God, Jesus, Mary, the Pope and Richmal Crompton, you are on our side after all.

It's the Nazi officer who was the dental patient. The one who wants my African story for his kids. I pull my notebook from my shirt and rip out the pages with the African story on it. It's only half finished, but these are tough times and I'm sure he'll understand.

I start to go over to him.

Barney grabs me. 'If you leave a queue in a place like this,' he says, 'you get shot.'

'Sorry,' I say.

That was stupid, I wasn't thinking.

'Excuse me,' I yell at the Nazi officer, waving the pages. 'I've got your story. Over here.'

He doesn't hear me at first, but I shout some more until Barney stops me, and when a soldier comes over and starts yelling at me even louder and pointing his gun at my head, the officer looks up and sees the pages I'm waving and comes over himself.

He orders the soldier away.

'Here it is,' I say. 'The story you wanted.'

I hold the pages out to him. He takes them, looks at them, smiles, folds them up and puts them in his pocket.

'Also,' I say, 'there's something else.'

I point to the locket hanging round Zelda's neck.

Barney puts his hand on my arm. I remember the Nazi officer doesn't speak Polish.

The officer is staring at the locket. Barney lifts it up so he can see it better and starts speaking to him in German.

'That's my mummy and daddy,' says Zelda quietly to the Nazi officer. 'They're dead. The Polish assistance killed them.'

The Nazi officer looks at the photo for a long time. Then he looks at Zelda and at Barney and at me and at the tent.

He points to Zelda and Barney and then points to the railway yard gate.

Yes.

He's saying they can go.

Barney speaks to him some more in German, pointing to me and the other kids, who are peering out of the tent. He must be asking if we can go too.

The Nazi officer shakes his head. He points to Zelda and Barney again.

'Go with Zelda,' I say to Barney.

He ignores me. He says more things to the Nazi officer. I don't speak German, but I can tell he's pleading.

The Nazi officer shakes his head again. He's starting to look angry.

'Go with Zelda,' I beg Barney. 'I'll look after the others.'

The other kids start screaming. Nazi soldiers have grabbed

them and are dragging them towards the train. One starts dragging me.

As I'm being lifted up I see Barney push Zelda's hand into the Nazi officer's hand. Barney comes running after us, yelling at the soldiers to leave us alone. Zelda struggles to get away from the Nazi officer, kicking and screaming.

'Felix,' she yells. 'Wait.'

Now I can't see her. I'm in one of the train boxcars, lying on the floor and on other people. I grab my glasses. Henryk lands on top of me. Other kids as well. Ruth is crying. Chaya is holding her bad arm. Jacob is holding little Janek to his chest. Other people are being thrown on top of us.

Through the tangle of people I see Barney climbing into the boxcar, crawling towards us, asking if we're alright.

'Zelda,' I yell, hoping she can hear me in the total confusion. 'Goodbye.'

But it's not goodbye. A soldier throws Zelda into the boxcar on top of us. Then he slides the door closed with a crash.

'Zelda,' I moan. 'Why didn't you stay?'

'I bit the Nazi,' she says. 'Don't you know anything?'

I put my arm round Zelda and we lie here shivering.

Outside people are screaming and dogs are barking and soldiers are shouting but the loudest noises are the gunshots.

Bang. Bang. Bang.

Suddenly I realise they're not gunshots. I realise what the soldiers are doing. They're nailing the train door shut.

Once I went on my first train journey, but I wouldn't call it exciting, I'd call it painful and miserable.

There are so many of us in this boxcar that most of us have to stand up. Every time the train lurches, we lurch too and squash each other.

'Sorry,' I say each time to the people around me.

At least the little kids have got a space to sit down. Not all the people wanted to make room at first, because it meant the rest of us were more squashed, but Barney had a word to them and then they did.

'Sorry.'

Barney's got all the kids doing a lice hunt, which is a really good idea. We're packed in so tight here we could be giving each other lice without knowing it. Plus nothing passes the time on a long journey like a lice hunt.

Zelda isn't doing it, she's asleep.

Please God and the others, let her get better.

'Sorry.'

I try and make myself thinner to give some of the old people more space. It must be terrible for them. I'm young and I'm used to going without food and water and space.

'Sorry.'

'For God's sake,' yells a man near me. 'Stop saying sorry.'

Barney gives the man a long look.

'He's just a kid,' says Barney. 'Give him a break.'

The man looks like he's going to explode.

'A break?' he says. 'A break? Who's giving us a break?'

I know how the man feels. We've been travelling for hours and this train hasn't stopped once for a toilet break. People can't hold it in for ever, which is why we've had to start going in the corner of the carriage.

Well, Ruth and Moshe and three of the other people have. Everyone else is desperately trying to hold it in because there isn't any toilet paper.

'Are we there yet?' says Henryk, looking up from Ruth's hair.

'Be patient,' says Barney softly. 'Don't let those lice get away.'

'Will we be there soon?' says Jacob, looking up from little Janek's wispy hair and blinking hopefully.

'Shhhh,' says Barney.

I know what he's worried about. People who hate 'sorry' probably hate 'are we there yet' just as much. Specially people who are trying not to think about two other words.

The two that Barney used once.

Death camp.


'Sorry,' says an elderly woman as she struggles through the rest of us to the toilet corner. 'Sorry, I have to.'

We all turn away, those of us that can, to give her some privacy.

Poor woman.

Having no toilet paper isn't so bad when you're young and you've lived in an orphanage a long way from the shops and you're used to sometimes just letting poo dry on you and then getting on with things. But for older people who are used to tradition it must be awful.

I start thinking about poor Mum and Dad and whether they had to go without toilet paper when they made this trip.

I don't want to think about them making this trip. About them arriving and getting off the train and . . .

Please, I beg my imagination. Give me something else to think about. I can't help Barney look after the kids if I'm a weeping wreck.

Suddenly an idea hits me.

Of course.

I reach into my shirt and after a struggle because a couple of other people's elbows are in my chest I manage to pull out my notebook and rip out a couple of blank pages.

'Here,' I say to the woman in the corner. 'Use this.'

The other people pass it over to her and when she sees what it is she starts crying.

'It's alright,' I say, 'I haven't written on it.'

Barney squeezes my arm.

'Well done, Felix,' he says.

Lots of other people hold their hands out for toilet paper and I rip pages out for them as well. Now I've only got pages left with stories on them. Stories I wrote about Mum and Dad.

I look over at the people crouching in the corner, at the relief on their faces.

Mum and Dad would understand.

I rip the rest of the pages out of my notebook and wriggle past everyone to the toilet corner. I grab a metal bolt poking out of a plank in the wall. If I push the bolt through the pages, they'll hang there and people can tear off a page or two as they need them.

The bolt comes away in my hands.

The wooden plank is rotten.

I kick at it and part of my foot goes through.

'Barney,' I yell.

People are looking at what I've done. A couple of men pull my foot out of the plank and start kicking at the wood themselves. Their big boots make a much bigger hole.

Barney and the men pull at the side of the hole with their hands and more bolts fly out of the wood and suddenly the whole plank comes away.

I can see green countryside speeding past.

One of the men tries to squeeze through.

'Wait,' says Barney. 'We need to make the hole bigger. If you roll out you'll fall on the track. You need to be able to jump clear.'

Everyone squashes back to give Barney and the men more room. Barney jams the plank into the hole and the men push till their faces are bulging.

A second plank splinters and the men kick it out.

They do the same with a third.

'That's enough,' yells one of the men. He takes a couple of steps back and dives out through the hole. The second man follows him.

'Come on,' yells someone else. 'We're free.'

More people fling themselves through the hole.

I grab Barney.

'Won't the Nazis stop the train and catch them?' I say.

Barney shakes his head. 'They won't let anything interfere with their timetable,' he says. 'They don't need to.'

We all freeze, startled, as gunshots echo through the train.

Lots of gunshots.

'They've got machine guns on the roof,' says Barney, hugging the little kids to him. 'Easier for them than stopping the train.'

People are peering out of the hole, trying to see what happened to the ones who jumped.

'Look,' screams a woman. 'Some of them have made it. They're running into the woods. They're free.'

I grab Barney again.

'We've got to risk it,' I say.

I can see Barney doesn't agree. I can see why. Henryk and Janek are in tears. Ruth and Jacob are clinging to each other, terrified. Moshe has stopped chewing his wood.

I crouch down and in as calm a voice as I can, I tell them a story. It's a story about some kids who jump off a train and land in a soft meadow and a farmer comes and takes them home and they live happily on the farm with his family and get very good at growing vegetables and in the year 1972 they invent a carrot that cures all illnesses.

I pull Zelda's carrot out of my pocket to show them it's possible.

But I can see that most of them aren't convinced.

'Felix,' says Barney. 'If you want to risk it, I won't stop you. But I have to stay with the ones who don't want to.'

'No,' I say, pleading. 'We all have to jump.'

'I don't want to,' says Ruth, clinging to Barney.

'I don't want to,' says Jacob.

'I don't want to,' says Henryk.

'I don't want to,' says Janek.

It's no good. I know I'm not going to change their minds. You can't force people to believe a story. And I can see Barney isn't going to try. Some people would make kids risk machine gun bullets and broken necks when they don't want to, but not Barney.

'I want to,' says a voice, and a warm hand squeezes mine.

It's Zelda.

'Are you sure?' says Barney, feeling her forehead.

'Yes,' says Zelda.

'You're sick,' says Ruth.

'I'm better,' says Zelda.

Barney looks like he's not sure.

'She wants to risk it, Barney,' I say.

'See,' says Zelda. 'Felix knows.'

Chaya hands little Janek to Barney.

'I want to risk it too,' she says.

Barney looks at her for a moment.

'Alright,' he says quietly. 'Anyone else?'

The rest of the kids shake their heads.

I check that Mum and Dad's letters are safely inside my shirt. And my toothbrush. Then I hug Ruth and Jacob and Henryk and Janek and Moshe.

And Barney. Now I've got my arms round him, I don't ever want to let go.

But I have to.

'If you see my mum and dad,' I say, 'will you tell them I love them and that I know they did their very best?'

'Yes,' says Barney.

His eyes are as wet as mine.

'Thank you,' I say.

I touch his beard for a moment and behind us I can hear some of the other people in the boxcar crying.

Barney hugs Zelda and Chaya. They hug the other kids.

'Only two wishes this time,' I say to the ones who are staying. 'But at least we got to choose.'

Moshe, chewing again, smiles sadly.

I take hold of Zelda with one hand and Chaya with the other, and we jump.

Once I lay in a field somewhere in Poland, not sure if I'm alive or dead.

You know how when you jump off a moving train and Nazis shoot at you with machine guns and you see sharp tree stumps coming at you and then you hit the ground so hard you feel like you've smashed your head open and bullets have gone through your chest and you don't survive even though you prayed to God, Jesus, Mary, the Pope and Richmal Crompton?

That's what's happened to poor Chaya.

She's lying next to me on the grass, bleeding and not breathing.

I reach out and touch her face. When I feel a bit better I'll move her away from the railway line to somewhere more peaceful. Under that tree over there with the wild flowers near it.

Zelda is lying next to me too. We cling on to each other, and watch the train speed away into the distance.

'Are you alright?' I say.

'Yes,' she says. 'Are you?'

I nod. My glasses are alright too.

'We're lucky,' she says sadly.

'Yes,' I say. 'We are.'

I think about Barney and what was in his jacket pocket when I hugged him just now.

Metal syringes.

I know he won't let the others suffer any pain. He's a good dentist. He'll tell them a story about a long peaceful sleep, and it'll be a true story.

I don't know what the rest of my story will be.

It could end in a few minutes, or tomorrow, or next year, or I could be the world's most famous author in the year 1983, living in a cake shop with a dog called Jumble and my best friend Zelda.

However my story turns out, I'll never forget how lucky I am.

Barney said everybody deserves to have something good in their life at least once.

I have.

More than once.

*Then*

Then we ran for our lives, me and Zelda, up a hillside as fast as we could.

Which wasn't very fast.

Not even with me holding Zelda's hand and helping her up the slope.

You know how when you and two friends jump off a train that's going to a Nazi death camp and you nearly knock yourself unconscious but you manage not to and your glasses don't even get broken but your friend Chaya isn't so lucky and she gets killed so you bury her under some ferns and wild flowers which takes a lot of strength and you haven't got much energy left for running and climbing?

That's how it is now for me and Zelda.

'My legs hurt,' says Zelda.

Poor thing. She's only six. Her legs aren't very big. And she's wearing bedtime slippers which aren't very good for scrambling up a steep hill covered with prickly grass.

But we can't slow down.

We have to get away before another Nazi train comes along with machine guns on the roof.

I glance over my shoulder.

At the bottom of the hill, the railway track is gleaming in the sun like the shiny bits on a Nazi officer's uniform.

I peer up the slope.

At the top is a thick forest. When we get up there we'll be safe. We'll be hidden. The next Nazi train won't be able to see us as long as Zelda doesn't yell rude things at them.

If we can get up there.

'Come on,' I say to Zelda. 'Keep going. We mustn't stop.'

'I'm not stopping,' says Zelda indignantly. 'Don't you know anything?'

I know why Zelda's cross. She thinks I'm lucky. I am. I'm ten. I've got strong legs and strong boots. But I wish my legs were stronger. If I was twelve I could carry Zelda on my back.

'Ow,' she says, slipping and bashing her knee.

Gently I pull her up.

'Are you OK?' I say.

'No,' she says as we hurry on. 'This hill is an idiot.'

I smile, but not for long.

Suddenly I hear the worst sound in the world. The rumble of another train in the distance, getting closer.

I peer up the slope again.

The forest is too far. We won't get there in time. If the Nazis see us on this hillside we'll be easy targets. My shirt's got rips in it that are flapping all over the place. Zelda's dress is lots of colours but not camouflage ones.

The train is getting very close.

'Lie flat,' I say, pulling Zelda down onto the grass.

'You said we mustn't stop,' she says.

'I know,' I say. 'But now we mustn't move.'

'I'm not moving,' says Zelda. 'See?'

We're lying on our tummies, completely still except for a bit of panting. Zelda is clinging on to me. Her face is hot against my cheek. Her hands are gripping my arm. I can see that one of her fingernails is bleeding from pulling up ferns for Chaya.

The noise of the train is very loud now. Any second it'll be coming round the bend below us. I wish we had ferns to hide under. Near us is a rabbit hole. I wish me and Zelda were rabbits. We could crouch deep in the hillside and eat carrots.

But we're not, we're humans.

The Nazi train screeches round the bend.

Zelda grips me even tighter.

'Felix,' she says. 'If we get shot, I hope we get shot together.'

I feel the same. I squeeze her hand. Not too tight because of her fingernail.

I wish we were living in ancient times when machine guns were really primitive. When you'd be lucky to hit a mountain with one even up close. Instead of in 1942 when machine guns are so super-modern they can smash about a thousand bullets into an escaping kid even from the top of a speeding train.

Below us the Nazi train is clattering like a thousand machine guns.

I put my arm round Zelda and pray to Richmal Crompton to keep us safe.

'Zelda isn't Jewish,' I tell Richmal Crompton silently. 'But she still needs protection because Nazis sometimes kill Catholic kids too. Specially Catholic kids who are a bit headstrong and cheeky.'

Richmal Crompton isn't holy or anything, but she's a really good story-writer and in her books she keeps William and Violet Elizabeth and the other children safe even when they're being extremely headstrong and cheeky.

My prayer works.

No bullets smash into our bodies.

'Thank you,' I say silently to Richmal Crompton.

Down the hill I see the train disappearing round the next bend. I can tell it's another death camp train full of Jewish people. It's got the same carriages our train had, the ones that look like big wooden boxes nailed shut.

On the roof of the last carriage there's a machine gun, but the two Nazi soldiers sitting behind it are busy eating.

'Come on,' I say to Zelda as soon as the train is out of sight.

We get to our feet. At the top of the hill the forest waits for us, cool and dark and safe.

I don't know how long till the next train, so we have to move fast. We might not be so lucky with the next one. The Nazi machine gun soldiers might not be having an early dinner.

I grab Zelda's hand and we start scrambling up the slope again.

Zelda trips on a rabbit hole and almost falls. I save her but accidentally almost yank her arm out of its socket.

'Sorry,' I say.

'It's not your fault,' says Zelda. 'It's the rabbits' fault. Don't you know anything?'

She lets go of my hand and holds her shoulder and her dark eyes fill with tears.

I put my arms round her.

I know her shoulder isn't the only reason she's crying. It's also because of what's happened to our parents and our friends. And because the most powerful army in the history of the world is trying to kill us.

If I start thinking about all this I'll end up crying myself.

Which is not good. People who are crying can't climb hillsides very fast. I've seen it happen.

I try to think of a way to cheer us both up.

'In the next valley there might be a house,' I say. 'With a really kind cook. Who's made too much dinner and who's looking for people to help eat the extra platefuls of delicious stew.'

'Not stew,' says Zelda. 'Sausages.'

'OK,' I say. 'And boiled eggs.'

'And marmalade,' says Zelda. 'On bread fingers.'

It's working. Zelda has stopped crying. Now she's pulling me up the hill.

'And bananas,' I say.

'What's bananas?' says Zelda.

While we climb I tell her about all the exotic fruit I've read about in stories. That's another way I'm lucky. I grew up in a bookshop. Zelda didn't, but she's still got a really good imagination. By the time we get to the top of the hill, she's fairly certain the cook has got mangoes and oranges for us as well.

We plunge into the forest and hurry through the thick undergrowth. It feels really good to be in here with the ferns and bushes and trees sheltering us. Specially when I suddenly hear a scary sound in the distance.

Machine guns.

We stop and listen.

'Must be another train,' I say.

We look at each other. The machine guns go on and on, not close but still terrifying.

I don't say anything about train people trying to escape, in case they're getting shot dead. There's only so much getting shot dead a little kid like Zelda can take.

'Do you want to rest?' I say to her.

What I actually mean is does she want to hide, but I don't say that either because I don't want her to feel even more scared.

'No,' says Zelda, pushing ahead. 'I want my dinner.'

I know how she feels. Better to get further away from the railway line. Plus it's almost evening and we haven't eaten all day.

I follow her.

At last the distant shooting stops.

'The house is this way,' says Zelda, scrambling through a tangle of creepers.

That's the good thing with stories. There's always a chance they can come true. Poland is a big country. It's got a lot of Nazis in it, but it's also got a lot of forests. And a lot of houses. And quite a few sausages.

'Has the cook got chocolate?' says Zelda after a while.

'Maybe,' I say. 'If we think about it really hard.'

Zelda screws up her forehead as we hurry on.

By the time we get to the other side of the forest, I'm pretty sure the cook has got chocolate, a big bar of it.

We pause at the edge of the trees and squint down into the next valley. My glasses are smudged. I take them off and polish them on my shirt.

Zelda gives a terrified squeak, and grabs me and points.

I put my glasses back on and peer down at what she's seen.

Zelda isn't pointing at a distant house belonging to a kind cook, because there aren't any houses. She's pointing at something much closer.

A big hole in the hillside. A sort of pit, with piles of freshly dug earth next to it. Lying in the hole, tangled up together, are children. Lots of them. All different ages. Some older than me, some even younger than Zelda.

'What are those children doing?' says Zelda in a worried voice.

'I don't know,' I say.

I'm feeling worried too.

They look like Jewish children. I can tell because they're all wearing white armbands with a blue blob that I'm pretty sure is a Jewish star.

Trembling, I give my glasses another clean.

'This wasn't in your story,' whispers Zelda.

She's right, it wasn't.

The children aren't moving.

They're dead.

That's the bad thing with stories. Sometimes they don't come true and sometimes what happens instead is even worse than you can imagine.

I try to stop Zelda seeing the blood.

Too late.

She's staring, mouth open, eyes wide.

I go to put my hand over her mouth in case she makes a noise and the killers are still around.

Too late.

She starts sobbing loudly.

Directly below us on the hillside, several Nazi soldiers jump to their feet in the long grass. They glare up the hill towards us. They throw away their cigarettes and shout at us.

I know I should get Zelda back into the undergrowth, out of sight, but I can't move.

My legs are in shock.

The Nazi soldiers pick up their machine guns.

**Then** the Nazi soldiers started shooting at us and suddenly I could move again.

And think.

Grab Zelda.

Get away.

Hide.

Bullets are cracking into the tree trunks all around us. Bits of flying bark are stinging us in the face.

We turn and run back into the forest, jumping over logs, crashing through bushes, weaving around brambles, slithering in and out of tangled undergrowth, scrambling over rocks.

I try not to think about Zelda's poor feet in their bedtime slippers or about the poor dead children in their pit.

Hide.

'Over there,' I say to Zelda. 'That big clump of bushes.'

We wriggle under thorny branches and through thick layers of ivy. With my hands I dig down into last year's leaves, which are damp and soft and even a bit warm when you get deep enough.

Zelda digs too and doesn't complain once about her sore finger.

We don't stop until we've made a secret place that is dark and quiet where we lie trembling and listening.

Zelda holds my hand.

I can hear Nazi soldiers shouting. Their boots are thudding as they run around in the forest looking for us. Nazi dogs are barking.

You know how when you're living in a secret cellar in a city ghetto with lots of other kids and you all make a tent with your coats and snuggle inside and try to feel cosy and safe even though outside the streets are full of Nazis?

That's what me and Zelda are doing in this burrow, except we haven't got our coats any more.

We haven't got our friends from the cellar either. I say a silent prayer to Richmal Crompton. I ask her to protect our friends who are still on that terrible train. Please don't let them end up in a pit too.

Suddenly, thinking about that makes me not want to stay cosy and safe in this hole.

I want to jump out and find a sharp stick and creep up on those Nazis and stab them hundreds of times until their guts are hanging out and they beg for mercy and promise never to shoot people ever again. But I wouldn't show them mercy, I'd keep stabbing them and stabbing them and –

'You're hurting me,' whispers Zelda.

I realise I'm squeezing her hand really tight.

'Sorry,' I say, letting go.

I don't tell her what I was thinking. She's seen enough killing and violence today without me going on about more.

I feel ashamed and push the angry thoughts out of my mind.

Zelda holds my hand again.

'It's OK,' she says. 'I'm frightened too.'

In the distance the soldiers are still shouting. I don't speak German, but you don't have to understand the words to know when somebody wants to kill you.

'Don't worry,' I whisper to Zelda. 'The Nazis won't find us.'

I hope I'm right.

I can't see Zelda in the gloom, but I know she's thinking about something. I can tell from her serious breathing in my ear.

'Felix,' she says at last. 'Those children who were shot. Where are their mummies and daddies?'

I have to wait a bit before I reply because just thinking about those children makes me feel very sad and upset. I try to imagine them covered up with ferns and wild flowers, but it doesn't help.

'I don't know,' I say quietly. 'I don't know where their mummies and daddies are.'

It's the truth. They could be dead with bullets in them like Zelda's parents, or sent to a death camp like mine, or they could be alive and just discovering the terrible thing that's been done to their children.

I don't say these things out loud. Zelda is still trembling and I don't want to upset her even more.

'Did some Nazis make those children dead?' asks Zelda.

I hesitate again.

I know why she's asking.

'Probably,' I say. 'But we can't be certain. We didn't actually see them do it.'

Zelda's breathing is even louder now and I can tell she knows they did.

'I hate Nazis,' she says.

Poor thing. She must feel awful. Her mum and dad were Nazis before the Polish resistance killed them. I've seen the photo of her father in a Nazi uniform in the locket round her neck. When I think about my mum and dad being dead, at least I know they were Jewish and innocent. Poor Zelda has to think about her parents being part of a gang of brutal murderers.

'Your mummy and daddy loved you very much,' I say to her gently. 'Try to remember that.'

'I can't,' says Zelda.

'Try to think about a happy time you had with them,' I suggest.

It's what I do when I'm feeling bad about Mum and Dad, but it doesn't always work.

'When I was little,' says Zelda, 'we had chickens. Not Nazi chickens, nice chickens.'

She starts crying.

I try to think of something else to say. Something to help Zelda have happy memories of her parents. But I can't think of anything.

'I wish I was little now,' she sobs.

Poor thing. It must be terrible to not have a family when you're only six. It's bad enough when you're my age.

'You've still got a family,' I say quietly to Zelda.

I reach out in the darkness and give her a hug so she knows I mean me.

Zelda doesn't say anything, but she snuggles closer and cries into my shirt so I'm pretty sure she does know.

'Felix,' she says when she's finished crying. 'Will you always be my family?'

'Yes,' I say.

'Will you stay with me for ever and ever?' she says.

I think about this. I remember how Mum and Dad promised to come back one day and they never did. But I know they wanted to. That's the important thing with a promise. You must want to keep it.

'I promise,' I say.

'I promise too,' says Zelda.

She snuggles into me.

I listen for the soldiers again.

Nothing, just forest insects and the wind in the trees. But the Nazis might not have gone yet. They could be back at the pit, smoking more cigarettes and covering the children with dirt.

'I think we should hide here till morning,' I say to Zelda.

'Alright,' she says.

'We haven't got any dinner,' I say. 'Sorry.'

There aren't even any weeds in this burrow, just old leaves. We daren't eat those in case there's mould on them that gets into our brains and makes us think we're opera singers. I've seen it happen.

'That's OK,' says Zelda in a small voice. 'I'm not hungry.'

I know she is because I am.

I hug her even tighter. Sometimes love from your family can make your tummy not hurt quite so much.

'Go to sleep,' I whisper to Zelda.

'Tell me a story,' she says. 'One where nobody gets dead.'

I tell her a story about two children called Felix and Zelda who meet two other children called William and Violet Elizabeth.

122

They all live together with some very friendly chickens who give them lots of eggs to eat. To say thank you to the chickens, Felix and Zelda invent a machine that feeds them automatically.

'That's silly,' murmurs Zelda. 'Machines can't feed chickens.'

'It's in the future,' I say. '1965.'

'Alright,' says Zelda.

Richmal Crompton doesn't set her William stories in the future, but I'm sure she wouldn't mind.

The wind in the trees is getting louder now and the air is getting colder. Carefully I scoop some more leaves onto Zelda to keep her warm.

'More story, please,' she murmurs.

'One of the chickens falls in love with Zelda,' I say. 'It wants to be her pet. She calls it Hubert.'

'Don't you know anything?' says Zelda sleepily. 'My pet chicken's name is Goebbels.'

'Sorry,' I say.

I tell her the next part of the story, about how Goebbels can juggle eggs.

Finally Zelda's soft breathing lets me know she's asleep.

I wish I could doze off too, but I can't. There are busy insects in these leaves and they tickle.

My brain is busy as well, wondering what we're going to do next. If we don't get food soon, we're in big trouble. There's not much point being snug and safe in a secret burrow if you're dead.

We need a safe hiding place that has food.

The only safe place I know in the whole of Poland that definitely has food is the Catholic orphanage where Mum and Dad hid me. But it's hundreds of kilometres away. We'd have to get past about a million Nazis to even find it.

Zelda's bedtime slippers just wouldn't last the distance. Neither would our tummies.

We need somewhere local.

Which means I'll have to ask a grown-up for help.

But asking for help can be risky these days. A lot of grown-ups aren't very good at listening to kids, specially not while they're shooting them.

Then I fell asleep and the next morning me and Zelda went to find some new parents.

Slowly.

Carefully.

Watching out for Nazis.

'Why?' says Zelda sleepily, rubbing her eyes as we creep along the forest path. 'Why do we need new parents?'

'To keep us safe,' I tell her. 'To look after our sore fingers and give us breakfast.'

Zelda thinks about this. We're both shivering in the cool damp morning air. We haven't had anything to eat or drink for a whole day and two nights. I can see she likes the idea of a hot breakfast as much as I do.

While I keep my eyes peeled for Nazi soldiers in the under-growth and Nazi dive-bombers above the trees, I tell her my plan.

She listens quietly.

But not for long.

'No,' she shouts, and plonks herself down at the side of the path.

I knew Zelda wouldn't like this part of the idea. The part that involves going back to the big hole with the dead children in it.

I don't like it either, but it's a vital and important part of the plan.

I try not to get irritated with Zelda. Hunger and thirst can make you really grumpy if you're not careful.

'You won't have to see the children,' I explain to her. 'They'll probably be covered up with earth. A grave is a really good place to meet new parents. If the mums and dads are still alive, sooner or later they'll want to visit the place where their kids are buried. And we'll be there, offering ourselves as replacements.'

Zelda frowns as she thinks about this.

I glance nervously around the forest. I'm hoping she'll agree it's a really good plan, but I'm also hoping she'll do it quietly.

'What does replacements mean?' says Zelda.

'Parents with dead kids sometimes adopt new ones,' I explain. 'It's no trouble for them, they've already got the bedrooms set up and everything.'

Zelda slowly stands up.

I can see she's starting to understand what a good idea this is.

But before she can tell me how grateful she is to have such a clever family as me, there's a snapping and crackling nearby and something hurtles towards us out of the undergrowth.

For a panicked second I think it's a Nazi dog, one of those big vicious killer brutes trained to bite you even through your clothes.

I try to get between Zelda, who's cowering and whimpering, and the vicious killer brute.

Except now I can see it isn't a vicious killer brute.

It's another kind of dog, big and floppy and panting with untidy brown fur like an old armchair with the stuffing showing. And big sad eyes that stare up at me while it licks a bare bit of my tummy through a rip in my shirt.

'Stop that,' says Zelda sternly to the dog. 'It's rude to lick tummies.'

I don't mind. Mum used to lick my tummy when I was little.

The dog turns and starts licking Zelda's arm.

She stops frowning and starts chuckling.

I look around for the dog's owner. I have a feeling he or she probably isn't a Nazi, but you can't be too careful. Before I can spot anybody, a whistle echoes through the trees and the dog gives Zelda one last lick and runs off into the undergrowth.

I still can't see anybody.

'Pity,' I say to Zelda. 'A person who owns a dog like that is probably nice.'

Zelda thinks about this.

Suddenly she yells as loud as she can.

'Hey, dog man or dog lady. We're over here. Felix and Zelda. Two kids who need breakfast and a mummy and daddy.'

In a panic, I put my hand over Zelda's mouth. Every Nazi in Poland probably heard that.

Zelda pulls my hand away.

'I was going to say please,' she mutters, glaring.

Before I can remind her we're in a war zone, I hear more sounds coming through the trees.

Thudding sounds.

Rattling sounds.

Getting closer.

I grab Zelda and look frantically around for a hiding place in the ferns and creepers. Somewhere marching Nazi soldiers with machine guns won't spot us.

I see a place.

'Come on,' I hiss at Zelda.

She doesn't move. I love having her as my family, but sometimes I wish she wasn't so stubborn.

'Look,' she says pointing, her eyes going big.

I turn and look. Coming round a bend in the forest path is a wooden cart, rattling and squeaking, pulled by a plodding horse with thud-thudding hooves.

The driver is an old man.

I check to see if the nice dog is riding on the cart or running alongside. It doesn't seem to be.

The old man sees us and winks.

Zelda is still staring at him with big eyes.

'The kind cook,' she whispers.

He doesn't have oranges piled up in his cart, or chocolate. But he's got something almost as good. A huge mound of crisp fresh turnips. Suddenly I can taste them and I feel weak with hunger.

Normally I don't like turnips, specially raw, but now the thought of that turnip juice running down my throat makes me desperate to have some.

The old man stops the cart.

I can't see the nice dog anywhere.

'You kids lost?' says the old man.

'No,' I say.

'Yes,' says Zelda. Right now she'll say anything for a turnip.

The man looks at us thoughtfully.

'Get on,' he says. 'I'll give you a lift.'

I hesitate.

'Where are you going?' I ask.

'To my farm,' says the man.

I think about this.

'Did you grow those turnips?' I say.

The man nods.

I put my arm round Zelda. I'm pretty sure the man isn't telling the truth about where he's going. I don't know much about farming, but where I come from if a person grows turnips on his farm, the reason he puts them in a cart is to take them to town. And in my experience towns are where Nazi soldiers have their headquarters.

'Actually,' I say, 'could we just have a turnip?'

'Or some sausages,' says Zelda.

The man smiles, but there's something a bit strange about the way he does it.

'Hop on,' he says. 'You can eat as much as you like on the way.'

Zelda starts to climb onto the cart.

The man reaches behind him and lifts her up. I step forward to pull her back down, but I'm so hungry I'm starting to feel dizzy and my tummy's making me have second thoughts.

Maybe we should go with the man. He might be telling the truth. He might be going back home to get something he's forgotten, like more turnips. He might give us stew and let us work for him and even offer to be our new parent or grandparent.

If he's lying, we can always jump off the cart and hide before we get to town.

I grab onto the side of the cart and begin to climb up after Zelda.

And stop.

Nailed to the side of the cart, right next to my face, is a tattered paper notice with printing on it. At the top is one word in big letters.

*JEWS.*

I read the rest of the notice.

*Reward*, it says. *For each Jew captured and handed over. Two hundred (200) zloty and one (1) bottle of vodka.*

Suddenly I'm not hungry any more. I'm thinking clearly again. This is why the man wants to take us to town. To get a Nazi reward.

I drop back onto the ground.

'Zelda,' I yell. 'Jump off.'

Zelda glares down at me and shakes her head. Her cheeks are bulging and she's got mud and turnip juice round her mouth.

'Zelda,' I scream. 'It's a trap.'

The horse rears up. The old man swears at me. The cart lurches forward. The old man doesn't try to stop it. He obviously thinks one reward is better than nothing.

I run after the cart. The back flap is held in place by two big rusty metal pins. I grab them and twist them out. The flap drops and hundreds of turnips roll off the cart and knock me over.

Zelda rolls off the cart too.

'Ow,' she says as we lie on the ground with the turnips. She takes her knee out of my mouth. 'That hurts. Don't you know anything?'

I'm not thinking about knees, not even Zelda's hurting one. I'm thinking about the horrible thing I glimpsed in the cart, after the load started spilling and before my glasses got knocked off.

A boy, half-buried in turnips, not moving, covered in blood.

The old man must already have caught one Jewish kid today and bashed him unconscious and hidden him under the turnips.

The cart has stopped and the old man has jumped down and is picking up turnips and yelling angrily at us. For a fraction of a second I wonder if I should try to rescue the boy.

No.

Get Zelda to safety.

You have to look after your family first. Plus the boy could already be dead.

I find my glasses and scramble up and grab Zelda's hand and drag her into the forest without looking back at the cart.

'Run,' I pant at her and we both do. We run until we're out of breath, which happens pretty quickly when you're weak from no food.

We flop to the ground behind a big tree. I'd like to be further away from the man, but I'm hoping he won't want to leave his cart in case somebody steals the Jewish boy to get the reward.

When my breathing quietens down, I listen carefully.

It doesn't sound like the man is following us.

'He wasn't a kind cook, was he,' whispers Zelda.

I shake my head.

'Sorry,' she says sadly. 'I didn't get you a turnip.'

'That's OK,' I say.

Looking at Zelda's kind concerned face, I feel a glow inside that makes the hunger seem not so bad.

'I know what we can do,' Zelda says. 'After the man's finished picking his turnips up and he's gone, we can go and see if he's missed one.'

'Good idea,' I say.

I don't tell her that no matter how hungry I am, I'm not sure if I could eat a turnip that's had blood on it.

Zelda gives me a hug.

'Thanks for saving me, Felix,' she says. 'I'm lucky to have you as my family.'

I'm about to tell her I'm lucky to have her as my family too, but I don't get the chance.

Twigs snap.

I try to spin round.

Too late.

'Run and you're dead,' says a gruff voice.

Strong hands grab us.

**Then** I knew me and Zelda were doomed. I knew what would happen next. We'd be bashed and thrown back onto the cart. Taken into town. Handed over to the Nazis. Made to lie down in a hole in the ground and . . .

I was wrong.

You can be sometimes when your eyes are watering with hunger.

It's not the turnip man who's grabbed us, it's the dog lady.

I think she's a farmer too, judging by her clothes. And how strong she is. She's gripping my collar in one hand and there's no way I can get free. In her other hand she's got Zelda's arm and she's not letting go of that either, even though Zelda is trying to bite her on the finger.

'Stop that,' says the dog lady.

I stop wriggling. The big floppy dog is licking my tummy again. I look into its sad eyes. And at the friendly dribble hanging from its friendly mouth. This dog is definitely not a Nazi. Which means its owner probably isn't either.

I glance over at Zelda.

She's still wriggling.

'Kind farmer,' I mouth at her.

Zelda frowns. Either she doesn't understand what I'm saying, or she thinks I'm wrong.

I think I'm right. Now that I'm having a closer look at the woman, I can see she's got sad eyes like her dog. Her face isn't particularly friendly, but she's got the same sort of mouth as Mum, one that's kind at the corners. Her hair is shorter than Mum's though. You probably have to have short hair on a farm or the cows chew it. Mum was a bookseller so she didn't have that problem.

'Stop wriggling,' the woman snaps at Zelda.

'You're not the boss of me,' says Zelda fiercely.

'It's OK,' I say to Zelda. 'She's friendly.'

I'm wrong about that too.

'You stupid Jews,' says the woman.

I stare at her, not sure if I heard right.

'You yids are meant to be smart,' says the woman. 'I don't call staying around here smart. Not after what happened to your lot yesterday.'

I did hear right. Only people who hate Jews call us yids. Suddenly the woman's mouth doesn't look so kind after all.

'We don't want to stay around here,' I say. 'If you let go of us, we'll leave.'

The woman doesn't stop gripping my collar or Zelda's arm.

'Don't even think about it,' says the woman.

She starts pulling me and Zelda away through the forest. My collar is twisted and she's half choking me. She must know about the reward.

'You're hurting my arm,' says Zelda.

The woman ignores her.

Zelda finally manages to get her teeth into the woman's hand.

The woman lets go of my collar, slaps Zelda's face, and grabs my collar again before I can do anything.

Zelda cries.

The dog whimpers.

'I'm reporting you to the police,' I yell at the woman, but straight away I know that's a dumb thing to say because the police are all Nazis too.

The woman drags us both down another forest path. As we stumble along, I give Zelda a look to let her know I'm sorry I couldn't defend her. And that I'm trying to think what to do next.

The woman is too strong to fight. I used to think Mum and Dad were strong from lifting books, but this woman's got arm muscles like thick ropes.

'Listen,' I say to her. 'My parents have got thousands of books from their bookshop stored away. If you let us go, you can have them all. They're worth much more than four hundred zloty and two bottles of vodka.'

It's not true, but sometimes to try and save your family you have to make up stories.

'You Jews have certainly got imaginations,' says the woman.

She doesn't let us go.

'I'd probably do the same if I was an orphan,' she says. 'Make up lies about my parents.'

I look at the woman.

How does she know I'm an orphan?

Suddenly we all jolt painfully to a stop. Zelda has grabbed a tree trunk with her free arm and is clinging to it.

'We're not going with you,' she yells at the woman. 'You're horrible. You hurt people.'

The woman pulls Zelda away from the tree.

'And you're a naughty little girl,' she says angrily to Zelda, 'who by rights should be in that pit with your friends.'

She steers us along the forest path again, fast.

My brain is going fast too.

The woman thinks me and Zelda escaped from the group of children who got shot yesterday. That's why she's in such a hurry to take us to town. So she can hand us over to the Nazis and they can finish the job.

Desperately I try to think of another plan to get away.

Before I can, we come to the edge of the forest. It's a different place to where we were yesterday, with a different valley. I can tell because it doesn't have a children's grave. Just lots of farms. And in the distance I can see a town.

I can't see any Nazis in the town, but I know they're there.

Now I'm panicking.

I'm panting almost as hard as the dog.

Zelda is still crying. I don't blame her. Anyone would cry with a hurting arm and a hurting face both at once.

Suddenly I know what I have to do.

'Zelda's not Jewish,' I say to the woman. 'I am, but she's not. Take me, but let her go, please.'

I look at the woman pleadingly.

Zelda stops crying. She gives me a glare.

'Felix is wrong,' she says to the woman. 'I am Jewish.'

I can't believe it. Why is Zelda saying this? It's not true.

'Don't listen to her,' I say.

'I'm Jewish just like him,' Zelda says to the woman. 'I want to be Jewish and I am.'

I realise what Zelda's doing. She's saying this so we can stay together.

My head is bursting.

Doesn't Zelda realise staying with me could kill her? Has she forgotten about the poor children in the pit?

'Zelda's parents weren't Jewish,' I say frantically to the woman. 'Look at the photo in the locket round her neck. You'll see.'

We stop. Without letting go of my collar or Zelda's arm, the woman peers at Zelda's neck.

I do too.

The necklace with the locket isn't there.

'Where's the locket?' I shout at Zelda.

'I'm Jewish now,' she shouts back. 'You can't stop me.'

Suddenly I understand. Zelda must have left the locket in our burrow. So she doesn't have to think about her parents being Nazis.

I try to explain to the woman.

She's not listening.

'Both of you,' she says angrily. 'Be quiet.'

I give Zelda a look to let her know that the last thing I want is to be separated from her but I can't think of what else to do.

Zelda stares back at me, angry and hurt.

'You promised,' she says.

She's right, I did.

I feel terrible.

The woman marches us down into the valley, towards the town, towards the Nazis.

At least I can keep my promise now. Whatever happens next, at least it will happen to me and Zelda together.

**Then** the woman did a surprising thing. Instead of dragging me and Zelda into town and handing us over to the Nazis, she took us to a farm.

I think it's her farm.

You know how when you've been expecting something awful to happen and it doesn't, a field of cabbage stumps sparkling with morning dew can look even more beautiful than usual?

This field we're tramping through now looks like that.

My empty tummy gurgles with hope as the woman hurries us along the track towards a farmhouse.

Maybe she's a kind farmer after all.

OK, she's not exactly behaving like one. She's still gripping Zelda's arm very hard. I can tell from poor Zelda's face how much it hurts. And instead of dragging me by my shirt collar, she's dragging me by my left ear, which also hurts.

Why are we going so fast? We're almost trotting now. Zelda's little legs can hardly keep up.

'My feet hurt,' says Zelda.

Poor thing. They must hurt a lot. On the way here the woman marched us through a field of cut hay. The stubble frayed Zelda's bedtime slippers to bits. Her feet are bleeding.

'Stop complaining,' says the woman. 'We're nearly there.'

I should point out to the woman that Zelda is only six and is walking very fast for her age, but I can't get the words out. My throat is too dry and my mouth is too weak with hunger.

Only one thing is keeping me going.

The trickle of smoke coming out of the farmhouse chimney.

Smoke can mean cooking. That might be why the woman is hurrying. And why the dog has rushed ahead and is barking at us.

He might be letting us know that the sausage stew is done.

Just the thought of stew is giving me extra energy. Stew and boiled cabbage. I bet the cabbages on this farm are as beautiful as their stumps.

'Cooking,' I whisper to Zelda, pointing to the smoke so she can get extra energy too.

I notice something else very exciting about the farmhouse. It's got two windows. That means it's probably got two rooms. So if the woman lets us live with her, we won't be overcrowded and getting on her nerves all the time.

I send a silent message to Zelda.

Please don't bite the woman again. People don't invite you to live with them if you bite them.

Zelda doesn't bite the woman.

Even so, the woman doesn't invite us to live with her.

Instead we all stop outside a low barn built from lumps of stone. The woman lets go of my ear, takes a key from her trouser pocket, unlocks a big padlock and pulls the barn door open.

Several chickens rush out.

Zelda grins, which is pretty amazing for someone who's hungry and thirsty and in pain.

The woman doesn't grin. She pushes me and Zelda into the gloom.

'I don't want to hear a squeak,' she says sternly, and locks me and Zelda in.

For a long time we sit on a pile of straw, too worn out to speak.

Finally Zelda does.

'I know why that woman locked us in here,' she says.

I hope Zelda isn't thinking the same thing as me. That the woman couldn't be bothered dragging us all the way to town just for two bottles of vodka and four hundred zloty. So instead she's sent a message for the Nazis to come and get us.

'She did it as a punishment,' says Zelda. 'Because you broke your promise.'

I sigh, but I don't argue. It's better if Zelda isn't thinking about Nazis. She's too young to be hungry and thirsty and scared all at the same time.

'I'm sorry,' I say. 'I was just trying to protect you.'

'Leaving me isn't protecting,' says Zelda. 'Hiding me is protecting.'

'You're right,' I say. 'Let's hide now. Under the straw.'

It's our only hope. If the Nazis arrive and can't see us, maybe we'll have a chance to run for it.

We burrow deep into the straw.

'See?' says Zelda. 'This is good protecting.'

'We have to practise being very quiet,' I whisper.

'I don't need to practise,' she says. 'I'm good at being quiet. Don't you know anything?'

A loud snuffling fills the barn.

'Shhh,' I whisper.

'It's not me,' says Zelda.

The snuffling turns into wheezing.

Zelda grabs me.

It's dark in our hiding place and I can't see her, but I know she's thinking the same as me.

That we're not the only ones in this straw.

'Hello?' I whisper. 'Is anyone there?'

Maybe the farm woman has captured another Jewish person so she can get six hundred zloty and three bottles of vodka. Or maybe there's a Nazi soldier already here in the barn waiting for us.

I stop breathing.

The wheezing turns into grunting.

'That's not me,' whispers Zelda.

Suddenly there's a violent movement next to us and most of the straw isn't over us any more.

I blink in the faint haze of daylight coming under the barn door.

I'm staring up at a strange face. Two beady black eyes and a pink bald head and a big snout dripping with snot.

It's a pig.

'Naughty pig,' says Zelda. 'You're too noisy.'

The pig shuffles back a few steps.

'It's alright,' I say to Zelda. 'I think it's just lonely.'

I peer around the barn. I can't see any other pigs. I know I'd get lonely, stuck in a barn on my own all day without any family. With just a few chickens who don't even tell me when my nose is running.

I pat the pig.

Zelda grabs me. Outside, somebody is unlocking the barn door. We dive back into the straw. But before we can cover ourselves, the door swings open and the woman comes in. She puts a bowl of food onto the floor, and a bowl of water.

'Go on,' she says. 'Get it into you.'

I hesitate. Does she mean me and Zelda, or the pig?

The woman doesn't wait to explain. She steps out of the barn, slams the door shut and locks it again.

The pig doesn't wait either. It sticks its snout into the food and starts gobbling.

Me and Zelda hurry over and grab some.

The pig doesn't seem to mind.

'Thanks for sharing,' I say to the pig, my mouth full of delicious cold mashed potato and cabbage stalks.

'That's OK,' says Zelda.

Her mouth is so full her cheeks are bulging.

You know how when you're really hungry all you can think about is food, but as soon as you've eaten all you can think about is how thirsty you are?

That's happening to me.

I take my glasses off and stick my face in the water bowl and drink and drink.

Zelda does too.

So does the pig.

We all drink and drink and keep drinking until the Nazis arrive.

★

As soon as we hear the truck coming towards the farm, me and Zelda scramble back under the straw and make sure we're completely covered. Except for a tiny peephole so I can pick the right moment for us to run.

The barn door bangs open. I squint out through the straw. The woman comes in. She's wearing a dress now, and makeup, and she's brushed her hair. She takes a handful of something from her dress pocket and flings it around the barn.

What is she doing?

Outside the barn, men are yelling at each other in Nazi and slamming the truck doors. Suddenly my nose tingles painfully and I know what the woman is scattering.

Pepper.

The woman wants me and Zelda to start sneezing so much we can't run. So we'll be helpless and the Nazi soldiers can grab us and she'll get her reward.

She's not a kind farmer, she's a horrible one.

Well, me and Zelda aren't going to sneeze. I press my fingers against my top lip and I press my other fingers against Zelda's.

'I can do it myself,' Zelda whispers indignantly, pushing my fingers away.

My hand brushes against something small and hard lying in the straw. I grab it. I can feel a chain. And a hinge. Zelda's locket. She must have had it in her pocket all the time. It must have fallen out when she was diving in and out of the straw.

I keep my eye at the peephole.

A Nazi soldier comes into the barn. He's got a rifle with a bayonet. A second soldier comes in with a dog. Not a floppy dog with sad eyes and comfy armchair fur. A vicious killer Nazi dog that's straining at its lead, desperate to bite people.

If it sniffs out me and Zelda, we're finished.

The Nazi dog coughs. The woman glances towards me and Zelda.

Oh no. I think she knows exactly where we are. She must have spotted our hiding place when she brought the food in.

It's too late to run. I squeeze the locket tight in my hand. When the woman drags us out of the straw and hands us over, I'm going to give the locket to the soldiers. When they see the photo of Zelda's father in Nazi uniform they'll have to show Zelda mercy.

Sometimes you have to break a promise if it's the only way to save your family.

That's weird. The woman isn't dragging us out and handing us over. She's standing very close to the soldiers, who are sniffing the air and frowning.

'Do you like it?' says the woman. 'My perfume?'

She gives them a cheeky grin, like Mum used to give Dad when she was up the ladder in the shop getting a book from the top shelf and Dad used to kiss her on the ankle.

The Nazi soldiers glance at each other.

The woman holds her wrist under their noses. They both sniff it. She gives them another cheeky grin. They both grin back.

I don't get it. If she wants to be romantic with Nazis, why doesn't she hand me and Zelda over first? That'll make them like her even more.

The Nazi dog sneezes.

Suddenly I have an amazing thought.

What if the pepper isn't for us? What if it's for the dog? What if the woman is doing some good protecting?

'Hope you find those two Jew kids,' says the woman to the soldiers. 'So you can finish the job. I reckon the little vermin are hiding in the forest somewhere. You'll know them when you see them, they'll look like that.'

Chuckling, she points to the pig, who's in the corner, trembling, as far away from the Nazi dog as it can get.

The soldiers frown again. Is it because they don't like seeing an animal scared?

Probably not. It's probably because they don't speak much Polish.

Oh no.

The soldier with the rifle is coming over to where we're hidden. The woman looks like she wants to stop him, but she doesn't. The soldier stabs his bayonet into the pile of straw next to ours.

Should I jump out and show him the locket?

Too late, now he's raising his bayonet over our pile.

I want to put my arms round Zelda, but I daren't move. I pray she won't make a noise. I pray I won't either, not even if that bayonet slices into me.

Help us, Richmal Crompton, please.

The bayonet blade hisses into the straw just past my head. And again just near my chest. I can't see where it goes after that, but Zelda isn't making a sound.

The soldier stops stabbing.

He gives the woman a shrug and a grin. The woman stops biting her lip and gives a half-grin back. But when the soldiers both turn away, she glances over towards me and Zelda again.

She looks very worried, like she really doesn't want us to be stabbed.

Yes.

My insides do a dance.

Except I'm feeling worried too.

Zelda still isn't making a sound.

The Nazi soldiers go out of the barn. The woman follows them. Just before she steps out the door, she forces a smile back onto her anxious face.

'Felix,' whispers Zelda in my ear. 'Are you stabbed?'

I've never been so happy to hear her voice.

'No,' I say.

'I'm not stabbed too,' says Zelda.

I put my arms round her and say a silent thank you to Richmal Crompton.

The Nazi soldiers are driving away. The woman is shouting friendly things after them, but I can tell she's only pretending.

Zelda's heart is going as fast as mine.

I'm not surprised.

It's pretty exciting when you get a new parent.

**Then** me and Zelda crawled out of the straw and the woman checked us over for stab wounds and was very relieved we didn't have any and took us into her house and gave us hot food including cabbage leaves and a whole turnip and a bath.

She also told us her name, which is Genia, and the dog's name, which is Leopold.

Zelda is first for the bath, but she doesn't want to get in.

'Come on, Zelda,' says Genia. 'This water won't stay hot for ever and I'm not heating any more.'

Zelda is staring at the kitchen floor, sticking out her bottom lip.

'You slapped me,' she says.

At first I can see Genia isn't sure what Zelda is talking about.

'In the forest,' says Zelda.

Now Genia remembers. She crouches down in front of Zelda.

'You bit me,' says Genia. 'So let's make a deal. If you don't bite me, I won't slap you.'

Zelda thinks about this.

She nods and gets into the bath. The deal works. Zelda doesn't bite Genia, and Genia is very gentle with Zelda's cut feet.

Now it's my turn.

My face is burning. Not from the water, because I'm standing up and it doesn't even reach my knees. My face is hot because Genia is staring at my private part like it's the most annoying thing she's ever seen.

I look away and pretend not to notice.

I was right about this house. It's got two rooms. There's the kitchen we're in now, and a completely separate bedroom. The house is made in a clever way. The wood stove is in the middle wall, so it heats both the rooms.

Genia is still staring at my private part.

Now she's sighing loudly.

'It's rude to stare,' says Zelda. 'Don't you know anything?'

'You Jews,' says Genia. 'Only Jews would do that to a kid.'

Of course. Now I know why she's staring. But it's not Mum and Dad's fault. They didn't want to have me circumcised.

'It wasn't my parents' fault,' I say to Genia. 'It was my grandfather. He was still alive when I was a baby and he made them do it. He said he'd get ill if they didn't do it.'

'Do what?' says Zelda.

'Chop off a perfectly good foreskin,' says Genia.

Now Zelda is staring at my private part too.

But only for a moment. She gives me the towel and a sympathetic look.

Genia isn't being sympathetic.

'What a very clever grandfather,' she says, taking the towel off me and drying my back. 'Now every Nazi Jew-killer can spot you a mile off.'

'He was religious,' I say.

You have to stand up for your grandfather even if he did accidentally put your life at risk.

'Religious,' says Genia scornfully. 'That's not my idea of religious.'

For a moment I wonder if she prays to Richmal Crompton too. But I don't say anything about that because there's something even more important I need to ask her.

'If you hate Jewish people so much,' I say, 'why didn't you hand me over to the Nazis?'

'And me?' says Zelda.

I wait anxiously for Genia's answer. It's a risky question to ask a person you hope is going to look after you and protect you and give you more turnips.

Genia chews her lip and rubs her head like some people do when a question is difficult. Szymon Glick used to do it in class all the time.

'You're right,' says Genia. 'I don't like Jews. I never have. It's how I was brought up.'

My insides sink.

Zelda is glaring. I can see she's trying to think of an insult to say back at Genia.

'But,' says Genia, 'there are people I dislike much more than Jews.'

'Nazis?' I say.

'Oh yes,' says Genia. 'I hate Nazis a lot.'

I remind myself to make sure that Genia never sees Zelda's locket, which I've hidden in my boot.

'But most of all,' continues Genia, 'I hate anyone who hurts children.'

Now, with her eyes fierce, she looks even more like Mum. Even with her short hair that's sticking up from where she was rubbing it.

'When I heard a rumour the Nazis had killed the Jewish orphans,' says Genia, 'I prayed it wasn't true. That's why I was in the forest, seeing for myself.'

She screws up her face at the memory and smacks the bathwater, splashing me and Zelda.

Leopold gives a yelp and jumps back.

'Those kids have lived in this district all their lives,' says Genia. 'What sort of monsters would do that to them?'

I'm not sure if she wants an answer, so I stand quietly while she dries me and Zelda again.

Genia stops frowning and looks at us both.

'How did you manage it?' she asks. 'How did you escape from the shooting?'

I can see she does want an answer to this. But I'm not sure what to say. She thinks we're local orphans and we're not. If I tell her the truth, will she still want to look after us?

'We didn't escape from the shooting, we escaped from the train,' Zelda says to her. 'Don't you know anything?'

Genia stares at us in surprise.

I wait for her to ask us to leave.

She doesn't.

'A train from the city,' I say quietly. 'On its way to a death camp.'

Genia puts her hand on my face, just for a moment, and I can tell from her expression that it's going to be alright.

Zelda is frowning.

'If you're going to be our new mummy,' she says to Genia, 'you have to like Jewish people.'

Genia nods slowly, puffing out her cheeks as if it's a very difficult thing to think about.

'Felix can't help it,' says Zelda, pointing towards my private part.

Genia gives a long sigh.

'Neither of you can,' she says. 'Come on, kneel down so I can do your hair.'

We both kneel down with our heads over the metal bathtub.

'Keep your eyes closed,' says Genia.

She wets our hair and rubs something onto it that smells horrible. And hurts.

'Ow,' says Zelda. 'That shampoo stings.'

'It's not shampoo,' says Genia. 'It's bleach.'

I don't know what bleach is, but when I finally open my eyes I see what it does.

Zelda's hair isn't black any more, it's yellow. And Zelda is staring at me with an amazed expression, so my hair must have turned yellow too.

I know why Genia has done this.

'It's so we blend in with the straw, isn't it?' I say to her. 'For when we hide in the barn.'

Genia smiles.

'Good thought, Felix,' she says. 'But you won't be hiding in the barn any more.'

I stare at her. I don't like the sound of this. Has she decided it's too risky to have us that close to the house?

'Where will we be hiding?' I ask anxiously. 'In a haystack?'

'Out in the open,' says Genia.

I stare at her even harder.

How can we hide out in the open?

'Are you good at stories, Felix?' asks Genia.

'Yes, he is,' says Zelda. 'He's very good. Specially funny ones and sad ones.'

'Excellent,' says Genia. 'Because from now on you both have to tell people a story about yourselves. How you're two Catholic children from Pilica. How your parents were killed. How you've come to stay with your aunty, who from now on is me.'

I try to take this in.

Zelda is thinking about it too.

I'm not sure how I feel about this.

'Wouldn't the barn be safer?' I say.

Suddenly the barn doesn't seem so bad. We could play with the pig. And the chickens. I try not to think about Nazi bayonets.

'Only Jews hide in barns,' says Genia. 'And from now on you're not Jews.'

For a moment I think Zelda is going to argue, but she doesn't.

I don't either, but I'm still not sure.

'Which would you prefer?' says Genia. 'Being stuck in a barn the whole time, or being able to run around and play outdoors and sleep in a bed?'

'A bed,' I say.

'A bed,' says Zelda.

It's a good point. We haven't slept in a real bed for ages.

I'm starting to see that hiding in the open could be better, except for one problem. I look down at my private part.

Genia sees me looking and nods her head.

'That is the weak link in our plan,' she says.

I wish it wasn't. But I do have one hopeful thought.

'When I was younger,' I tell Genia, 'my parents hid me in a

Catholic orphanage. I told the other boys I'd been circumcised for medical reasons because I'd had an illness of the private part.'

Genia shakes her head.

'Good story,' she says. 'But the Nazis have heard it a million times before.'

We all look at my private part.

'Only one thing to do,' says Genia.

'What?' I say, hoping it won't be painful.

'Don't show it to anybody,' says Genia.

I nod. I'll have to hope no Nazis want to see it.

'I'll make sure he doesn't show it to anybody,' says Zelda.

'Good girl,' says Genia. 'Now, we have to find new names for you.'

Zelda's eyes light up.

'William and Violet Elizabeth,' she says.

Genia thinks about this.

'They're names from our favourite stories,' I explain. 'Our favourite story-writer Richmal Crompton is English. When her stories are changed into Polish, the names stay English.'

'English names aren't a good idea,' says Genia. 'The Nazis are at war with England.'

'We like those names,' says Zelda fiercely.

Genia rolls her eyes.

'Alright,' she says. 'But we have to make them Polish. Wilhelm and Violetta.'

Zelda grins.

I'm happy too. Now it's almost like Richmal Crompton will be helping Genia look after us.

This bed is comfortable and warm, and Genia doesn't snore that much, and she's left a lamp burning low so we won't be scared.

But I just can't get to sleep.

Neither can Zelda.

'Felix,' she says, nudging me in the ribs. 'Tell me a William and Violet Elizabeth story.'

'You mean Wilhelm and Violetta,' I whisper. 'And don't fidget. You'll pull the covers off Genia and wake her up.'

It's very kind of Genia to let us share her bed. Luckily there's space because her husband's away.

Zelda lies very still and I whisper a story to her. It's about how Wilhelm and Violetta are rescued by a kind lady called Genia. They live happily ever after with Genia, and with her friendly dog who likes to be tickled, and with a nice pig who likes to be tickled too, and with some very loyal chickens. Sometimes Wilhelm and Violetta play hide-and-seek with the chickens, and at no stage do the chickens betray them to the Nazis.

By the time I've finished the story, Zelda is asleep.

'Good story,' whispers Genia.

I'm startled. I hadn't realised she was listening.

'Can you tell another one?' she says. 'About a Polish man who's forced to go to Germany to work for the Nazis and who comes home safely.'

I look at her, confused. I'm not sure if I know enough to tell a story like that.

'He likes to be tickled,' says Genia.

While I'm waiting for my imagination to come up with something, I see the sad smile on her face and I realise who she's talking about.

'Does he come home at weekends?' I ask. 'Your husband.'

Genia shakes her head.

'I haven't seen him for two years,' she says quietly.

'That's terrible,' I say.

I tell Genia the story she asked for, but while I'm telling it I'm also thinking about something else.

Why do people start wars when they know so many sad things are going to happen?

I don't get it.

After I finish the story, me and Genia talk for a while. She doesn't get it either.

Finally she says, 'I must let you sleep. Good night, Wilhelm. And thank you.'

'Thank you,' I say. 'For protecting me and Zelda. I mean me and Violetta.'

We're both lying here, breathing quietly, Zelda asleep between us.

I don't know Genia very well, but I can guess what she's thinking.

The same as me.

We're both hoping our stories come true.

Then me and Zelda lived happily with Genia for more than a week without any sad things happening.

We also lived happily with Leopold the dog and Trotski the pig.

And a bit less happily with the chickens, who won't stay still long enough for us to feed them with our automatic chicken-feeding machine.

'Stop running away,' says Zelda crossly, waving her arms at them and chasing them all over the barn. 'You have to line up.'

I'm not surprised the chickens are a bit scared. They've probably never seen a gherkin tin nailed to a rafter before. Specially not one with a string hanging down that you have to pull with your beak to make the tin wobble and the grains of wheat fall through the holes in the bottom.

New inventions are always a bit confusing and scary. I remember how nervous Mum and Dad were at home when we first got a tin-opener. You can't blame these chickens for feeling the same.

'Give them time to get used to it,' I say to Zelda.

But Zelda grabs a chicken and staggers with it over to the chicken-feeding machine. She holds its beak and tries to make it pull the string. The chicken spits the string out, squawks indignantly and flaps out of her arms.

'Idiot,' Zelda yells at it. 'You have to pull the string. Don't you know anything?'

I smile to myself.

When Zelda asked me to build the automatic 1965 chicken-feeding machine from our story, I had a feeling it might be a bit too advanced for these 1942 chickens. But I didn't care because it was such fun inventing and making it. Nothing takes your mind off sad war things like an automatic chicken-feeding machine.

For a while, anyway.

'You're all idiots,' Zelda is yelling at the chickens. 'And Nazis.'

Leopold the dog and Trotski the pig are cowering in the corner of the barn.

The chickens are looking pretty stressed too, which I'm now remembering isn't a good thing.

Before Genia went into town this morning, she explained that these days eggs are so precious they're like money. In fact, eggs are Genia's only money. Which is why instead of us eating them, she takes them to town to swap for things.

When she gets home this afternoon I don't want her to find all the chickens have stopped laying eggs because Zelda has been calling them Nazis.

I decide to give the chickens a break.

'Let's play hide-and-seek,' I say to Zelda.

She looks at me like I'm an inventor who's not taking inventing seriously enough. But after a few moments she grins.

'Alright,' she says.

We help Leopold hide in his kennel and we give Trotski a hand to lie down behind an old horse harness. After that we burrow down into the straw.

'Come and find us,' Zelda calls to the chickens as she snuggles next to me.

I'm not sure if the chickens will be any better at this than they are at feeding themselves automatically, but it doesn't matter. It's fun here in the straw with no Nazis around.

'Felix,' whispers Zelda. 'I like it here. Can we stay here for ever?'

At first I think she means in the straw, which would get a bit itchy after a while because of the insects.

'On this farm,' says Zelda.

'I hope so,' I reply, but before I can explain that it's up to Genia, the barn door gives a loud creak.

I blow the dust off my glasses and peer out through the straw.

The barn door was shut to keep the chickens in, but not locked. Now somebody, I can't see who, is slowly pulling it open.

'Shhh,' I whisper to Zelda.

We hold our breaths.

Leopold barks.

I pray it's just Genia home early and I wait for her to step inside.

She doesn't.

Instead, a lump of something is tossed through the doorway and lands with a splat on the dirt floor.

A lump of raw meat.

I stare at it.

This is incredible. Meat is even more precious than eggs. Who would throw a lump of meat onto the ground?

'Good boy,' I hear a voice whispering from outside. 'Good boy, Leopold.'

Leopold comes panting out of his kennel and goes straight to the meat and starts eating it.

I can't believe what I'm seeing. Leopold is an important family member and we love him a lot, but you don't give meat to a dog, not in wartime, not when people are lucky if they have it once a month.

I'm tempted to crawl out of the straw to remind Genia about this, but before I can, somebody comes into the barn and it's not Genia.

It's a kid.

He's about my age with dark hair and old grown-up clothes that are too big for him. He kneels down next to Leopold, who's still scoffing the meat.

'Good boy,' he says in a gruff voice, and gives Leopold a hug.

Gently I squeeze Zelda's arm to let her know we should stay hidden until I can work out who this kid is. We can't be too careful. Kids like rewards too, even if they don't drink vodka.

Zelda is stiff with fright. I know what she's hoping. That the chickens don't suddenly get good at hide-and-seek and find us.

Wait a minute, that kid looks a bit familiar.

Have I met him before?

While I'm trying to think if I have, Trotski the pig goes over to the meat and starts gobbling it too.

Leopold doesn't mind, but the kid does.

'Get lost,' he says, and smacks Trotski on the head.

Before I can stop her, Zelda is on her feet, straw flying everywhere, striding towards the kid.

I stand up too.

The kid jumps back, startled, dark eyes glaring.

'Don't hit Trotski,' Zelda yells at the kid. 'He doesn't like being hit. He only likes being tickled.'

Zelda puts her arms round Trotski, who looks slightly dazed by all the attention.

The kid grabs Zelda and gets one arm round her neck. In his other hand he suddenly has a knife close to her throat.

There's blood on the knife.

Please, I beg silently, let it be blood from the meat.

'Stop being a bully,' squeals Zelda.

I take a step towards them. The kid moves the knife even closer to Zelda's throat.

'Let her go,' I say. 'We're Leopold's friends too.'

The kid doesn't reply. Just glowers at me with the angriest eyes I've ever seen.

'Leopold isn't your friend,' Zelda says to the kid. 'Bite him, Leopold.'

Leopold growls, but stays with the meat. I don't think he likes fighting.

I'm going to have to grab the knife. I don't like fighting either and I haven't really done much, but I can't think of any other way.

The kid looks like he's done a lot of fighting. He's got a big scab on his forehead.

Here goes.

But before I can fling myself at him, the kid suddenly mutters some swear words and pushes Zelda away and runs out of the barn.

I let him go.

'Are you alright?' I ask Zelda, helping her up and checking her for stab wounds.

'Children shouldn't play with real knives,' she says tearfully. 'Doesn't he know anything?'

I hug her. Leopold licks her. Trotski burps in a sympathetic way. The chickens run around clucking excitedly, but I think that's just because they've found us.

We creep to the barn door, but there's no sign of the kid.

'Let's chase after him,' mutters Zelda. 'With sticks.'

But we don't. We're not the sort of people who go looking for trouble, not even when we're angry.

I hope we never see that kid again.


After a while Genia arrives home from town.

She's got things she bought with the eggs. Trousers for me and a dress and shoes for Zelda and warm underwear for us both.

In the kitchen, while we try them on, we tell Genia about the horrible kid. She examines the last bit of the meat we've saved as evidence.

'Rabbit,' she says. 'I could have made a stew with that.'

'Or a pet,' says Zelda.

Genia frowns, thinking.

'That boy must have escaped,' she says.

'Escaped from where?' I say.

'The orphanage,' says Genia. 'Apart from you two, the only other kids who ever made friends with Leopold were the orphans. The ones the Nazis murdered.'

I look at Genia, surprised.

She used to hate Jewish people. Why did she let them be friends with her dog?

'The Nazis made the orphans do farm work,' says Genia. 'Growing food for the German army. The kids helped me plant my fields earlier this year. They did a good job. Beautiful crop of cabbages I had, before the Nazis took them.'

Zelda is frowning now.

'If the Jewish orphans were good at Nazi cabbages,' she says to Genia, 'why didn't the Nazis let them keep being alive?'

Genia scowls.

'Who knows why those slugs do anything,' she says. 'I heard a rumour they needed the orphanage building for something else.'

I'm shocked. Killing innocent children just to get their bedrooms.

I'm also shocked to hear that the kid with the knife is Jewish. A Jewish orphan whose friends are all dead except for Leopold.

I wish I'd known that.

Perhaps me and Zelda and the chickens could have been a bit friendlier.

**Then** Genia helped me and Zelda to be Wilhelm and Violetta. She got us fake Wilhelm and Violetta identity cards from a priest in exchange for eggs. She told us all about the place where Wilhelm and Violetta were born. For two weeks she tested us on our Wilhelm and Violetta childhoods.

'What did your father do?'

'He had a shop selling lamp oil,' I say.

'What was your mother's first name?'

'Jadwiga,' says Zelda.

'What street was your school in?'

'Poznod Street,' I say. 'Next to the bank.'

'What pets did you have?'

'A chicken called Goebbels,' says Zelda.

'No,' says Genia. 'Not Goebbels. That was your pet chicken when you were Zelda. Now that you're Violetta, your pet chicken was called Kranki, remember?'

Poor Zelda. Genia is a tough questioner. I think she could be a Nazi herself if she wanted to be. Luckily she doesn't.

'Remember?' she says to Zelda again.

'Yes,' sighs Zelda.

I hope Zelda can remember. Specially this morning, because we're on our way into town for the first time. So far, as we walk along the road past the local farms, we haven't met anybody. But I can see somebody coming in the distance.

Suddenly I don't feel ready.

'Genia,' I say. 'Can we go home and practise some more?'

'No,' says Genia. 'People want to meet you. They've seen me buying things for you and they're getting suspicious. We can't put it off any longer.'

Yes we can, I want to say. But how can you argue with someone as kind and generous and caring as Genia? Look what she's doing for us, and she doesn't even like Jewish people that much.

'Kranki,' Zelda is repeating sternly to herself as she clomps along the road in her new shoes. 'Kranki.'

The person coming towards us is a big woman with a grey headscarf and a red face.

I'm shivering with nerves now, even though the sun is shining and my hair is gleaming yellow because Genia put more bleach on it this morning.

'You'll be fine,' Genia whispers to me and Zelda. 'Just don't drop those eggs.'

We're carrying eggs in boxes. They're packed in straw, but mine are wobbling around because I'm trembling so much.

'Good morning, Mrs Placzek,' says Genia in the same fake friendly voice she used with the Nazi soldiers.

'Good morning,' says the scarf woman. She smiles at Genia for about one second, turns, and looks at me and Zelda.

Suddenly I know what an egg feels like. My disguise feels about as strong as a very thin shell.

'These are the children I was telling you about,' says Genia. 'Wilhelm and Violetta.'

Mrs Placzek clucks sympathetically.

'Poor orphans,' she says, reaching out.

For a moment I think she's going to touch my hair to see if the yellow comes off, but she doesn't. Instead she grabs my cheek and gives it a squeeze.

'Your poor dead mummy and daddy,' she says.

'Jadwiga,' says Zelda.

'My father had a shop selling lamp oil,' I say.

Genia is looking a bit concerned. I think it's because we're answering Mrs Placzek's questions even before she's asked them.

'What have you got there?' says Mrs Placzek, pointing to my egg box.

I can't think what to say. We haven't practised this one. But after a moment my brain clears.

'Eggs,' I say.

'Lucky boy,' says Mrs Placzek. 'I love eggs. Delicious.'

Once again I'm not sure what to say. I haven't eaten an egg since I was little. I can't even remember what they taste like.

'Eggs are good for us,' says Zelda to Mrs Placzek. 'Goebbels told me.'

Mrs Placzek frowns.

Zelda's eyes go wide as she realises what she's just said.

'I mean Kranki,' she blurts out.

Genia is frowning too now.

Mrs Placzek laughs.

'Children,' she says to Genia. 'What imaginations. It must be a joy having them around.'

'It is,' says Genia, smiling, but still sort of frowning at the same time.

I don't care. Mrs Placzek hasn't run off to fetch the Nazis. She's smiling and waving to us now as we say goodbye and walk away.

Our disguises are working.

A horse and cart is approaching, but I'm feeling much more confident. I stay feeling more confident until I recognise the old man driving the cart.

It's the turnip man.

Zelda recognises him too, I can tell from the little squeak she gives.

As the cart gets closer, I see the reward notice still stuck to the side. The cart doesn't have any turnips in it today, probably so he can fit more Jews in.

'It's OK,' I whisper to Zelda. 'He won't recognise us.'

I hope I'm right.

'Good morning, Mr Krol,' says Genia.

Mr Krol doesn't stop the cart. His only reply is a grunt. But as he rumbles past, he stares at me and Zelda for a long time, not smiling.

I feel a desperate urge to tell him my father had a shop selling lamp oil.

I manage not to.

'Bad-tempered old turnip,' mutters Genia once he's gone.

I agree, but at least he didn't try to get us into his cart. Our disguises are working even with somebody we've met before.

I think we're going to be OK.

After a couple of minutes I glance over my shoulder. I can still see the cart in the distance. Mr Krol is turned round in his seat, still staring at us.

It's alright, I tell myself. He's probably just thirsty for a drink of vodka and he's wishing me and Zelda were Jews.

**Then** we got to the town and it wasn't alright.

At first I felt at home. The stone houses and slate roofs and cobbled streets were a bit like the ones in the town where I lived when I was little. When I was Felix, not Wilhelm.

But in the town square there's something I've never seen before.

Big wooden posts with dead people hanging from them.

'Don't look,' says Genia to me and Zelda. She tries to hurry us across the square.

But we are looking. You have to. It's terrible. The hanging people with ropes round their necks aren't soldiers, they're just people. A lady in a green dress. An older lady wearing an apron. Several men in shirts. One in pyjamas.

The other people in the square aren't looking. They're hurrying past, staring at the cobbles. Which is what Genia is trying to make us do.

'Are those people dead?' says Zelda, pointing. She's starting to get upset.

'Yes,' whispers Genia. 'They were sheltering the Jew in the green dress. The Nazis caught them and killed them and everyone else in their family.'

That's awful. And it's extra awful just to leave them there like that.

The Nazis must be doing it as a warning.

To people like us.

'I hate Nazis,' says Zelda bitterly.

Genia gives her an anxious look as we cross the square.

I see why. A group of Nazi soldiers are strolling towards us. A couple of them are looking at us.

'Come on, Wilhelm and Violetta,' says Genia loudly. 'Be careful with those eggs.'

I'm finding it hard to be careful with the eggs. I'm having too many feelings all at once. That could be me and Zelda and Genia hanging there. And if it was, Genia would be dead for looking after me, and Zelda would be dead for being my friend, and it would all be my fault.


Genia takes us to a shop on the other side of the square.

On the door is a sign.

*NO DOGS OR JEWS.*

I hesitate.

'Don't dawdle, Wilhelm,' says Genia. 'You're blocking the doorway.'

I go in, trying to look like I couldn't care less about the sign.

'That sign isn't fair,' says Zelda loudly. 'Our dog Leopold would have hurt feelings if he saw that sign.'

Behind the counter is a big woman with her sleeves rolled up. She does the sort of laugh people do when they're not really amused.

'My dog already got hurt feelings,' she says. 'Right around the time I decided not to waste any more food on it.'

Zelda stares at the woman, shocked.

'Wilhelm and Violetta,' says Genia hastily, 'this is Mrs Szynsky.'

'Hello,' I say politely.

'Hello,' mutters Zelda.

Mrs Szynsky doesn't reply. She just looks me and Zelda up and down.

'Must have a lot of food to spare,' she says to Genia. 'Oh well, your loss.'

She fiddles with her blonde hair for a while, then points to our egg boxes as if she's only just noticed them.

'How many eggs?' she says.

'Fourteen,' says Genia.

We all put our boxes on the counter and Mrs Szynsky counts the eggs, picking each one up and peering at it closely.

'What do you want?' she says, not looking at Genia.

'A coat and a hat for each of the kids,' says Genia. 'When they were bombed out in Pilica they lost all their winter clothes.'

Mrs Szynsky looks scornful.

'For fourteen eggs?' she says. 'Not a chance. You can forget the hats for a start.'

'Ten eggs for the coats,' says Genia. 'With scarves.'

While Genia and Mrs Szynsky haggle, I peer around the shop. It's full of amazing things. Furniture and piles of clothes and unusual shoes and stuffed animals and paintings and decorated plates and glass cases full of jewellery.

Genia is holding Zelda's hand, but not mine.

I wander around the shop, gazing at everything.

Up the back, next to a pile of clocks, I find a polished wooden box.

Inside are the shiniest knives and forks and spoons I've ever seen. Even shinier than the ones we used to have when I was little.

I take out one of the spoons.

I wish I could buy it for Genia. She's only got wooden ones.

'Put it back,' hisses a voice.

Guiltily I put the spoon back.

A boy of about my age leaps out from behind a rack of hanging suits and snatches the box.

'No touching the goods,' he says in a bossy voice.

That doesn't seem fair. Next to us two burly farmers are trying on shiny red waistcoats. I open my mouth to point out that they're touching the goods. But I remember I'm Wilhelm, not Felix, and close it again.

'This is my family's shop,' says the boy. 'You were going to steal that spoon, weren't you?'

He's glaring at me, his lips wet and his face pink. His hair is so fair I can even see the pink skin on his head.

'No,' I say. 'I wasn't. Honest.'

I can feel my face going pink too, with panic. If he calls the police . . .

The boy gives me a wet grin.

'Only kidding,' he says.

I stare at him, stunned.

'Can't you take a joke?' he says, looking a bit offended.

I pull myself together.

'Course I can,' I say, dizzy with relief. I hold out my hand. 'I'm Wilhelm Nowak.'

I shake the boy's cold damp hand.

'I'm Cyryl,' he says.

Suddenly he leans towards me like I'm his best friend.

'Hey,' he says, tapping the cutlery box. 'Guess how much this cost.'

I haven't got a clue. Thousands of zloty probably. Millions.

'Two eggs,' says Cyryl.

I wait for him to tell me he's only kidding again.

'From the dumb Jews,' he says, grinning. 'My dad takes eggs and milk and bread over to that other part of town, you know, where we put all the Jews, what's it called . . .?'

'I don't know,' I say.

I do, it's called a ghetto. But I don't tell Cyryl that. If he doesn't know, Wilhelm shouldn't.

'Anyway,' says Cyryl, pointing around the shop, 'the dumb Jews swapped all this stuff for bits of food.'

'Perhaps they were hungry,' I murmur, and immediately wish I hadn't.

But Cyryl hasn't noticed. He's grinning at me and licking his lips. His teeth are crooked and he's got a dribble problem.

'What's the difference between a Jew and a rat?' he says.

'Don't know,' I say, trying to be Wilhelm.

'Once you've got them out from under your floorboards,' says Cyryl, 'who cares?'

I can feel my face going pink again. With anger this time.

Don't do anything silly, I beg myself. Like opening the cutlery box. And doing something to Cyryl with a fork.

'Hey,' says Cyryl, stepping close to me again like he's sharing another big secret. 'When Jews say their prayers, it makes cheese go mouldy. My dad told me.'

I struggle to be Wilhelm.

Cyryl looks at me for a moment.

'You're new,' he says. 'I haven't seen you before.'

'We just moved here,' I say. 'From Pilica.'

'If you want,' says Cyryl, 'you can join my gang.'

I don't know what to say. I wouldn't join Cyryl's gang if you gave me a whole box of cutlery and an uncircumcised private part.

I'm saved by a yelling voice.

'Cyryl, come back here, you haven't finished this job.'

A teenage girl with blonde pigtails is sticking her head out of a back room and glaring at Cyryl.

His shoulders slump and he gives her a sulky look.

'Sisters,' he says to me, scowling. 'They're worse than Jews.'

I nod. I don't trust myself to actually say anything. Cyryl doesn't notice. He's too busy being indignant.

'I do everything around here,' he says. 'I have to sort through all the new stuff that comes in. Half of it's junk. The Jews are always trying to cheat us.'

'Cyryl,' yells his sister, furious.

'That's all Jew junk there,' says Cyryl, pointing to a big wooden crate as he walks off.

I wait till Cyryl's in the back room before I look in the crate. Perhaps there'll be something cheap in there that Genia needs. She might be able to add it to the coats for the same number of eggs.

The stuff in the crate doesn't look like junk to me. There are cooking pots, shoes, ornaments, all sorts of things. A bit scuffed but not bad. There's even a book. OK, it looks like it's been in a fire, some of the pages are a bit burned and . . .

I pick it up and glance at the cover.

My heart jolts.

It's a Richmal Crompton book. In Polish, just like the ones I used to have, except this is one I've never read.

I try to be Wilhelm and drop it back into the crate, but I can't help it, I'm Felix and I stuff it inside my shirt.

Cyryl said this was all junk so I'm not really stealing.

Yes I am, but I don't care.

Suddenly I do care.

A voice is screaming at me. A voice so angry I can't even make out the words.

Is it Cyryl? His sister? Mrs Szynsky?

I turn, weak with fear.

And go even weaker.

It isn't any of the Szynsky family, it's a Nazi soldier.

He's got a rifle and he's pointing it at my head.

**Then** the Nazi soldier started waving his rifle. I still didn't understand any of the Nazi words he was yelling, but I could see he was ordering me out of the shop.

I felt sick.

What's the Nazi punishment for stealing a Richmal Crompton book? Getting hanged from a big wooden post in the town square with the other dead people?

I walk slowly towards the door of the shop.

Once I'm outside I'll run. It's all I can do. The book is inside my shirt, so I can't pretend I was buying it.

I don't look at Genia and Zelda. If I ignore them, maybe the Nazi soldier will too.

But Genia doesn't ignore me. She grabs my hand.

'Don't,' I whisper. 'The Nazi soldier will think you're in on it.'

Genia gives me a puzzled look. She doesn't let go of my hand.

'Come on, Wilhelm and Violetta,' she says. 'The soldier is ordering everybody outside to watch the Hitler Youth parade.'

She drags me and Zelda towards the door.

Everybody else in the shop is leaving too. Customers, Mrs Szynsky, shop assistants, Cyryl and his big sister.

Outside, hundreds of people are standing around the edges of the town square. We join them.

At first I'm not sure what's going on. I'm just dizzy with relief at not getting arrested.

'I can't see any parade,' says Zelda loudly.

'Shhh,' says Genia.

I realise why Genia wants Zelda to behave herself. Nazi soldiers are strutting about, bossing people and making everyone stand neatly.

Faintly, in the distance, I can hear the sound of marching boots.

Everybody is looking towards the far end of the square. The sound gets louder. A column of Nazis appears, marching in rows of four into the square.

There's something strange about them.

Compared to the other Nazi soldiers, they look a bit small.

As they get closer, I see why. They're boys about my age, maybe a couple of years older. All wearing Nazi uniforms and gleaming Nazi boots. They don't have guns, which is a good thing. Most of them have really sneering expressions. They don't look like the sort of people who would handle guns responsibly.

Genia jabs me with her elbow.

'Lower your eyes,' she hisses.

I see that all around the square, people are taking off their hats and looking at the ground.

I bow my head. But I keep watching from under my eyebrows as the marching boys get closer.

I've heard about the Hitler Youth. Adolf Hitler, the leader of the Nazis, started the Hitler Youth for German kids who are too young to join the army but want to strut around full of themselves anyway.

I've heard they can be very violent, even without guns.

'What fine young men,' says Mrs Szynsky, who's standing next to us. 'You could join them, Cyryl, if you weren't such a slob.'

'They're German,' says Cyryl. 'I'm not German.'

'You're still a slob,' says his sister.

I stop listening to Cyryl and his sister bickering because a thought hits me.

'Genia,' I whisper, my head still bowed. 'Is that why the Nazis wanted the Jewish orphans' bedrooms? For the Hitler Youth?'

I look sideways at her.

She nods.

The Hitler Youth have almost reached us now and everybody is bowing their heads even lower.

Except Zelda, who is glaring at the Hitler Youth and poking her tongue out.

'Don't,' I hiss at her in panic.

Genia sees what Zelda is doing.

She grabs Zelda and tries to hide her by standing in front of her.

But it's too late.

Cyryl also sees what Zelda is doing, and he starts giggling loudly.

One of the Hitler Youth at the front of the marching column yells something to the others and they all stop.

Right next to us.

Four of the Hitler Youth step out of the column and stride towards us. Behind them, a Nazi soldier raises his gun like he's keen to join in.

My insides are throbbing with fear.

I get ready to throw myself at the Hitler Youth if they touch Zelda.

But it isn't Zelda they touch. It's Cyryl. They grab him and slap him and punch him really hard. His mother lets out a shriek, but when they turn to her she smothers her mouth with her hand.

They punch and slap Cyryl some more.

I get furious.

I can't help it. When I see how much those Hitler Youth thugs are enjoying what they're doing, I stop being Wilhelm and take a step towards them.

As soon as I do, I come to my senses. What am I doing? I'm not a fighter. I can't protect Cyryl. All I'm doing is getting my family into trouble.

Genia grabs me and pulls me back.

The jolt makes the Richmal Crompton book fall out of my shirt onto the ground. For a moment I think I'm sprung. I brace myself to be arrested.

But nobody notices.

Mrs Szynsky is too busy helping Cyryl to his feet. The Hitler Youth thugs are too busy taking their places back in the column.

I crouch down to grab the book.

Just before my hand makes contact with it, the Hitler Youth leader yells something again.

I look up. He's not yelling at me, he's yelling at the column to start marching again, which they do.

But as the column marches off, one of the other Hitler Youth, not one of the thugs, stares at the book on the ground in front of me.

And does an amazing thing.

He grins at me. And with a small movement of his hand, so the other Hitler Youth can't see him, he gives me a thumbs up.

I blink. Did he really do that?

Is he telling me he's a Richmal Crompton fan too?

I grab the book and stuff it back inside my shirt and stand up and try to look like nothing has happened.

Nobody seems to be looking at me.

Well, hardly anybody.

The Hitler Youth column is halfway across the square now, but the boy who saw the book is still throwing glances back in my direction.

Somebody else is looking at me too.

Cyryl.

His mum is trying to wipe away the blood that's trickling out of his nose. He keeps moving his head. He wants her to leave him alone so he can do something else.

Stare at me and Zelda with total hatred.

I look away, but my insides stay knotted with worry. This is the last thing me and Zelda need.

An enemy with a gang.

**Then** me and Zelda and Genia went home. We didn't say much on the walk back. Genia didn't lose her temper till we were in the house.

'That was very foolish,' she yells.

At first I think she's angry with me for stealing the Richmal Crompton book. Except I don't think she saw it when I dropped it in the town square and it's been hidden in my shirt ever since.

'Very foolish and very naughty,' yells Genia.

I realise it's Zelda she's telling off.

'Poking your tongue out at Nazis,' yells Genia. 'What were you thinking, Violetta?'

'She's only six,' I say.

I agree Zelda was foolish, but I can see she's scared at how cross Genia is, and sometimes you have to look after your family even when they have been naughty.

'You're old enough to understand what Nazis are like,' Genia says to Zelda. 'You saw what they did to the poor Jewish orphans. And the orphans weren't even rude to them.'

'If they try to take our bedroom,' says Zelda. 'I'll be very rude to them.'

She isn't looking scared any more.

Genia sighs.

'I hate Nazis,' says Zelda.

I want to explain to Genia that this isn't the way to protect Zelda. That giving angry examples of how bad the Nazis are isn't going to make Zelda behave herself in public. It'll only make her worse.

Suddenly I know what I have to do. On the way home I was trying to decide, but now I know it's for the best.

So Genia understands.

So we can help Zelda.

I go into the bedroom. Next to the wall in the corner is a crack between two floorboards. I squeeze my fingers in and pull Zelda's locket out of its hiding place.

I take a deep breath.

This is risky, but sometimes you have to take a risk to protect your family.

I go back into the kitchen.

'Genia,' I say. 'You know how you said I couldn't help being Jewish?'

Genia nods.

I can see she's wondering what I'm on about.

'Well,' I say, 'here's something Zelda can't help.'

I show Genia the locket.

Zelda is staring. She thought she'd lost her locket in the barn. I'm pretty sure she didn't ever want to see it again.

Genia is staring too, at the tiny photo inside the locket. The photo of a Nazi dad in uniform and a Nazi mum gazing at him adoringly.

'Zelda's parents,' I say.

I want Genia to understand. To see why Zelda has bad feelings about Nazis, apart from them being vicious thugs and killers. To understand that some of her bad feelings are about her mum and dad.

Genia looks at the photo for a long time.

She gives a big sigh and looks at me.

'Why didn't you tell me?' she says.

'You hate Nazis,' I say. 'I didn't want you to hate Zelda.'

Genia sighs again. She puts one arm round Zelda and the other round me.

'Neither of you can help who your parents are,' she says quietly. 'Do you understand that, Zelda? Your mummy and daddy aren't your fault.'

Zelda pulls away from Genia.

'They aren't my mummy and daddy,' she says crossly. 'I'm Violetta. Don't you know anything?'

I wait for Genia to get angry again, but she doesn't, she just nods.

'Good girl,' she says, putting both arms round Zelda. 'You're learning.'

They look so content, hugging like that.

I don't like to interrupt.

But I have to.

'Genia,' I say. 'About Zelda's real parents. There's another problem.'

Genia looks at me over the top of Zelda's head. She leans across and ruffles my hair and puts her finger to her lips.

'Zelda's trying to forget about her parents,' she says. 'We have to help her do that.'

I sigh.

Genia doesn't understand.

Kids like us don't forget our real parents.

Not ever.

And until Zelda feels better about hers, she's going to keep poking her tongue out at Nazis.

**Then** I helped Zelda have happy memories of her real parents so she wouldn't be so cross and upset about them being Nazis.

Leopold helped too.

Well, we tried.

'Zelda,' I say as we sit in front of the wood stove. 'Give Leopold a hug. See if it brings back any happy memories.'

Zelda looks at me as if I've got leaf-mould madness. But she does it anyway because hugging Leopold is one of her favourite things to do.

Leopold likes it too. His tail is whacking the kitchen floor just at the thought.

Zelda puts her arms round him and buries her face in his neck fur.

'I love you, Leopold,' she says, her voice muffled.

'Any happy memories?' I say softly after a while.

Zelda keeps her face buried, thinking.

'Yes,' she says. 'I can remember when I hugged Leopold this morning before breakfast.'

I try to think of something that will help her have earlier happy memories.

'Your daddy had whiskers like Leopold,' I say.

Leopold looks a bit offended.

'No he didn't,' says Zelda, still muffled. 'My daddy's whiskers were short. And he didn't lick my ear.'

Leopold stops licking Zelda's ear and gives me an apologetic look.

'It's alright,' I say to him. 'You're doing a good job helping Zelda.'

I give Leopold a pat and he gives me a loving look and suddenly, gazing into his gentle eyes, I'm having memories of my own.

Dad giving me a bath and drying me on our kitchen table.

Mum blowing raspberries on my tummy.

'You're helping me too,' I whisper to Leopold.

I try to feel happy but it's not easy.

Zelda looks up, concerned, and watches me for a moment.

'See?' she says. 'Memories aren't happy, they're sad. Don't you know anything?'

Every day it's the same.

I do my best, but Zelda is a very stubborn person.

Like today. We're doing drawing in the barn.

Or rather, I'm letting Zelda do most of the drawing because there's only one pencil.

Earlier, when it was my go of the pencil, I did a diagram of how the automatic chicken-feeding machine works.

Now I'm nailing the diagram to the wall under the gherkin tin so the chickens can see what they have to do.

Leopold and Trotski are staring at me. They're looking a bit disappointed, possibly because there aren't any dogs or pigs in the diagram.

I give them both a tickle.

'Don't worry,' I say to them. 'Me and Violetta will invent automatic feeding machines for you next.'

Animals get very anxious in wartime. If the humans get killed, who's going to feed them?

I go over to Zelda to see how her drawing's going.

'That lady's got a very pretty hat,' I say, pointing to the person Zelda has drawn. 'Who is it?'

'It's Violetta's mummy,' says Zelda. 'She wears her pretty hat when she kills Nazis.'

The paper Zelda's drawing on is old shop paper that has been wrapped round face powder or something. There's a pink stain in the middle which Zelda turns into a dead Nazi's brains leaking out.

I stare at the drawing, worry nagging inside me. If I can't find a way to help Zelda feel better about her parents, I hate to think what's going to happen next time she meets a Nazi.

'Zelda,' I say quietly. 'Why don't you do a picture of your real mummy and daddy? From when you were little. When they took you on holiday or gave you a present or did something fun with you.'

Zelda looks at me. She doesn't say anything, but I can see she doesn't like the idea much.

Leopold and Trotski come over. Leopold licks Zelda's knee. Trotski blows some snot in her direction. I can see they're both trying to help. It's their way of telling Zelda they'd like to see a nice picture of her real mummy and daddy too.

Zelda moves the pencil to another part of the paper and starts a new drawing.

'Thanks,' I whisper to them both.

While Zelda draws, I tell a story to inspire her.

It's about a friend of William and Violet Elizabeth's called Zelda. Zelda's parents accidently drown her collection of ants while they're watering the garden. Zelda is very angry, but her parents say they're sorry and cuddle her and Zelda feels better.

'And then do some other ants kill her parents?' says Zelda.

I sigh. It's not a very good story, but I'm doing my best.

'Maybe,' I say. 'But Zelda discovers that even when her parents do bad things, they still love her.'

'How can they still love her if they're dead?' says Zelda.

I sigh again. I'm getting confused now. Stories always work best when you don't try to tell people what they're about.

I see that Zelda has drawn a happy child holding hands with two happy grown-ups.

'Is that your real mummy and daddy?' I say hopefully.

'No,' says Zelda.

Suddenly I can't stand it any more. Why can't Zelda see how important this is?

'Just draw a picture of your real mummy and daddy,' I say to her crossly.

As soon as I've said it, I feel awful. I know how sad I get thinking about my parents. And I'm ten. How sad must it be for a little kid?

Zelda is looking at me, frowning. She holds up her drawing.

'This is Wilhelm's mummy and daddy,' she says. 'They've come to cheer you up cause you're unhappy.'

I don't know what to say.

Zelda puts the drawing down and gives me a hug.

'They love you very much,' she whispers. 'They don't mind that you're Jewish.'

I hug Zelda tight. I can't believe how lucky I am to have her as my family.

'Leopold and Trotski and the chickens don't mind that you're Jewish either,' whispers Zelda.

She doesn't have to tell me that because I can tell from the way Leopold is licking my hand and Trotski is dribbling snot onto my boots and the chickens are pecking at my bootlaces.

But it's a very kind thing to say. Zelda may be only six but she's got the kindness of a ten-year-old.

'Sorry I got cross,' I say.

'That's alright,' she says.

I take a deep breath. I mustn't give up. I must find a way. I must do everything I can to protect Zelda and her loving heart.

Suddenly I hear the distant growl of a truck engine.

Leopold barks.

I rush to the barn door and peer out across the fields.

Oh no.

'Quick,' I say to Zelda. 'Into the house.'

I grab her hand and her pencil and paper and we run across the farmyard into the kitchen.

Genia is in the bedroom having a rest. I bang on the door.

'Genia,' I yell. 'Wake up. The Nazis are back.'

Then Genia told me and Zelda to stay in the house while she went out to see what the Nazi soldiers want.

Suddenly it hits me.

The Richmal Crompton book, I bet that's what they want. Cyryl probably complained to the Nazis about me stealing the book from his family's shop and they've come to get it.

And me.

I peer through the kitchen window. It's the same two Nazi soldiers from the first day when me and Zelda were hiding in the barn.

But Genia isn't wearing any makeup or perfume this time. When I yelled about the Nazis, she jumped up from her bed and went straight outside.

Next to me Zelda is watching the Nazi soldiers through the window too. And poking her tongue out at them.

'Zelda,' I whisper frantically. 'Stop that.'

Luckily the Nazi soldiers aren't looking in our direction. They're both turned towards Genia. But they aren't grinning and sniffing her wrist this time.

They're shouting at her.

'I hate them,' mutters Zelda.

One of the soldiers grabs Genia and pulls her over to the barn. They push her inside and go in after her.

My mind is racing.

Of course. They must think I've hidden the Richmal Crompton book in the straw. When they don't find it, they'll get even angrier with Genia. And they won't take long to discover it's not there. Nowhere near long enough for Genia to put on makeup and perfume.

I dart into the bedroom, pull the book from its hiding place under my side of the mattress, and head for the kitchen door.

'Wait here,' I say to Zelda.

I hurry outside with the book.

This is all I can do. Give the book to the soldiers and say I'm sorry. Explain that Cyryl told me it was junk. Hope that when they see my Polish Wilhelm identity card, they'll have mercy.

At least they haven't got their killer dog with them today.

I crouch outside the door of the barn. I don't want to just barge in. Everyone knows you never creep up behind a horse or a Nazi.

I peep through a crack in the door so I can choose a moment when the soldiers haven't got their heads in the straw.

My eyes get used to the gloom and I blink with surprise and alarm.

The Nazis aren't doing a book search at all. One of them is grabbing the chickens and stuffing them into a sack. The other is putting a rope round Trotski's neck.

Trotski isn't happy. He's trying to bite the soldier. The soldier is swearing.

Genia is very upset.

'You can't take them,' she's yelling. 'You can't.'

One of the Nazi soldiers has got his gun pointed at Genia, but apart from that they're ignoring her.

Leopold is very upset too. He's barking and growling. Genia is holding him by his collar, but he's jumping and leaping, trying to get at the soldiers.

I know I should be doing the same. Or at least pleading with them.

Before I can move, I hear a voice calling out.

'Hey, Nowak.'

At first I don't understand what that means. I'm too numb to think. But slowly I realise.

That's me.

I turn round.

Cyryl and three other boys are walking towards me across the farmyard. Cyryl is grinning, but not in a friendly way. As he gets closer, I see that his face is badly bruised from when the Hitler Youth bashed him the other day.

I hurry forward to meet the boys so I can find out what they want before they get too close to the barn.

'This is my gang,' says Cyryl, pointing to the other boys, who aren't looking very friendly either.

Now I'm thinking fast. Cyryl must have decided to come here in person to report me to the Nazis for book stealing. And Zelda as well probably. So he can gloat while the Nazis arrest us. And there's nothing I can do. I've got the book in my hands. He must have seen it already.

Cyryl and the other boys come and stand very close to me. But Cyryl isn't even looking at the book.

'Do you want to join my gang?' he says.

I stare at him, surprised. I don't know what to say. I just want to get back to the barn.

'We want you to join,' says Cyryl.

The other boys all nod.

My thoughts are whirling. Maybe his gang do a lot of stealing and that's why they're inviting me. Maybe if I'm in his gang he won't press charges about the book.

'Alright,' I say, stuffing the book inside my shirt.

'And me,' says another voice. 'I want to join too.'

It's Zelda. She's standing next to me, hands on her hips, looking sternly at Cyryl.

'Go back to the house,' I plead with her.

'Not unless you do,' she says.

Cyryl scowls at Zelda.

'No girls,' he says. He turns back to me. 'Before you can join, you have to do the test.'

'What test?' I say.

'Pull your trousers down,' says Cyryl.

I don't understand. But after a couple of seconds I do. Fear starts to churn inside me.

'You're rude,' says Zelda to Cyryl.

Cyryl ignores her.

'It's the entrance test for the gang,' he says to me. 'You have to prove you're not a Jew.'

My insides are quivering. I try not to show it.

'That's stupid,' I say. 'I've changed my mind. I don't want to join.'

'Too late,' says Cyryl. 'You said you did. If you don't pull your trousers down, we will.'

The other boys take a step towards me.

Cyryl is looking me right in the eye, his wet lips gleaming. I can see exactly what he's thinking.

He's hoping I've got a Jewish private part.

He can't wait to show the Nazi soldiers.

If my trousers come down, we haven't got a chance. The Nazis'll take me into town and kill me on a post. Same with Genia for hiding me. And Zelda doesn't stand a chance either. Even Nazi kids get executed if they protect Jews.

You know how when you're trapped and terrified and your insides are squeezed up with fear, you get an urgent need to do a poo?

I'm getting that now.

'Pull his trousers down,' says Cyryl.

The boys all grab at my trousers and start to undo the buttons. I try to fight them, but two of them hold my arms.

'Get off him,' yells Zelda.

Cyryl pushes her away. She sprawls onto the ground. I kick and struggle but it's no good. The boys have got two of the buttons undone already.

There's only one thing I can do. It's my last chance for us to survive.

I let the poo out.

Cyryl has got his hands on the back of my trousers, trying to drag them down.

'Urghh,' he says. 'What's that smell? Yuck, it's warm.'

183

I don't say anything.

He'll realise.

He does.

'Arghh,' he yells, jumping back. 'He's pooed his pants.'

The other boys jump back too.

I look down. I don't want to see their faces and what they think of me.

'Disgusting,' says one of the boys.

'Filthy maggot,' says another.

They're right, but what choice did I have?

Zelda is scrambling to her feet.

'You made him do it,' she yells at the boys. 'He doesn't usually do it.'

She puts her arms round me.

'It's not your fault,' she says. 'Sometimes poo just comes out.'

The barn door bangs open. One of the Nazi soldiers appears, carrying a sack full of squawking chickens.

Cyryl runs over to him, crowing loudly, pointing at me.

'He pooed his pants.'

Maybe he hopes the Nazi soldier will shoot me for being disgusting.

The Nazi soldier isn't in the mood. His hands and face are covered with chicken scratches. He swipes at Cyryl and almost knocks him over.

'Get lost, all of you,' he yells at us in bad Polish.

But we don't.

Cyryl stomps back towards me and I can see he's determined to get my pants down, poo or no poo.

Zelda is staring at the sack of chickens, horrified, and I can see she's determined to rescue them.

I step forward to try and stop them both.

I'm still moving forward when something else happens.

Something even worse.

Inside the barn, loud and terrible.

A gunshot.

184

# Then we froze.

Me and Zelda and Cyryl and the other boys.

A gunshot can do that. Make your whole body go cold and rigid, even if the bullet doesn't actually hit you.

The Nazi soldier with the sack of chickens doesn't freeze. He just tosses the sack into the back of the truck. He doesn't even look concerned. He probably hears a hundred gunshots a day, most of them probably killing innocent people like Genia or innocent pigs like Trotski.

Suddenly, with a jolt of panic, I come back to life.

So do Cyryl and his gang. They stop gawking at the barn and swap scared looks.

'I haven't finished with you, Nowak,' Cyryl snarls at me, and I can see he means it.

He and the other boys sprint away.

Zelda is storming towards the chickens.

I lunge forward and grab her just as the other Nazi soldier comes out of the barn. He's putting his pistol back into its holster and dragging an angry Trotski at the end of the rope.

More panic hits me.

If it wasn't Trostski who was shot . . .

'Let that pig go,' Zelda yells at the soldiers. 'And those chickens.'

I put my hand over her mouth.

Before I can see what terrible thing has happened in the barn, I have to keep Zelda safe.

'Be a good girl, Violetta,' I say loudly, just like Genia would. 'The officers are just collecting food for the Nazi army.'

Zelda bites my hand.

I try not to let the soldiers see I'm in pain. I pretend I'm wiping dirt from round Zelda's mouth. While she grunts into my hand, I smile and wave with my other hand to the soldiers. They grunt too as they lift Trotski up and dump him in the back of the truck.

Please understand why I can't rescue you, I beg Trotski silently.

I keep smiling and waving while the Nazis drive away. It's incredibly hard, smiling with full pants and fear in your guts and an aching heart, but I do it for Zelda.

'You let them take Trotski,' Zelda yells at me when I finally take my hand off her mouth. 'You let them take the chickens.'

I try to explain but I can't speak. Zelda probably thinks it's because I'm ashamed, which I am.

But mostly it's because of what might be waiting for us in the barn.


I stop in the barn doorway, not wanting to look. From inside I hear sobbing.

A person can only sob when they're alive.

'Genia,' I whisper, weak with relief.

But my relief doesn't last long. My eyes get used to the gloom. What I see isn't a relief at all.

Leopold is lying on the ground. Not barking. Not growling. Not even moving.

Genia is kneeling next to him, her face in her hands.

'Leopold,' screams Zelda, rushing past me.

She flings herself down next to Genia and tries to lift Leopold, but his head just flops against her chest.

'Leopold,' sobs Zelda. 'Don't be dead.'

Genia looks at me and Zelda. Her eyes are red and her face is wet.

'I tried to hold him back,' she says, her voice croaky with grief. 'But his collar snapped. So they shot him.'

Now I can see how red the fur on his neck is.

Zelda is shaking with sobs, pressing her face against Leopold's limp body.

I crouch down and gently close his eyelids and stroke his soft untidy fur.

'Good boy,' I whisper.

After that I have to close my own eyes because they're so full of tears.


We bury Leopold at sunset in a corner of the cabbage field.

'It was his favourite field,' says Genia.

We lay some wild flowers and ferns onto the mound of soil.

'Why are Nazi monsters so mean and horrible?' says Zelda.

Genia and me don't reply. We don't know the answer. Instead we stand quietly by Leopold's grave and say some prayers for him.

I ask Richmal Crompton, out loud so Genia and Zelda can hear, if she can arrange for Jumble, the dog in her books, to end up in the same part of heaven as Leopold. I think they'll like each other.

'Jumble will like Trotski and the chickens too,' says Zelda.

I smile at her through my tears.

'He will,' I say.

Zelda rummages around in her coat pocket and pulls out a folded piece of paper. She unfolds it and gives it to Genia.

It's a drawing of Leopold and Trotski and the chickens all being fed automatically.

'So you can remember them,' says Zelda.

Genia looks at the drawing for a long time.

'Thank you,' she says softly. 'Both of you.'

She takes a deep breath and turns to me.

'Wilhelm,' she says.

'Yes?' I say nervously.

I'm worried about what Genia's going to say next.

While she was washing my trousers earlier she didn't say anything. Not about the poo or about how my private part nearly got us killed. But I could see her thinking about things.

What if she's decided now she simply can't protect such a dirty and dangerous boy?

Genia gives me a hug.

'I'm proud of you,' she says. 'What you did this afternoon was very brave and very quick-thinking.'

I'm a bit dazed, but glowing too.

'He can do it any time he wants,' says Zelda, hugging me from the other side. 'Any time he sees a Nazi, he can just do a poo.'

We stand with our arms round each other for a long time and I don't ever want to stop because I'm so lucky to have a family like Zelda and Genia.

Finally we walk back towards the house.

'We're going to be hungry this winter,' says Genia, looking sadly towards the barn. 'The Nazis have taken everything now. All I've got is a few cabbages and a few potatoes and a few onions.'

'And a few turnips,' says Zelda.

Genia smiles and gives her a squeeze.

'You're right, Violetta,' she says. 'We mustn't forget the turnips.'

Poor Genia. If she didn't have to feed us, at least she'd have a bit more for herself.

That's when I decide to do it.

I may not be big or tough or muscly enough to be a fighter, but there is one thing I can do.

Get more food for my family.

Then I racked my brains about where you can get food in this part of Poland with winter coming on and all the fields empty because the Nazis have stripped them bare.

Grow cabbages in the barn?

Catch birds?

Boil up acorns?

I try everything, but it's no good. You need sunlight for cabbage seeds to grow. Candles just aren't bright enough. And you can't catch birds when they've all gone to Africa to get away from the cold. And boiled acorns taste yucky and give you a belly ache.

'What about mushroom soup?' says Zelda one morning.

I look at her hopefully.

'Have you found mushrooms somewhere?' I ask.

'No,' she says, handing me a piece of paper. 'But I thought about them really hard. Like we did that time with chocolate. And I remembered what they looked like.'

I stare at a drawing of mushrooms.

'Be careful,' says Zelda sternly. 'They might be poisonous.'

In bed one night I suddenly remember the rabbit holes. That hillside me and Zelda climbed up when we were escaping from the Nazi train was full of rabbit holes.

Rabbit holes mean rabbits.

Tender juicy rabbits.

Perfect for winter stews.

I wait till Genia and Zelda are asleep. Carefully I slip out of bed. In the darkness I put on my boots. I leave my coat, I can move faster without it.

I creep into the kitchen.

I've never killed a rabbit before, so I'm not sure exactly what I'll need.

A net?

A rope to strangle them?

A knife?

I can't find a net or a rope, so I borrow Genia's vegetable knife. On my way to the door, I have another thought and I borrow her shopping bag too. It's a nice one made of string.

I'll try not to get blood on it.

I creep out of the house.

It's a cloudy night, but as I hurry across the cabbage field, the moon comes out. The cabbage stumps gleam white in the moonlight.

Shame the rabbits don't know they're here. I bet rabbits love cabbage stumps. A field of rabbits on my doorstep would make my job a lot easier.

Well, a bit easier.

I'd still have to kill them.

'Wish me luck, Leopold,' I whisper as I pass his grave.

I'm sure he does. And I know he'd come with me if he could.

There's a chill breeze whipping across these fields, but I'll stay warm as long as I move quickly. In the distance I can see the hills, and the ragged line of forest that runs along the top. That's where the rabbit holes are, in those hills.

I try not to think about what's also there.

The poor dead children in their grave.

I reach a lane and go along it in the direction of the hills. But the lane isn't straight. It's got bends and turns. And corners. There's a high hedge on both sides and now the moon is back behind a cloud and I'm not sure any more which direction I'm going.

I leave the lane and cut across a field towards what I hope are the hills looming in front of me. I start climbing a slope. Except, as I climb, I can't see any rabbit holes. Or any trees.

Suddenly I hear voices talking loudly in the distance.

I fling myself to the ground, praying that the moon will stay hidden so I can too. Now, as I peer ahead, I can make out a faint haze of lights.

More voices.

The growl of engines.

The moon comes out. I have to find a better hiding place than this open hillside.

I crawl up the rocky slope, hoping to find a bush or a burrow. What I see at the top is so amazing I forget all about bushes and burrows.

I even forget about rabbits.

Down the slope on the other side is a big house. About fifty times bigger than Genia's place. There's even an upstairs. Plus other buildings that look like stables or garages. Lamps are burning in just about all the rooms. A motorbike is sitting out the front with its engine running even though it's not going anywhere.

These people must be very rich.

I can see some of them, walking around outside, dark against the lit-up windows. They're talking and laughing and . . .

. . . wearing uniforms.

I wipe the sweat off my glasses and look again.

Nazis.

Now I can see trucks with swastikas on them. And guards at the gate. And machine guns.

I know I should run as far away as I can, but I can't stop looking.

I've heard how the Nazis always take the best country houses for themselves. The big ones with wine cellars and bathrooms. Which explains why they haven't moved into Genia's place.

'Don't move.'

A voice hisses at me from behind.

I feel a cold sharp blade prick the skin on the back of my neck.

A bayonet, probably.

'Turn round,' hisses the voice. 'Slowly.'

I turn round. And find myself facing a kid.

It's a kid I've seen before. I recognise the scar on his forehead.

He's Leopold's Jewish orphan friend and he's holding the same knife as when he visited the barn. I see he has cleaned the blade. It glints in the moonlight as he points it at my chest.

He stares at me with angry, unfriendly eyes.

'How's Leopold?' he asks.

My mind races. I want to tell him the truth, but I don't want to upset him more.

'I think he's probably missing you,' I say.

I can see the kid doesn't like this answer. I wonder if I'm going to have to fight him. My knife is in my pocket, wrapped in Genia's shopping bag.

Even if I could get to it, I don't think it would do me much good. The kid is wearing a thick coat that reaches almost to the ground. I'm not sure a knife could stab through it.

I need to try something else.

I have an idea. It's risky, but I can't think of a less risky one.

'I'm Jewish too,' I say.

The kid doesn't move. Or lower the knife. Or stop looking at me suspiciously.

I don't really blame him. It's very hard to trust people in the modern world. I need to give him some proof.

'Don't be alarmed,' I say. 'I'm going to pull my trousers down.'

He doesn't even blink.

Very slowly, so he can see there's no trick involved, I pull my trousers down.

The kid looks at my private part.

'What's your name?' he says.

'Felix,' I say. 'But I'm pretending to be Wilhelm.'

There. I've said it. Now he's got two ways to kill me. He can stab me, or he can tell the Nazis I'm Jewish.

'What's yours?' I say.

The kid doesn't answer. But he lowers the knife.

'What are you doing here?' he says.

'Hunting rabbits,' I say as I pull my trousers up. 'I got lost. What are you doing here?'

For a few moments he looks like he's not going to answer that question either. But he does.

'I come here a lot,' he says quietly. 'I used to live here.'

My mind races again. This big house must have been the Jewish orphanage. The one the Nazis wanted empty so the Hitler Youth could move in.

Poor kid.

All his friends murdered.

We both stare down at the house. I can't see any Hitler Youth here at the moment. They must be in bed. But there are several Nazi soldiers and officers strutting around, wasting lamp oil and not caring about the dead children they shot last month.

Suddenly I want revenge.

I want to do something to them that will make them go back to Germany and never shoot another dog or child or hang another grown-up from a post ever again.

Something that will hurt them a lot.

I take deep breaths and tell myself to stop being silly. Who am I kidding? What could one boy do with a vegetable knife and a shopping bag?

Even two boys with two knives.

I turn away.

Anyway, I say to myself, we're not like them. We only kill for food.

Suddenly I remember Leopold's rabbit meat. This kid must know how to hunt rabbits.

'Hey,' I say to him. 'Let's go hunting.'

The kid shakes his head, not taking his eyes off the Nazis in the orphanage.

I get the feeling he doesn't mind the idea of hunting, just not with me.

**Then** I asked the kid more questions like where was he from originally and how did he escape being shot with the other orphans and where is he living now but he won't answer so I say goodbye and head off to hunt rabbits.

On my own.

When I finally make it to the forest, I stand in among the dark trees, wondering which way the railway line is.

Richmal Crompton hears my prayers. She helps me choose the right direction.

Also a train clatters past in the distance to give me an extra clue.

I crouch in the ferns, looking down at the hillside covered in rabbit holes. The moon is out and so are the rabbits, peeking out of their tunnels as the sound of the train dies away.

I check that the vegetable knife and the shopping bag are still in my pocket.

This is going to be the difficult part.

Catching a wild rabbit will be hard. I'll have to be very fast.

Cutting its throat will be even harder. I'll have to try and make myself into a killer. Just for a few seconds. For my family.

Alright . . .

Here goes . . .

I plunge my hands into a rabbit hole.

Oh no. I've got one. A live rabbit, kicking and struggling in my arms. Warm and quivering. I slide my hand up to its throat and reach for the knife. I can feel the veins in its throat throbbing and now it's looking at me with big dark eyes . . .

What was that?

Gunshots.

I've been seen.

I drop the rabbit and dive back into the thick ferns, waiting for bullets to smash into me, imagining Zelda waking up not knowing where I've gone, never finding out why I didn't come back, thinking I broke my promise.

The shooting stops.

The rabbits have all dived for cover too, except for a few who are twitching and dying.

Voices boom out from the trees. Nazi soldiers, several of them, with torches and guns, slide and slither their way down the slope. They pick up the dead rabbits and examine them in the torchlight.

I'm almost weeping with relief.

It wasn't me they were after.

But that's not the only reason I'm relieved. I can still feel that rabbit's veins, throbbing frantically. My head is throbbing now in just the same way.

I couldn't have killed it.

Not even to feed my family.

I don't know how Leopold's friend can do it.

I stay hidden and watch the soldiers. I can't understand what they're saying, but their voices don't sound very happy. I'm not surprised. There are four of them and only three dead rabbits.

As they climb back up the hillside, they're arguing about something.

Suddenly I understand one of the words.

*Fische.*

It's one of the few German words I know. When I was little, a German tourist came into our bookshop and asked where he could catch fish in our local river and Dad told him.

The Nazi soldiers seem to be agreeing about *Fische* now.

I think it sounds like a good idea too. I think I'll be better at catching fish than killing rabbits.

The Nazi soldiers head off through the forest.

I follow them.

*

I didn't know there was a river in these parts.

It's not as big as the river I grew up near, but it's big enough for fish, I can see that even from behind these bushes.

The Nazi soldiers are standing on the river bank. One of them is fiddling with something in a bag. I wonder what it is? The bag doesn't look big enough for a fishing rod.

Suddenly the soldier throws something, a dark lump, and it splashes into the river.

They can't be trying to kill fish with rocks, that's crazy. Perhaps they're using rabbit meat as bait.

The other soldiers duck.

An explosion erupts out of the water.

A huge one.

I'm deafened and drenched even over here. As I wipe the water off my face and glasses, my dazed mind tries to make sense of what's happening. Is this a battle? Are we being bombed?

The Nazi soldiers are all in the river, yelling excitedly and waving fish at each other. I can see other fish floating in the water.

Now I get it.

They're fishing. That thing they chucked into the river must have been one of those bombs you throw with your hand, what's it called . . .

'Hand grenade,' says a voice in my ear.

I nearly pass out with shock.

It's Leopold's friend, crouching next to me in the bushes. He must have crept up while the hand grenade was going off.

'Keep your head down,' he mutters.

We watch the soldiers splash around, gathering up dead fish and tossing them onto the shore.

Silently I beg them to leave a couple for me and Zelda and Genia. And one for the kid.

'You still want to go hunting?' says the kid quietly. 'You and me?'

I look at him, surprised. Does he mean fish or rabbits?

I nod uncertainly.

The kid reaches into the big pockets of his coat and pulls out a few things and puts them on the ground in front of us.

The first thing I see is his knife.

There's blood on it again.

But it's the other two things that really shock me.

Guns.

Two big dark shiny hand guns.

I stare at them. The kid picks one up and holds it out to me. I don't know what to say.

'W-what are we hunting?' I stammer.

The kid doesn't answer. Just squints at the Nazi soldiers, who are still gathering up stunned and dead fish.

I feel like a stunned fish myself.

Does he mean . . .?

I stare him. He can't mean that. We're kids.

He looks at me, waiting.

After a few moments he gives a snort and puts the weapons back in his pocket.

'Forget it,' he says, and disappears into the dark undergrowth.

Suddenly I want to get out of here.

But the soldiers haven't finished yet. They clamber out of the water and the one with the bag grabs another grenade. He throws it into the river. The other three soldiers put their hands over their ears and turn away.

I'm about to do the same when I see something near the grenade-throwing Nazi that makes me freeze, even though I know I'm about to be deafened and blinded again.

The kid.

He's stepping out from behind a tree.

Holding one of the guns in both hands.

Pointing it at the back of the Nazi's head.

I stop breathing.

For a moment everything else seems to stop. But only for a moment. Now the water is exploding again, as loud as before.

'Don't,' I yell at the kid.

But I can't hear my own voice, so I'm sure he can't either.

The kid's arms twitch and the Nazi soldier falls forward onto the river bank.

My head is ringing and my glasses are covered with spray. The kid is just a blur now, but he seems to be bending down, reaching for something.

When I finish wiping my glasses, he's gone.

So has the grenade bag.

The other Nazis see their friend on the ground. They run to him, shouting at him and at each other and turning him over.

I've only got a few seconds before they realise it wasn't the grenade that got him. A few seconds before they start hunting for a culprit.

I run.

**Then** I realised that running was stupid.

Soon the whole area will be full of troops looking for the kid who killed the Nazi soldier. There'll be dogs. Trucks. Maybe even planes.

I stop running. I have a better idea. I'll hide in the one place they probably won't look.

The river.

I'm a fair way along the river bank from the dead Nazi. I find a place where low branches dip into the water. I slide down the muddy bank under the leaves.

This is a good hiding place. The water is up to my chin and the branches hide my head from view. Only two things worry me, apart from being found and killed. The water is very cold and Genia's good shopping bag is very wet.

The minutes tick by, lots of them. After a while I can hear troops and trucks and dogs. I pass the time thinking about the kid.

How could he do it?

Shoot another person in the head?

I couldn't even kill a rabbit.

He must be very strong and very determined. And very stupid. Doesn't he know that Nazis will do anything for revenge? Didn't he stop and think that he was putting every child for miles around in serious danger?

Leopold could have told him.

I think about Zelda, sleeping peacefully and not even knowing that by tomorrow she could be on a Nazi revenge death list.

A dead fish floats towards me, eyes dull in the moonlight.

'I won't let them get her,' I say to the fish.

The fish doesn't reply, but it doesn't need to. I know what I'm going to do.

I wait until the trucks and the dogs have finally gone and I pull myself and the fish out of the water and start heading back to Genia's.

The sky is clear now. The air is cold. I move fast so I don't freeze.

With the help of the moon and Richmal Crompton and the distant engine sounds of trucks being parked, I manage to avoid the Hitler Youth orphanage.

I find the lane.

I find Leopold's cabbage field.

I'm feeling tired and exhausted as well as cold and wet, but the sun will probably be up in a couple of hours so I don't have any time to waste.

I hurry into the barn. Genia doesn't bother keeping it locked now that Trotski and the chickens are gone.

Inside the barn I put the fish down, take my wet clothes off, find a spade and start digging.


'Wilhelm, what are you doing?'

You know how when you've been working on a hole for ages and you've got used to only hearing the sound of the digging, chunk, chunk, chunk, and suddenly somebody startles you and you nearly slice into your foot with the spade?

That just happened to me.

'Wilhelm,' says Genia sternly. 'What is going on?'

I look up. She's standing at the edge of the hole in her nightdress and coat. The early morning sun is milky through the open barn door behind her.

Now I've stopped digging, I realise the hole is getting quite big. I'm standing in it and only my head is above ground level.

Good.

It's nearly deep enough.

'Come out of there,' says Genia, frowning.

I can see she's wondering why I'm naked.

She reaches down and grabs my hand and hauls me up. Now that I'm standing next to her, even through my sweaty glasses I can see what a mess I've made. Dirt is scattered all around the barn.

'Sorry,' I say. 'I'll clean it up.'

Genia is staring at me with the expression people get when somebody has dug a hole in the floor of their barn and they don't understand why.

'It's for Zelda,' I explain. 'I mean Violetta. An emergency hiding place. In case the Nazis come for her. I've made it big enough so she can lie down. We can put straw in the bottom and Leopold's kennel over the top.'

I stop talking to give Genia a chance to take it all in.

She's looking at me as if she thinks I'm a bit mad. Oh well, at least she's not staring at my private part. And she won't think the hole is a crazy idea when I tell her about the killer kid at the river.

But before I can, Genia speaks first.

'Wilhelm,' she says softly. 'It's a very kind idea, but think about it. Can you honestly imagine Violetta staying still and quiet and hidden for more than two minutes? You know what a fidget she is.'

A chill runs through me, even though I'm hot and dripping with sweat.

I hadn't thought of that.

'I'm not a fidget,' says an indignant voice. 'I'm just lively. Don't you know anything?'

Zelda is standing in the doorway, rubbing her eyes sleepily. She comes to the edge of the hole and looks down into it.

'It's too small,' she says. 'Only one person can hide in there, not two of us.'

I hadn't thought of that either. I forgot about me. My brain must be addled because I haven't slept all night.

Zelda's face is a mixture of crossness and such loving concern that I want to hug her.

I don't because I'm covered in sweat and mud. And Genia is staring at my pile of wet clothes. And the fish. And the things from the kitchen. She's looking like she might explode.

'Wilhelm,' she says quietly. 'Have you been to the river?'

I nod.

I can see from her face she's struggling to control herself. Probably because she doesn't know whether she should thank me for getting food or yell at me for getting her shopping bag wet.

I confess everything. The rabbits. The Nazis fishing with grenades. Leopold's killer friend.

When I've finished, Genia doesn't speak for a long time.

Zelda does.

'I want Leopold's friend to teach me how to do it,' she says quietly as she stares at Leopold's kennel. 'How to shoot a Nazi.'

Genia gives her a look.

Zelda sticks out her bottom lip, stubborn and determined.

'The Nazis will take revenge for tonight,' says Genia. 'People will die. But if you really did get away without being seen, Wilhelm, there's no reason any of us will suffer.'

I sag with relief.

'I did,' I say.

'Good,' says Genia. 'I want you to promise me you'll never do anything like that again.'

I think about how upset I felt when the kid shot the Nazi and how cold I was in the river and how worried I've been ever since.

'I promise,' I say.

Genia nods. I can see she believes me.

'If the Nazis come for revenge,' says Zelda, 'I'll shoot them.'

Genia frowns. I think she's starting to see the problem we have with Zelda and Nazis.

Then Genia and Zelda went out while I was sleeping and found some delicious herbs and made a fish stew.

It's the best one I've ever tasted. The last one was about six years ago, but Mum only had caraway seeds for herbs and I didn't like the taste of them much. I could probably get to like them now, though. If Genia can get to like Jewish people, anything's possible.

'Would you like some more stew?' says Genia.

'Yes, please,' I say.

There's nothing like a herb and fish stew to stop you worrying about Nazi revenge attacks. For a while, anyway.

'Yes, please, thank you very much,' says Zelda.

Genia goes over to the stove to get the pot.

Zelda is making a picture on the table with her fish bones. Little stick figures with fish-bone arms and legs. They look happy.

I wish Genia looked happy. She's been frowning and biting her lip ever since she got back with the herbs. I hope she's not having regrets about using all the fish in the stew instead of saving some.

She could have preserved some of the fish with salt and stored it in the wardrobe like I suggested. Preserving is a really good way of keeping food for winter. Mum used to do it with carrots. I bet in the future they invent lots of ways of preserving food. I bet by the year 1970 we'll be able to eat cherries in winter if we want, or lettuce.

Genia gives a big sigh.

On second thoughts I think she's worried about something more important than preserved fish. I think she's worried about Zelda, like me.

I look at Zelda's fish-bone figures again. Both of them have got fish-bone smiles. I'm glad she's doing a happy picture.

'Is that your real mummy and daddy?' I say to her.

As usual I'm hoping it is. The sooner she gives up this crazy idea that she's Jewish, the less likely she'll have to use the emergency hole in the barn.

'Your mummy and daddy look happy,' I say to Zelda. 'I know why. It's because they've still got you as their daughter and they love you very much. Love is like preserved carrot. It never goes off.'

'Wilhelm's right,' says Genia quietly. 'A person doesn't have to be here to love you.'

Zelda puts fish-bone whiskers on the faces of her figures.

'They're rabbits,' she says to me. 'They're happy because you didn't stab them.'

I sigh. I'm happy I didn't stab them. But I'd be happier if Zelda could forgive her parents.

I glance over at Genia. She's still at the stove. She's staring at the photo of her husband she keeps in a frame on the shelf.

She's been staring at it a lot today.

Suddenly I realise why she's unhappy.

Of course. Here's me so worried about Zelda, I'm forgetting Genia's got someone she cares about just as much.

'You must really miss him,' I say to her.

Genia looks at me with a guilty expression, like she didn't want me to see her staring at the photo.

'Yes,' she says.

Poor Genia. She hasn't seen her husband for two years. She must be missing him a huge amount.

'I had some news about him today,' Genia says.

I feel a jolt of concern. It couldn't have been good news, not with her looking so worried.

'Has something bad happened to him?' I say, hoping I'm wrong.

'No,' says Genia. 'Nothing bad.'

I feel relieved. Except why is she looking so miserable?

Genia comes over with the stew pot and puts it on the table. She looks at me and Zelda as she slowly spoons more fish stew into our bowls.

'You know I told you how Gabriek was forced to go to Germany to work for the Nazis?' she says.

I nod.

Zelda glares indignantly. 'Nazis shouldn't force people,' she says.

'He's coming home,' says Genia. 'Probably in a few days.'

At first I'm happy for her. And for her husband.

'Hooray,' yells Zelda, clapping her hands.

But Genia isn't cheering or clapping. She isn't even smiling.

I don't get it.

Why wouldn't a person be happy that her husband is coming home? I can only think of two possible reasons. Either she doesn't like him any more, or she's worried about what will happen when he gets here.

I can't sleep.

It's partly because I slept for half the day. And also because I'm worried.

Zelda can't sleep either. I can feel her tossing and turning next to me in the darkness.

'Don't fidget,' I whisper to her. 'You'll drag the covers off Genia.'

'I'm not fidgeting,' whispers Zelda, turning over again. 'I'm thinking.'

Luckily Genia is a deep sleeper because Zelda is the noisiest thinker I know.

'Felix,' says Zelda. 'After Genia's husband gets here, will there be enough food for us all?'

'Don't worry,' I say. 'I'm sure there'll be enough. He can help us get more if we need it.'

Zelda is so clever. Only six and she's thinking about grown-up things like that. I'm ten, so it's natural for me to worry. Specially now I know the real reason Genia is so unhappy.

Genia told me earlier, when I was helping her clear up.

'It's alright,' she said to me. 'Gabriek won't mind you being here. It'll be fine.'

That's all she said but I know what she meant.

Genia's worried that when her husband gets back and sees what the Nazis are doing to people who protect Jews, he might think it's too risky for me and Zelda to stay here.

Too risky for him and Genia.

I haven't said anything to Zelda yet. I don't want to worry her. Little kids should be protected from worry as much as possible. Now that Leopold and Trotski and the chickens have gone, poor Zelda hasn't got anything to take her mind off the war except for one pencil and some fish bones.

I close my eyes and try to think of a good side to Gabriek coming home.

For example, if he doesn't throw us out, Zelda will be able to see him and Genia being loving to each other and that might bring back happy memories of her real mum and dad.

That makes me feel better.

I'm not going to think any more negative thoughts about Gabriek.

I peer at Zelda in the gloom to see if she's getting sleepy.

She's still awake, and she's frowning.

'Felix,' she says. 'After Genia's husband gets here, what if he doesn't want us?'

**Then** the next day dawned, and the one after that, and quite a few more, and Genia's husband didn't arrive.

'He must be having trouble with his travel arrangements,' I say to Zelda.

We feel sorry for Genia, but relieved as well. We stay feeling relieved right up until the next morning, when the local police come round to all the farms with strict instructions.

Everybody be in the town square at ten o'clock on the dot.

By order of the Nazis.

We don't want to go, but we have to.

Everyone does.

We're all very gloomy as we trudge into town. It's drizzling and the road is muddy and the wind is cold. Me and Zelda and Genia have got our coats and hats on. Mrs Placzek is wearing two headscarves. She's so gloomy she doesn't even say hello, just stares down at the road as she walks past us.

This makes me feel worried. When you're a Jew in hiding and somebody stops being friendly, it could be serious. Or maybe Mrs Placzek is just worried like us. Maybe she doesn't know either why the Nazis want us in the town square.

'Genia, why are the Nazis making us be in town?' says Zelda for the hundredth time.

'Don't worry, Violetta,' replies Genia, also for the hundredth time. 'It'll be fine.'

But she doesn't look very sure.

Earlier, as we were leaving the house, Zelda whispered to me that maybe everyone was going to town to have a party to welcome Genia's husband home.

I told her I didn't think so. I also told her that he might not be home for a while yet because Germany is a long way away.

That cheered her up a bit.

Me too, for a couple of minutes. But now I'm worried again. Why do the Nazis want us in town? Revenge for what happened at the river?

I'm also worried we might bump into Cyryl and his gang. Even if the Nazis don't want revenge, I know Cyryl does.

'Genia,' says Zelda. 'Will the Nazis make us go shopping in town?'

Genia gives a big sigh, which can sometimes mean she's getting cross.

'I might as well tell you,' she says. 'You'll find out sooner or later. They're making us go there to mock Jews.'


Genia's right. That is why we're here.

Nazi soldiers and local police and Hitler Youth are making everyone stand on both sides of the town square. They're making us look at a straggling line of Jewish people shuffling past us.

I can tell the people are Jewish because they're all wearing white armbands with a blue star. The star reminds me of the one Mum has on her plate for special cakes.

Used to have, I mean.

I'm feeling very sad because these poor people are so thin and pale and their clothes are so ragged. A lot of them look ill. I don't know how they can walk. Specially the old people and the little kids. They probably wouldn't be walking at all if the Nazi soldiers weren't yelling at them and hitting them.

'Murdering Nazi scum,' mutters Genia softly, so only me and Zelda can hear.

'Where are those people going?' says Zelda in a loud concerned voice.

A man standing next to us chuckles in a not very nice way.

'Railway station,' he says. 'One way ticket to somewhere hot. And I don't mean Africa.'

I know where he means. A death camp where the Nazis burn people up after they kill them.

Some of the people around us are laughing. Others are disgusted. I'm not sure if they're disgusted with the man, or because some of the Jewish people are being sick onto the cobbles.

'Filthy vermin,' the man yells at the poor straggling prisoners.

So do quite a few other people.

I don't understand. Why do the Nazis want us to mock and insult the Jewish people? Aren't the Jewish people suffering enough?

I wish we could help them.

I wish we could at least give them some food or clothes from Mrs Szynsky's shop or something.

Genia nudges me.

'Shout at them, Wilhelm,' she whispers.

For a second I don't know what she means. Nazi soldiers are glaring at us and making it hard for me to think.

'Filthy vermin,' Genia yells at the Jewish people.

I'm not exactly sure what vermin are, but I can tell from the fierce look on Genia's face that it's not a nice thing to call people. I'm shocked until I see how sad her eyes are. Suddenly I realise why she's doing it and why she wants me to do it as well.

It's to make us look like we hate Jews, specially me.

'Go on,' Genia hisses at me and Zelda.

I can see Zelda doesn't want to. I can see from her frown that she wants to go home. But she can't because Genia is holding her hand very tight.

I'm worried by Zelda's frown. If she loses her temper, I know what will happen. She'll yell out something that will make the Nazis think that neither of us hates Jews.

I have to do it.

I take a deep breath, and I try not to look at any of the Jewish people, and I do my best.

'Filthy vermin,' I yell, but suddenly I'm thinking of Mum and Dad and their journey to their death camp and my voice goes wobbly and my eyes fill with tears and I wish I could be like Leopold's friend and point a gun at all the laughing faces and pull the trigger and . . .

I shut my eyes and make the thoughts go away.

I tell myself to think of Zelda.

I remind myself I must never do anything to put her in danger.

When I've calmed down, I open my eyes.

I'm too ashamed to look at the Jewish people. I look over their heads. That doesn't really help because now I'm staring at all the dead people hanging from the wooden posts. There are lots of them because the Nazis did take revenge for what happened at the river.

I look in another direction. And see somebody I recognise. Standing near us with his back to the Jewish people, helping the other Nazis supervise the onlookers, is the Hitler Youth boy who spotted my Richmal Crompton book.

Except he's not doing much supervising.

He's staring off into the distance like I was trying to do. He doesn't look stern and enthusiastic like the other Nazis, he looks sad.

'Filthy vermin,' yells Genia loudly.

I tell myself she's shouting it at the Nazis rather than at the Jews.

The Hitler Youth boy must have heard her, because he glances over. And sees me. And now he's coming over.

Is he going to bash me for not mocking the Jewish people enough?

No, he's grinning.

'Richmal Crompton,' he says to me. 'My favourite.'

I'm stunned. I've never met a Nazi Richmal Crompton fan before. Plus he speaks Polish with quite a good accent.

'Good stories,' says the Hitler Youth boy, still smiling. 'Very funny.'

I nod. I'm trying to smile back, but behind the Hitler Youth boy I can see a Jewish man and a Jewish woman, their thin arms round each other, helping each other stagger along.

They look like they're in so much pain.

Somebody pushes past me.

'Violetta,' I hear Genia yell frantically. 'Come back.'

I turn to see what Zelda's doing.

Genia must have been distracted by the Nazi Richmal Crompton fan too, because Zelda has pulled away from her and is darting past the Nazi supervisors.

She goes up to the Jewish man and woman.

'My mummy and daddy are dead,' she says to them. 'If you want, you can be their replacements.'

The man and the woman stare at her.

So do I. She learned that word replacements from me and I wish she hadn't.

'If you be my new mummy and daddy,' Zelda says to the man and woman, 'you can come and live with me and Wilhelm and our aunty Genia and you won't have to go to the hot place.'

A Nazi soldier grabs Zelda with one hand and raises his rifle.

He's going to smash her in the head with it.

I fling myself forward.

'No,' I shout. 'She's only little. She doesn't mean any harm.'

I'm scrabbling in my coat for Zelda's locket to show the Nazi she's one of them. But the pockets are full of fluff and my frantic fingers can't find it.

The Nazi soldier turns angrily to me and before I can plead any more, he jabs his rifle butt down and my head explodes.

Then I opened my eyes and I wasn't dead.

Just home.

In bed.

In pain.

Genia is staring down at me. Her face is shiny and worried in the daylight that's jabbing through the window.

'Thank God,' she says.

'Where's Zelda?' I croak.

It's all coming back to me. Zelda talking to the Jewish couple. Being grabbed by a Nazi. Did she get bashed too? Or worse?

Zelda's face pops up next to Genia's.

'I'm here,' she says. 'Don't you know anything?'

She looks fine, as far as I can see. I can't see very clearly because my head is throbbing and every time it does the whole room flickers.

I look around for my glasses. They're next to the bed and they don't seem to be broken.

'Are you injured?' Genia asks me anxiously. 'Can you move your arms and legs?'

I move everything a bit. When I do, my head hurts more.

'It's just my head,' I murmur.

'You were knocked out,' says Zelda. 'You came home in a cart.'

Genia is dabbing at my head with a damp cloth, which feels cool and soothing and very painful.

I squint at Zelda, trying to see if she has any injuries. She's very brave for her age and she might be hiding them so Genia won't be worried.

'Thanks for trying to rescue me,' says Zelda, squeezing my hand.

'Are you alright?' I say to her.

Zelda nods.

'Violetta's not hurt,' says Genia. 'Thanks to your Hitler Youth friend. He persuaded the soldier who hit you to let Violetta go.'

'He was nice,' says Zelda. 'He wasn't a murdering Nazi scum.'

I say a silent thank you to the Hitler Youth boy, whatever his name is. And to Richmal Crompton.

Genia is double-checking my arms and legs. She looks at me, puzzled.

'How do you know that German boy?' she says.

'We like the same books,' I say.

'Richmal Crompton books,' says Zelda. 'Richmal Crompton is English, but we don't mind.'

I lift my head off the pillow and squint at Genia, trying to see if she minds that I've got a Nazi friend. Grown-ups can sometimes go straight from being anxious to being cross when they realise kids aren't badly hurt.

She doesn't seem to mind.

I hope she's not cross with Zelda either.

'Violetta didn't mean to cause trouble,' I explain to Genia. 'What she said to that Jewish couple about being replacements, she got that idea from me.'

'It's alright,' says Genia gently. 'Violetta and I have talked about it. I'd have offered those poor people shelter myself if it was possible.'

'Our bed's not big enough,' says Zelda.

I flop back, relieved.

Genia dabs my head again.

'It's stopped bleeding,' she says. 'I don't think it'll need stitches. But you will have a big bruise.'

Zelda leans over and kisses my head.

'That's good for bruises,' she says.

'Thanks,' I say.

'Come on, Violetta,' says Genia. 'We have to let Wilhelm rest.' She looks at me again, still worried. 'Are you feeling any better?'

'Yes,' I say. 'I am.'

But it's not true.

I'm feeling worse. Not because of my throbbing head, because of the thoughts I'm having.

I try to make the thoughts go away. I try to sleep instead. But every time I hear Zelda's voice in the kitchen, the thoughts come back.

I'm thinking about how that Nazi soldier probably wouldn't have let Zelda go if he'd seen my private part. How he'd have assumed she was Jewish like me and shot us both.

I'm also having thoughts about how Genia's husband might let a non-Jewish kid live here, just not a Jewish one.

Thoughts about how Zelda will never be safe while I'm around.

Just thinking that makes a pain stab inside me worse than a hundred bayonets.

But it's true.

She won't.

I know now what I have to do. I've been pretending for ages that I don't have to do it, but I do.

It's what Mum and Dad did for me when they hid me in that Catholic orphanage. They didn't want to do it, but they had to. They went away and left me and stopped being with me to keep me safe.

That's what I have to do for Zelda.

I ask Richmal Crompton to help me have the strength to do it.

Richmal Crompton lets me cry for a while, because that can be a part of getting strength.

After I wipe my eyes, she helps me think about things. About how she's with me every day, in my thoughts and in my imagination, even though she's not actually physically here.

I can be with Zelda like that.

In her thoughts.

In her imagination.

After I've gone.

But first I have to make sure Zelda doesn't enrage any more Nazi thugs.

I'm still trying to get her to draw a happy picture of her real parents. So she'll feel better about them. So she won't hate Nazis so much in public. So she won't tell any more nutty stories about being Jewish.

'No,' says Zelda, scowling.

She flings the pencil down and throws herself onto the bed next to me.

The bed wobbles, which hurts my head, but I try not to show it. Genia only let Zelda come in here because I said I was feeling better after a sleep.

I think Genia knows now how important Zelda's feeling about her parents are. That's why she bought Zelda a new pencil.

'Let me have a go,' I say to Zelda.

I prop myself up and put my glasses on and squint at the wrinkled shop paper and draw a picture of Zelda's parents helping her look after a sick chicken.

In the picture Zelda is bandaging the chicken's head. Her mum and dad are holding the aspirin and lemonade.

'They were very kind, your mummy and daddy,' I say as I show Zelda the picture.

'Goebbels wasn't a boy chicken,' says Zelda. 'She was a girl chicken.'

I make Goebbels a girl chicken.

'That's not my mummy and daddy being kind,' says Zelda. 'That's Violetta's mummy and daddy being kind.'

She takes the pencil and draws two tiny figures on the horizon.

'Who's that?' I say.

'Don't you know anything?' says Zelda. 'That's my Nazi mummy and daddy. Shooting children.'

I sigh and my head hurts and not just because of the bruise.

I have to accept it. This plan isn't working. I need another way to keep Zelda safe after I've gone.


I ask Richmal Crompton to help me find another way.

While I'm waiting for her to get back to me, I light the lamp next to the bed and read myself a story from her book.

It's to help with the pain.

Not my head pain, the other one, the leaving-Zelda pain.

Except I'm finding it hard to concentrate. I'm reading each page three times and I'm still not sure what this story's about. I'm on the last page now and I haven't got a clue why William and his friends are throwing onions and potatoes out of his bedroom window at a grown-up.

It's no good. I'm too miserable for a story. And I've still got the sad pain in my chest.

Wait a minute.

Potatoes . . .

Reading about potatoes is reminding me of something Genia was talking about recently.

Something that might help protect Zelda.

Yes.

Richmal Crompton, thank you.


I climb high into the tree and don't fall out.

This is good.

If you can climb a tree only two days after being bashed on the head by a Nazi, you know he hasn't done any permanent damage.

I look out across the potato field.

Lots of people are bent over the furrows, picking potatoes and putting them in baskets. Adults as well as kids.

This is what Genia was talking about. The Nazis haven't got

any orphans left to pick the potatoes, so now they're making people from town do it.

Genia was right about something else too.

The potato pickers aren't just being guarded by grown-up Nazis, they're being guarded by Hitler Youth as well.

I peer down at the Hitler Youth boys in the potato field.

Please, I beg Richmal Crompton, let your fan be on potato duty. And please let me spot him quickly because I have to get home. Genia and Zelda will be back from their rabbit hunt soon and I'm not meant to be out of bed.

Yes.

There he is.

The only Hitler Youth Richmal Crompton fan in the whole world, supervising the potato pickers with his Hitler Youth mates. I'm pleased to see he's not swaggering quite as much as the others.

Excellent.

Tomorrow I'll get myself rounded up to do potato picking. Which will give me the whole day to have a quiet word with him.

I won't feel so bad if I know Zelda's got some Nazi protection after I've gone.

**Then** the next day I told Genia a lie. I told her I felt too ill to go rabbit hunting with her and Zelda. I told her I needed to stay in bed.

But I didn't.

After they left, I got up and put my Richmal Crompton book in my coat pocket and walked into town and waited to be rounded up for potato picking.

The potato trucks are in the town square now. The Nazi soldiers are ordering us to get onto them.

People don't like having to do potato picking for the Nazis, but most people don't try to run away. It's only for a few hours and it's better than being shot.

I clamber up onto a truck. I try to look annoyed like the other people I'm squeezed in here with. But not too annoyed. People who look like trouble-makers get hit.

I'm not here to make trouble, I'm here to help Zelda.

I know this is risky, letting the Nazis round me up, what with my private part and everything. But it's a risk I have to take. And I've got an emergency plan. I stopped myself doing a poo this morning in case I need it later.

As the truck jolts and rumbles along the road out of town, I spot the person I've come to see.

The Richmal Crompton fan. He's in a jeep with some other Hitler Youth. They speed past our truck and head towards the front of the convoy. The Richmal Crompton fan doesn't see me because I'm jammed in with so many other people, but that doesn't matter.

I've got all day.

Now there's only one other person I have to keep my eyes open for.

Cyryl.

I didn't see him in the town square, and he's not on this truck, and I don't think he's on any of the others.

So far so good.

You know how when you're doing potato picking for the Nazis and you're desperate to be seen by one particular Hitler Youth boy but he's over the other side of the field and you daren't go over to him because potato pickers have to stay in their own furrow so you pray to Richmal Crompton for help and she makes it rain?

That's happening now.

We're all running for shelter under the trees.

The Nazis don't do potato picking in the rain. They don't like the potatoes to get too wet because soggy potatoes go mushy when they're stored. I don't think they have recipes for mushy potatoes in German cooking.

I see the Richmal Crompton fan standing under a tree chatting with some other Hitler Youth. I go and stand under the next tree.

He hasn't seen me yet.

'Jew!'

Oh no.

Someone else has.

I know that voice.

Cyryl.

He must have been on one of the other trucks. Now he's pointing at me, his face pink with anger and his wet lips shining.

'This rat is a Jew,' he yells. 'Check his willy. I bet I'm right.'

I hear several loud clicks. I realise what the sound is. Nazi soldiers releasing the safety catches on their guns.

One of the soldiers puts his gun down and comes towards me. I see why he wants both hands free. He's planning to undo my trouser buttons.

I push hard in my guts.

The poo won't come.

It should come out easily because I'm terrified, but it's not coming out at all.

I must be too terrified.

I strain my guts one more time.

Nothing.

My insides are in a knot of panic. Suddenly I think of something else to try. My last hope. I stuff my hand in my coat pocket and feel around frantically under the Richmal Crompton book.

Yes.

Zelda's locket.

I pull it out and hold it up in front of the Nazi soldier. He takes it and looks at it, frowning. The other soldiers and Hitler Youth boys crowd round and peer at it too.

Please, I beg silently. Please think Zelda's parents are my parents.

The soldier holding the locket says something to me in Nazi, which I don't understand.

I panic even more. Will this give me away? If I was a real Nazi kid, even a Polish one, I should be able to understand some German.

There's only one person here who can help me.

I take the Richmal Crompton book from my pocket and hold it so the Hitler Youth boy can see it and remember who I am.

For a few seconds we stare at each other, but only for a few seconds.

The Hitler Youth boy steps forward, says something to the soldier in German, and turns to me.

'Listen carefully,' he says to me in Polish. 'The sergeant is asking you if the people in the locket are members of your family.'

I feel dizzy with gratitude.

'Yes,' I say. 'They are.'

Zelda is my family, so her parents must be too, sort of.

The Hitler Youth boy turns back to the soldiers and speaks to them again in German. He says a lot of things. The soldiers nod. Whatever he's telling them, they look like they're believing it. They lower their guns.

'He's a Jew,' yells Cyryl. 'He stole that book from my family's shop.'

The Hitler Youth boy steps over to Cyryl and punches him hard in the stomach. Cyryl keels over, clutching himself.

The Nazi soldiers and the other Hitler Youth all laugh and clap.

I look away.

I should feel glad that Cyryl's been punished. But I don't. In my experience, punches in the stomach just make enemies into bigger enemies.

The sergeant hands me Zelda's locket. He turns and starts shouting. You don't have to speak German to know what he's saying. It's stopped raining. We have to go back to work.

'My name's Amon,' says the Hitler Youth boy as we walk back to my furrow.

'I'm Wilhelm,' I say.

For a second I'm tempted to tell him my real name, but that would be crazy.

Amon smiles.

'Your parents must really like Richmal Crompton,' he says. 'To give you the same name as her hero.'

I nod. I feel guilty lying to Amon after he's saved my life, so I tell him as much of the truth as I can.

'My parents liked the William stories a lot,' I say. 'They used to read to me every night. But they're dead now.'

Amon gives me a sympathetic look.

The sergeant's still yelling. I know I haven't got much time to talk, so I say what I've come to say.

'Amon, I have to go away soon. After I've gone, will you look out for my sister Violetta like you did the other day? Sometimes she says things that aren't true. Things that upset your army.'

Amon thinks about this.

For a while I worry he's going to ask me why I have to go away. But he doesn't.

'Tell Violetta,' he says, 'if she gets into trouble, to ask for me. Amon Kurtz.'

'Thank you,' I say, weak with relief.

'The SS officers know me,' he says. 'I speak Polish. I translate for them sometimes when they're having drinks with women.'

I hold my William book out to Amon.

'This is for you,' I say.

He looks surprised. And pleased.

'Thank you,' he says.

Amon takes the book and looks at it for a moment. His face goes serious. He glances around the potato field to make sure nobody else is listening.

'I wish Richmal Crompton was in charge of Germany instead of Adolf Hitler,' he says quietly. 'If she was, I wouldn't have to be in the Hitler Youth. You and me, we'd both be at home with our parents. I wouldn't be sleeping in a dead kid's bed.'

He puts the book inside his jacket.

I want to talk with him more, but we're at my furrow now and I must get back to work.

There is one last thing I have to ask.

'Amon,' I say. 'What did you tell the others about me back there?'

Amon grins.

'I told them you were just like us Hitler Youth,' he says. 'A boy doing his duty.'

We look at each other for a few moments.

'Thank you,' I say.

Amon clicks his heels together and gives the Nazi salute.

'Heil Richmal,' he says quietly.

I'm late.

The Nazis made us pick potatoes till dark and by the time we were dropped off in the square the town clock was striking six and now I'm hurrying back to the farm as fast as I can.

Genia and Zelda will be frantic.

I have to think what to tell them. Why I've been away all day. I hate lying to them. But I can't tell them the truth, that I'm planning to leave.

What was that?

I stop and peer into the dark trees at the side of the road.

Is somebody following me?

No, it's just my imagination playing tricks. That happens when you have to live with a fake identity and make up untrue stories to tell the people you love.

I start walking again.

'I saw you,' says a voice.

I spin round.

A figure steps out of the trees and comes towards me.

Zelda?

Genia?

The figure steps into a patch of moonlight.

It's Leopold's friend. The kid who shot the soldier. He's still got his gun. He's pointing it at me now.

'I saw you this afternoon,' he says, scowling. 'I saw you talking and grinning with that Hitler Youth vermin.'

I don't know what to say.

I can't take my eyes off the gun.

Up close it looks too big for him. He's only a bit taller than me. But he's holding it in both hands and I know he can use it.

'You're a Nazi vermin spy,' says the kid, aiming the gun at my head.

**Then** I invited the kid with the gun home for dinner.

He stared at me and I could see from his stunned expression he wasn't sure if he'd heard right.

Dinner?

In the moonlight his dark angry eyes go narrow with suspicion.

His gun wobbles a bit.

I hope I haven't caught him too much by surprise. Some people go twitchy when they're caught by surprise, and Leopold's friend has still got his fingers on the trigger and the gun is still pointing at my head.

I try not to think about what happened last time I saw him point a gun at somebody's head.

The chill breeze is making the autumn leaves rustle in the trees. A leaf floats down near the kid. He sees the movement out of the corner of his eye, swings the gun towards the leaf, realises what it is and points the gun back at me.

He's twitchy alright.

I'll have to be careful.

'Genia's making rabbit stew,' I say, trying to sound relaxed and casual and like I invite people with guns home for dinner every night.

I don't, but this is too good an opportunity to miss.

If I can persuade the kid to stop killing Nazis, the Nazis will do less killings in revenge. Less innocent people hanged from posts. Less chance Zelda could be one of them after I've gone.

'You've met Genia,' I say. 'You helped her plant cabbages. She makes really delicious stew.'

I hope he remembers her. And what a kind person she is.

I'm guessing that a kid who goes round killing Nazis probably doesn't have much in the way of loving grown-ups in his life.

'She'll be really pleased to see a good friend of Leopold's,' I say.

I decide not to tell the kid yet what happened to poor Leopold. No point upsetting a person when you're trying to invite him to dinner.

I can see he's tempted. But he's still frowning.

'Why were you being friendly with that Nazi scum?' he says.

'It's not what you think,' I say. 'His name's Amon and he hates Adolf Hitler as much as we do. He's not like the others.'

The kid still looks doubtful.

'What were you both talking about?' he says.

'Books,' I say. 'Come on. We're late. I'll explain on the way.'

The kid doesn't move.

We stand looking at each other. I have a feeling he wants me to be telling the truth. But there's a world war on and hardly anyone tells the truth in a war.

'After I've explained,' I say, 'if you still think I'm a spy, you can shoot me.'

The kid thinks about this.

'Alright,' he says, lowering the gun.

We set off.


'Wilhelm,' shouts Genia as I come into the house. 'Where have you been?'

She's furious.

I have to move fast. If she scares the kid, anything could happen. He's still got the gun in his coat pocket.

'This is Dov,' I say. 'He's a friend of mine. And Leopold's.'

Dov steps uncertainly into the kitchen. Genia stares at him. I can see she's struggling with her feelings. She's still angry with me, but because she's good-hearted she doesn't want to upset a guest.

Zelda is also staring. She hides behind me.

225

'Children shouldn't play with knives,' she says sternly to Dov.

I don't blame her. The last time she saw Dov he was threatening her with one. I give her a look to let her know it won't happen this time.

I hope.

'This is Genia,' I say to Dov. 'And Zelda.'

'I'm Violetta, remember?' Zelda hisses.

'It's OK,' I say to her. 'Dov knows about us. He's Jewish.'

Zelda looks at Dov warily. 'So am I,' she says to him. 'Sometimes.'

I glance at Genia to see if she's realised who Dov is. I don't think she has.

'Dov is from the Jewish orphanage,' I say. 'He met Leopold when he was here helping with the cabbages.'

Genia is still staring at him, but with a gentler expression.

'I think I remember you,' she says. 'Hello, Dov.'

'Hello,' he mutters.

'I'm glad you're still alive,' Genia says quietly. 'Where are you living now?'

'Krol's place,' says Dov.

Now it's my turn to stare.

Mr Krol? The turnip man who tried to kidnap me and Zelda?

'Krol rescued you?' says Genia.

Dov nods.

'I thought as much,' she says. 'I had a feeling that sly old grump had someone hidden at his place.'

I try to take this in.

The reward notice on the cart must be just a disguise, to make the Nazis think Mr Krol hates Jews, so they won't suspect him of protecting one.

Incredible.

'Are you hungry, Dov?' says Genia.

'If there's not enough rabbit stew,' I say to her, 'he can have mine.'

Genia sighs.

226

'We're not having rabbit stew,' she says. 'We're having cabbage soup again.'

'We caught a rabbit,' says Zelda. 'But I wouldn't let her kill it.'

Genia gives me and Zelda an exasperated look. Sort of loving and cross at the same time. Like she's forgiving us but wondering where it will all end.

'Sorry there's no stew,' Zelda says to Dov.

'That's alright,' he says gruffly.

'I'm sure Dov understands,' says Genia to Zelda. 'If he's friends with Felix, he probably doesn't like the idea of killing things either.'

After we have the soup, Zelda shows Dov her drawings.

'This is Violetta's mummy and daddy being nice to chickens,' she says.

While Dov looks at the drawings, I try to think of a way of persuading him to stop killing Nazis.

As it turns out, I don't need to.

Genia is sweeping up. Dov's coat is on the floor where he left it. Genia moves it to sweep under it and the gun falls out with a clatter.

We all look at the gun.

Nobody says anything.

Dov just stares at the table and sort of hunches his shoulders.

Genia picks the gun up and puts it back in Dov's coat pocket. I can see she's thinking hard. When I got back from the river, I told her about seeing Leopold's friend shoot a Nazi. I think she's guessed that's who Dov is.

She comes and sits next to Dov at the kitchen table. Before she can say anything, he turns to her angrily.

'I came here to see Leopold,' he says. 'Where's Leopold?'

Genia hesitates.

This is the moment I've been dreading. I should have told Dov about Leopold on the way here, but I was worried he wouldn't want to come.

'Don't you know anything?' says Zelda quietly. 'The Nazis killed Leopold.'

Dov jumps to his feet.

I do too. For a second I think he's going to lash out at Zelda. But instead he just looks at Genia as if he's pleading with her to say it's not true.

Genia looks at him and nods sadly.

Dov grabs a wooden bowl and hurls it across the room. It bangs against the wall near the shelf. I hold my breath and wait for Genia to get angry. The bowl almost hit the photo of her husband.

She doesn't.

She just takes hold of Dov's hand and gently pulls him back down onto the bench next to her.

'We all miss Leopold a lot,' she says. 'Just like you must miss your parents. They used to run the Jewish orphanage, didn't they?'

Dov doesn't say anything. Just stares at the table.

'Felix and Zelda miss their families an awful lot,' Genia says quietly. 'I miss my sister and her children. We know how you feel, Dov.'

Dov is clenching his teeth, like he doesn't want to let any words out. But he does.

'No you don't,' he mutters.

Genia slowly reaches across the table and slides a clean piece of paper over in front of Dov. She puts the pencil on top of it.

'Show us,' she says softly.

For a long time Dov just sits there, staring at the paper.

Just when I think he's not going to touch it, he suddenly picks up the pencil and starts drawing. Not with careful little movements like Zelda does when she draws. With big violent slashes. Sometimes he tears the paper, but he keeps going.

Me and Zelda and Genia watch.

He's drawing a pit in the ground. I recognise what it is. The children's grave. There are lots of people lying in it and lots of people standing next to it and lots of Nazis shooting them.

A drop of liquid splashes onto the paper.

It's a tear.

Dov wipes his face with his hand.

'They took us into the forest,' he says, his teeth still clenched. 'Me and my mum and my dad and my brother and all the orphan kids. They shot us. We fell into the hole. I wasn't dead. People fell on top of me. I was buried in people. They were moaning. They stopped moaning. I climbed out. It was dark. I looked for my family. There were too many bodies.'

Dov drops the pencil onto the table and puts his hands over his face. His whole body is shaking.

'I couldn't find them,' he sobs.

Genia puts her arms round him and holds him tight.

We're all crying now, Genia included.

After a while, Zelda wipes her eyes. She picks up the pencil and starts drawing on a fresh piece of paper. When she's finished, she goes round to the other side of the table and gives the drawing to Dov.

I lean over to see what she's drawn.

It's very simple.

Two grown-ups with their arms round a child.

'This is my mummy and daddy,' says Zelda to Dov quietly. 'They're Nazis. They're saying sorry.'

**Then** it was time for Dov to leave. Genia went with him to Mr Krol's place to make sure he got there safely. I stayed at the kitchen table with Zelda.

She did another drawing.

Two grown-ups and a child. And some chickens. All dancing.

'This is me and my mummy and daddy,' says Zelda. 'We're not Jewish, but we still love each other.'

I smile at her.

'I'm glad,' I say. 'I'm glad you're not cross with your mummy and daddy any more.'

Zelda is looking sadly at the picture.

'They couldn't help being Nazis,' she says quietly. 'I couldn't tell them not to, I was too little.'

I give Zelda a hug.

After a long time she lifts her face from my neck and looks at me with a serious expression.

'Felix,' she says. 'Tell Leopold's friend I don't want to shoot Nazis any more.'

I smile again. I'm so happy for her and not just because she'll be safer now. When your mum and dad have been killed, it's even worse if you're angry with them.

I go to my coat and get Zelda's locket. I put it round her neck.

'Will you wear this now?' I say. 'To keep you safe?'

Zelda opens the locket and looks at the little photo of her parents.

She frowns.

'You keep me safe,' she says. 'And Genia does. And Richmal Crompton does.'

'We try to,' I say. 'But wearing this will help keep you even safer. It'll make the Nazis like you.'

She thinks about this for a long time.

'Even if the other Nazis do like me,' she says, 'I won't like them.'

But she leaves the locket on.

'Thank you,' I say.

'I'm going to do some more drawings,' says Zelda, picking up the pencil again. 'I'm going to do one now of when my mummy cooked me an egg.'

I give her another smile, but suddenly I'm full of sadness.

I know why. It's nearly time for me to go.

Zelda looks at me, concerned.

'It's alright,' she says. 'My mummy's cooking you an egg too.'

I think about how lucky I am to have Zelda, and that makes my sadness even stronger. But it's not time to go just yet.

While Zelda draws more pictures, I write a story. It's a long story about the things the Nazis have done to my family and Dov's family and all the other people they've hurt too.

When I've finished, me and Zelda go out to the barn.

Leopold's kennel is covering the hole I dug in the barn floor. I drag it to one side.

'What are you doing?' says Zelda.

I jump down into the hole and fold my story into a small square of paper and push it into the soft earth.

'I'm hiding my story,' I explain. 'When the war's over and the Nazis have been defeated, it will be evidence of what they did.'

Zelda thinks about this.

'Who's going to make them defeated?' she asks.

'The English,' I say.

I tell Zelda what Genia told me one time. How the English have still got an army and one day they're going to attack the Nazis.

'You mean Richmal Crompton?' says Zelda.

'She'll help,' I say.

Zelda kneels by the hole and hands me down some crumpled pieces of paper.

'Hide my evidence too,' she says. 'So Richmal Crompton's army will know that my mummy and daddy weren't bad Nazis.'

I look at the pieces of paper. They're her drawings of her parents dancing and cooking her an egg and bathing her knee when she cut it.

I fold the drawings and push them into the soil next to my story.

Zelda helps me scramble out of the hole and we brush the dirt off my trousers. While we do, I tell her about Amon, the Hitler Youth boy. I tell her how she must ask for him if she ever gets into trouble with the Nazis.

She stops brushing and looks at me.

'What about you?' she says. 'Why don't I ask for you?'

I take a deep breath.

'This is in case something happens to me and I'm not here,' I say.

Zelda puts her arms round my waist and hugs me tight.

'Nothing's going to happen to you,' she says. 'I'm not going to let it. Don't you know anything?'

Genia gets home and we all go to bed and I sleep the whole night with my arms round Zelda.

Not the whole night.

I wake up before dawn.

Was that a noise outside? I listen carefully. I have a fleeting thought that it's Dov creeping around out there in the farmyard, but it's probably just part of a dream I was having.

All I can hear is the wind.

I know this is the time I should go.

Genia and Zelda are both asleep. I should creep out now and leave them the note I've written telling them how much safer they'll be without me and how I promise I'll come back after the war and find them.

But I can't.

I just want to stay here a little bit longer.

I'll go in a while, before they wake up.

**Then** I opened my eyes again and Genia was gently shaking me.

'Wilhelm, wake up.'

I stare at her, confused. I fumble for my glasses and put them on. Genia's up and dressed. I must have slept in. Zelda appears next to her, up and dressed too.

'Mr Krol's giving us a ride into town,' says Zelda. 'To get you a birthday present.'

I'm even more confused.

It's November. My birthday isn't until January.

Genia and Zelda are both grinning at me. Genia holds my Wilhelm identity card close to my face and points to where it says *Date Of Birth*.

*29 November, 1931.*

'Today's the twenty-ninth,' says Genia. 'You're eleven today. Happy birthday, Wilhelm.'

I try to sit up. Genia gently but firmly pushes me back down into bed.

'You have to stay here,' she says. 'It's a surprise. I'm not using my last three eggs on a present if it's not going to be a surprise. Anyway, you need to rest and get better.' She strokes the bruise on my head. 'Promise me you won't go out playing like yesterday.'

'I promise,' I say quietly.

It's true. Travelling to another part of Poland and finding a place to hide isn't playing.

'See you later, birthday boy,' says Genia.

I sit up and throw my arms round her.

'Thank you,' I say, struggling not to cry. 'Thank you for looking after me and Zelda.'

Genia gives me a long hug.

'Thank you,' she whispers. 'I was turning into a miserable old turnip before you two came along.'

She stands up and goes out.

Zelda has gone out too.

I panic.

Before I can jump out of bed, Zelda runs back in, putting her coat on. She jumps up onto the bed, kisses me on the cheek, and jumps down again.

She stops in the doorway and turns to me with a grin.

'Happy birthday,' she says.

Then she's gone.


I don't hang around.

I have to keep busy.

If I stop and get sad I won't be able to do it.

I get up and put all my clothes on. My trousers and coat and boots and both shirts and all my socks.

I put the note on the kitchen table and write an extra bit thanking Genia and Zelda for the surprise birthday present whatever it is and asking them to keep it safe for me till I come back after the war.

Halfway to the door I stop and go back to the table and find a clean piece of paper and write something else.

The story of Zelda and Genia and their loving hearts.

It's the most important story I've ever written and it's very easy to write because it's already come true.

I'm going to hide it in the barn with the other evidence. So the whole world will know. In case something happens and I don't come back.


I drag Leopold's kennel off the hiding hole in the barn.

And almost faint with shock.

There's a man in the hole.

He's lying there on some straw. He's wearing a ragged suit and blinking up at me like he's been asleep.

He sits up and raises his arms like I'm going to attack him. But when he sees I'm just a kid he lowers them.

'Who are you?' he says.

'Felix,' I say. 'I mean Wilhelm.'

He looks at me for a long time.

I wonder if I should be running. Is he going to grab me for the reward? I think if he was, he would have done it by now. Plus he wouldn't have a kind face like this man.

He's nodding to himself.

'Now I understand,' he says.

I wish I did.

'I'm Gabriek,' says the man, standing up in the hole. 'Genia's husband. I got here in the middle of the night. When I looked through the window and saw somebody in bed with my wife, I . . .'

He doesn't finish the sentence, but I know what he's trying to say. In wartime, with people being killed every day, a lot of people end up in bed married to other people's husbands and wives.

'I decided to wait till morning,' says Gabriek. 'To find out who this person was and . . .'

'It was me,' I say. 'And Zelda. Genia's been protecting us.'

Best to get it out in the open straight off. So we both know where we stand.

Gabriek is nodding to himself again.

'I'm not surprised,' he says. 'My wife has a very big heart.'

I agree with him as he climbs out of the hole.

'Is she awake?' he says.

I explain how Genia's gone into town with Zelda.

'I'm sorry she's not here,' I say. 'It's sort of my fault. They've gone to get me a birthday present.'

Gabriek is looking sad.

But he still wishes me a happy birthday.

Later, after I've explained everything to Gabriek and he's read all the evidence in the hole and seen my note and examined Zelda's pictures, he looks at me, concerned.

'It's nearly winter,' he says, 'Where are you planning to go? Back to the Catholic orphanage?'

I shake my head.

'If I go to there,' I say, 'I'll be putting Mother Minka and the others in danger. I have to find somewhere I can hide on my own.'

Gabriek frowns as he thinks about this.

'I can't tell you what you should do, Felix,' he says. 'If you want to stay here with us, I'll do everything I can to protect you. But the final decision has to be yours.'

'Thank you,' I say.

What a brave and kind man. I can see why Genia chose him to marry. But his kindness has put my mind in a whirl.

I jump down into the hole and busily hide the evidence again, partly to give myself a chance to think.

Could Gabriek still protect Zelda if the Nazis discovered my private part? He'd have Amon to help him, but would that be enough? Or would he and Genia and Zelda all be killed for sheltering me?

I so much want to stay.

But the more I think about it, the more I know, for their sakes, I have to go.

Suddenly I see something glinting under the straw in the bottom of the hole. I pick it up.

Zelda's locket.

Her good protection.

She must have left it here last night as part of her evidence.

She's in town now, without it.

Now I know I definitely have to go, and quickly.

I must get it to her.

**Then** I said goodbye to Gabriek and ran into town, Zelda's locket hard and hot in my fist.

Oh no.

The town is already crowded.

It's market day. How will I find Zelda and Genia in among all these people?

I can only think of one place to start looking.

Cyryl's shop.

I push my way along the street, trying not to go too close to the groups of Nazi soldiers bullying the stallholders for bargains.

'Hey, Jewboy.'

I freeze.

You know how when you're in a crowd and there's one person you don't want to bump into and you suddenly hear his voice yelling at you and it feels like a bad dream?

That's happening to me now.

But it's not a dream.

Cyryl is pushing his way towards me, wet lips smirking.

'Your Hitler Youth friends can't help you now, Jewboy,' he says. 'The police have arrested your vermin family.'

I stare at him, panic and confusion like a huge noisy crowd in my head.

'Your stupid aunty and your stupid sister turned up at our shop with that Jew-lover Krol,' says Cyryl. 'The Nazis have had suspicions about him for ages. So when he walked in this morning and tried to buy clothes for a boy, my mother called the police.'

Dread slices into my guts like a bayonet.

'That aunty of yours is a thug,' says Cyryl. 'She hit my mother.

238

And your vermin sister bit a soldier. The Nazi police had to drag them away.'

'Where did they take them?' I say.

Cyryl does a big wet grin.

'Town square,' he says.

The town square is packed with people but I see Mr Krol straight away.

Oh.

Oh no.

Then I see Zelda and Genia.

I pray it's not really them. I pray that any second they'll come up behind me and give me a hug and Zelda will tell me off for having smudgy glasses and not being able see clearly.

She won't.

Because I can see clearly. Even with smudged glasses. Even with tears.

Oh Zelda.

Oh Genia.

The breeze turns them gently and now they're facing me.

Please, Richmal Crompton, do something.

If I go over there and lift them down from those posts and take those ropes from round their necks, it's not too late is it?

I close my eyes because I know it is too late.

I can't move.

I'm numb.

All I want to do is stay numb for ever. So I just stand here until some Nazi soldiers tell me to get lost and shove me away.

Then I'm not numb any more.

Then all I want to do is kill.

Then I went to Mr Krol's farm.

No sign of Dov in the house.

I call his name while I look for a cellar or an attic or a hole in the barn floor. Finally I find him in the turnip bunker.

I tell him what's happened and what I want to do.

He doesn't take it in at first. He's too busy staring at the wall and swearing and throwing turnips and crying and going on about what a good person Mr Krol was.

I tell him again.

'I want to kill as many of them as I can,' I say.

Dov looks at me.

This time he gets it.

He reaches under some turnips and pulls out a bag and unzips it.

I've seen that bag before.

'Alright,' says Dov. 'Let's do it.'

**Then** we did the planning and the preparations, and then we went to get our revenge.

I should be scared, I know.

We walk towards the Nazi orphanage through the darkness. The big house ahead of us is all lit up. I can see guards at the gates. Soldiers and officers strutting around inside. All with guns. All trained to fight. And Hitler Youth vermin who say they'll protect innocent kids but don't.

I should be scared, but I'm not.

All I'm thinking about is how many of them I can kill. And how many of their families I can hurt. Families suffer a lot when fathers and sons are blown to pieces. Sometimes they go mad. Sometimes they starve.

Good.

'Slow down,' hisses Dov.

I know what he's worried about. Us looking suspicious. Or slipping in the snow and going sprawling and showing the Nazis what we've got hidden under our coats.

I slow down.

We stroll up to the main gate. Dov says hello to the guard in German. The guard looks at us.

The blood on our Hitler Youth uniforms is on the back so the guard can't see it. Dov was clever, shooting them that way.

The guard says something to us and waves us in.

We stroll through the gate, trying not to look too fat. It's not easy when you've got six grenades taped to your chest and tummy.

My coat starts to slip off my shoulders and I yank it back on. I need it in position, partly to disguise the fatness and partly because of the other grenade in the side pocket.

The one I'll explode first.

The one that will make all the others on my chest explode.

We reach the house. Dov looks at me. I look at him. This is where we split up. Him in the front. Me in the back. Two human bombs in two different parts of the house.

That way we'll kill more of them.

Dov isn't crying now. His eyes are hard. Mine are too. He doesn't say anything. Neither do I. There's nothing to say.

Dov goes up the front steps.

I hurry round to the back of the house. I find an open door. Inside is a corridor. I go down it, listening for voices.

I want lots of voices.

I want a room packed with Nazis.

A thought hits me. What if Dov explodes himself before me? What if the Nazis in this part of the building all run away before I can blow them up?

I grip the grenade in my pocket, my finger through the ring of the pin.

Yes.

Voices.

I push open a door. A room full of Nazis. Some of them turn and stare at me. I hesitate. They're mostly Hitler Youth.

Doesn't matter.

I start to pull the pin.

'Wilhelm.'

A voice behind me.

Dov?

I stop. I turn.

It's Amon. He's staring at me, his face all upset. Does he know? Has he guessed what I'm here to do?

'Wilhelm,' he says in a strange voice. 'Come. I have your book.'

He grabs my shoulders and steers me back out into the corridor. I start to pull the pin again.

I hesitate again.

There's something about Amon's expression. He's not looking scared, he's looking sad. Plus he's closed the door behind us. Now it's just him and me in the corridor.

'I tried, Wilhelm,' he says. 'I tried to save your sister but they wouldn't listen to me.'

He's holding something up in front of my face. Something that glitters in the corridor lights.

'This was in your sister's coat,' he says. 'Wilhelm, I'm sorry.'

I take it from him.

A locket.

Not silver like Zelda's. A gold one.

It's open. Inside each half is a tiny drawing. A boy on one side, a girl on the other. They're facing each other. Under the girl is the letter Z. Under the boy is the letter F.

I stare at it.

My birthday present.

I stare at it for a long time.

Then I take my hand off the grenade in my pocket.

**Then** I grabbed Amon and dragged him down the corridor towards the back door.

'What are you doing?' he says.

I don't answer.

As we burst out into the night, a huge explosion smashes through the house.

Screams.

Frantic shouting.

Rubble falling.

I realise I'm lying on the ground with pain in my ears and gravel in my mouth.

I find my glasses and put them on. They're cracked, but I can still see.

Amon is on the ground too, staring at me in shock.

All around us, chaos.

Dust.

Panic.

People staggering around.

I pull the unexploded grenades off my chest and wriggle out of what's left of the Hitler Youth uniform.

Amon is saying something, but I can't hear what. I see the Richmal Crompton book I gave him, sticking out of his pocket.

I take it.

I still don't speak.

I get to my feet.

I run.

Then I came back here to the barn and climbed into the hiding hole and pulled the kennel over me and I've been here ever since.

Nearly eleven months.

The Nazis didn't come looking for me so I think Amon must have told them I was blown up with Dov. If he did, I'm grateful to him.

I'm even more grateful to Gabriek.

He brings me food once a night and takes my wees and poos away and washes me sometimes and we have very good talks and sometimes we read Richmal Crompton stories to each other.

He always calls me Felix.

Sometimes we talk about Genia, which makes us sad but also happy because of how lucky we were to have her.

My legs are a bit weak and so are my eyes. I don't get to use them much here in my dark hiding place.

But my memory is strong.

I've kept it strong by telling the story of me and Zelda in my head as I lie here on the straw. It's what I do all day. It's how I'm keeping my promise to Zelda. It's why I decided to live.

I'm Zelda's evidence.

She helps me. She stays in my mind all the time. I don't even have to ask her.

One day in the future, when Richmal Crompton's army defeats the Nazis, I'll climb out of here and be the best human being I can for the rest of my life.

To show people what Zelda was like.

'She was only six,' I'll say, 'but she had the loving heart of a ten-year-old.'

And if people carry on hating each other and killing each other and being cruel to each other, I'll tell them something else.

'You can be like her,' I'll say. 'Don't you know anything?'

Let's see what they do then.

*Dear Reader,*

*Once and its sequel Then are two parts of the same story, but they were written and first published as two separate books. In this edition they are published together for the first time.*

*Felix and Zelda's story came from my imagination, but it was inspired by a period of history that was all too real.*

*My grandfather was a Jew from Krakow in Poland. He left there long before that period, but his extended family didn't and most of them perished.*

*Fifteen years ago I read a book about Janusz Korczak, a Polish Jewish doctor and children's author who devoted his life to caring for young people. Over many years he helped run an orphanage for two hundred Jewish children. In 1942, when the Nazis murdered these orphans, Janusz Korczak was offered his freedom but chose to die with the children rather than abandon them.*

*Janusz Korczak became my hero. His story sowed a seed in my imagination.*

*I couldn't have written this story without first reading many other books about the Holocaust. Books full of the voices of the real people who lived and struggled and loved and died and, just a few of them, survived in that terrible time.*

I also read about the generosity and bravery of the people who risked everything to shelter others, often children who were not family members or even of the same faith, and by doing so sometimes saved them.

On my website is a list of some of the books I read. I hope you get to read some of them too and help keep alive the memory of those people.

This story is my imagination trying to grasp the unimaginable.

Their stories are the real stories.

Morris Gleitzman
July 2009


www.morrisgleitzman.com